John J. Maresca

The Taliban in Texas

A Joey Torino Adventure

John J. Maresca

THE TALIBAN IN TEXAS

Edition Noëma

Bibliografische Information der Deutschen Nationalbibliothek
Die Deutsche Nationalbibliothek verzeichnet diese Publikation in der
Deutschen Nationalbibliografie; detaillierte bibliografische Daten sind im
Internet über http://dnb.d-nb.de abrufbar.

Bibliographic information published by the Deutsche Nationalbibliothek
Die Deutsche Nationalbibliothek lists this publication in the Deutsche Nationalbibliografie; detailed
bibliographic data are available in the Internet at http://dnb.d-nb.de.

Cover image: Mosque at Sundown / istockphoto.com gm1162560002-318928030

This is a work of fiction. Any names or characters, businesses or places, events or incidents, are fictitious. Any resemblance to actual persons, living or dead, or actual events is purely coincidental.

ISBN-13: 978-3-8382-1762-8

Edition Noëma
© *ibidem*-Verlag, Stuttgart 2023
Alle Rechte vorbehalten

Das Werk einschließlich aller seiner Teile ist urheberrechtlich geschützt. Jede Verwertung außerhalb der engen Grenzen des Urheberrechtsgesetzes ist ohne Zustimmung des Verlages unzulässig und strafbar. Dies gilt insbesondere für Vervielfältigungen, Übersetzungen, Mikroverfilmungen und elektronische Speicherformen sowie die Einspeicherung und Verarbeitung in elektronischen Systemen.

All rights reserved. No part of this publication may be reproduced, stored in or introduced into a retrieval system, or transmitted, in any form, or by any means (electronical, mechanical, photocopying, recording or otherwise) without the prior written permission of the publisher. Any person who does any unauthorized act in relation to this publication may be liable to criminal prosecution and civil claims for damages.

Printed in the EU

"When strong winds blow, the wise take shelter."

Afghan Proverb

1. Blue Hill, Maine, March, 2001

The sun was just rising, visible through the trees to the East. Joey could sometimes see it as it emerged from the sea – a shimmering golden ball, slowly appearing at the distant line of the horizon. His house was at the top of a small hill, away from the coastline, but the elevation made it possible – just barely possible on a clear day – to catch a glimpse of the distant glowing sun. He often made a point of getting up early, for no other reason than to gaze at this unique scene, at this special moment, and he never regretted it.

The woods around his house were quiet at this time of day. Later there would be birds chirping, but also the muffled sound of distant cars, passing from time to time along the country road that curved around the hill to pass the entrance to his plain dirt driveway, half a mile away. This was the moment he savored, because it was the time when he felt most strongly the distance he had managed to put between himself and the rest of the world. Here he was in his own realm, far from the many pressures of his earlier life, in Washington and its many extensions.

Joey was not a cynical man – on the contrary. His view of the world, of his life experience, of what the future might hold – was simple and ... well ... simple. He was attached to the ordinary things – like this sunrise moment he enjoyed so much – which made up his straightforward life. He enjoyed the quiet, the subtle sounds of life in the forest, the rolling volume of waves as they curled across the sand, and all the varied whistles and squawks of the birdlife in the trees above him, against the silence of the air above.

He was a man who had tired of the busy, and dangerous, life he had led, and had simply decided to opt out. He was done with all that – the pressures of doing something that someone else wanted him to do, the risks of doing things he questioned, resented, or even disagreed with. And he had managed to escape that life, quietly, without fanfare or animosity, and with just enough income to be able to live, here in the northern forests of Maine, in the secluded, modest style he preferred. And he was happy in his simple life here.

Today was mail day – it was delivered once a week to his mailbox by the side of the road below, out of sight beyond the thick grove of trees and the wild shrubs which hid his cabin from the few cars that passed. The road below, in any case, went nowhere – coming to a dead-end at a small, unspoiled lake about a mile beyond. There were no houses there, and no beaches, so the only cars that followed that road were those that belonged to the rare summer fisherman, looking for a remote place to drop his line.

And so, after doing a few stretching exercises on the veranda he had added to the modest cabin, he set off down the hill, cutting through the trees toward the road, about a half-mile away, as he always did on the days when the mailman passed. He never used the driveway, but preferred to walk randomly, and silently, through the woods, stepping – instinctively and not deliberately – on the thick layer of pine needles that covered the ground. It was a habit he had formed years earlier, and which was just, well, his way. His way of walking through the trees was mostly silent, and even the birds continued to chirp and sing. He knew they would stop if he made a noise, just as he was alerted when someone approached his cabin, a modest natural alarm system, which he valued.

And there was a silence in the woods today, which he noticed immediately – the birds were not chirping as they normally did, and even the trees seemed silent. Joey instinctively went silent himself, and advanced slowly, cautiously, through the trees. There was little that he feared in his solitary life in the woods, but he did not appreciate surprises, which normally meant intrusions by outsiders into his solitary lifestyle. He advanced through the trees without hesitation, but with an increased degree of awareness, his senses noting every sound or stirring of the air above him.

After a few minutes he could see the road below, curving around the hill, and realized that there was a car parked there, alone on this remote hillside, where cars almost never passed. Joey paused for a moment, silently, to watch. Over the years he had learned that waiting, watching, was sometimes useful. He stood in the shadow of a tree, immobile and alert.

After a few minutes a man opened the door of the car, stretched, and stood by the side of the black vehicle to smoke a cigarette. He looked harmless – perhaps a bill collector or an inspector of some kind. Or a plain-clothes policeman. Joey quietly resumed his descent toward his mailbox, and emerged from the driveway onto the black surface of the road. The man saw him and snuffed out his cigarette, clearly indicating that he was there to see Joey. "Morning," he said.

"Can I help you?" Joey said as he continued toward his mailbox.

"Mr. Torino?"

"That's me."

"I have a message for you from Mr. Highsmith."

"Highsmith? He could have called me." Joey took a local newspaper and a couple of bills from his mailbox. He never got any letters.

"He wanted me to contact you personally. I think he wanted you to know it was important."

"Pen Highsmith," said Joey. He made a point of looking at the front page of the local paper, with its headline: "Town Taxes May Rise."

"He wants you to call him as soon as possible. As soon as it's convenient for you, of course. He's in Houston ... in Texas. I can give you the number. He said for you to reverse the charges." The man was clearly uneasy, feeling awkward in this situation. "I drove up from Boston to give you the message ... personally."

"Boston," said Joey.

"Yeah. My office." He was anxious to get back into his car and drive away. "Here's the number. I wrote it on the back of my card, in case you should need to call me." He handed Joey a calling card: "H.R.WILSON, Legal Advice".

Joey took the card and inspected it. "What business are you in, Mr. Wilson?" he asked.

"Legal Advice."

"Are you a lawyer, Mr. Wilson?"

"No."

"I see."

"He just wanted me to see you personally – and to make sure you understood that it was important, urgent. You know Mr. Highsmith!" The man tried to smile, but decided against it, feeling Joey's steady, somehow threatening, gaze.

"Well," he said, I guess I'll be going then … . Long drive back to Boston." He got back into the car. "Can I tell Mr. Highsmith that you'll be calling him?"

Joey nodded slightly.

"Okay, thanks! I'll tell him. I'll call him right away!" He started the engine, gave a kind-of salute out the window, drove off down the narrow road, around the curve, and disappeared. In the silence Joey could hear the car for a few moments, heading toward the main route back into town, to take the highway south to Boston.

Joey slowly turned back toward his house, reflecting silently on what Pen Highsmith might want, why he would be calling … after all this time. Whatever reason he had to call, whatever he wanted, it couldn't be good.

2.

Joey Torino valued his isolation, the woods which surrounded his house, the silence which was only broken by the sounds of the forest, the fact that his nearest neighbor was half a mile away. He appreciated the harsh winter weather and the short summer with its mild temperatures. Above all he welcomed the fact that people left him alone here – he had the company of the birds and a handful of animals which appeared from time to time – and that was all he needed or wanted. He left food for them in the winter, and listened for their sounds whenever he went out walking through the thick forest.

It was the winter, with its white isolation and its many challenges, that he loved the most – that seemingly endless period of short days and long nights, a kind-of natural testing of the human soul. He had spent much of his life among people, in cities and countries – often distant places – and now he felt at home. It was the place he preferred.

Some of his neighbors – the nearest was a mile away – thought he was a bit strange, and it was true that his manner was somewhat forbidding. But Joey had developed his view of life from his experience, and he had come to trust the natural world more than he trusted people. The animals of the forest were his friends. He understood them, and liked to think that they understood him. They knew he was not there to harm them, but just to live, side by side with them, in this wilderness. People, on the other hand, were – sometimes – his enemies. He had learned this over time, the hard way.

Now he reflected on what Pen Highsmith might want. He was not exactly a friend, but Joey knew that Highsmith valued his ... special abilities ... while understanding his attitude toward other people, toward the world, toward life in general. That made him almost unique. The two had been through a number of difficult episodes — not exactly "together," but somehow sharing the same circumstances, concerns, and risks. For better or worse, they knew each other, and to a certain extent they even respected each other.

Those episodes in Russia were long past now — they had occurred years ago. Joey had been asked by Highsmith to take on a difficult mission at that time; he knew that Joey had the "special skills" to carry it out. What else could you call Joey's skills? They were just ... "special skills." Joey knew that, if Highsmith was trying to reach him, it was because of his understanding and appreciation of Joey's ability to take on difficult problems — problems which would be daunting for anyone else.

So Highsmith had a problem — a "special" problem, Joey thought — a very difficult, very "special" — problem. And he was calling to see if Joey could help him. That would be the only reason he would call.

Joey would certainly call Highsmith back, he thought. But ... not right away. He put together a basic back-pack with some things to eat, a sweater and a rain jacket — just the essentials for a hike which would get him back to his house before nightfall. He would call Highsmith then. Anyway, he thought, if he's in Texas it is two or three hours earlier than it is here in Maine.

And on this thought he left on a long walk through the forest, to reflect on the call he would make ... later.

3. Houston

Several hours later, in Houston, Pendleton Highsmith III was in his office, anticipating a call from Joey. Outside it was hot and humid, and Highsmith had turned on the air conditioning in his car as his driver took him to the Wilde Oil Tower, the company's home base, earlier in the day. The Tower was a tall new office building, modern and distinctive, with floor-to-ceiling glass in the executive offices on the top floor, meant to convey a sense of modernity, prosperity and boundless wealth. This was important for the company, intended to give an impression of spectacular on-going profit – for the benefit of analysts, investors and potential competitors. A key element of the company's strategy, and its vision of itself, was to project an image of constant growth and profit – whether or not that was its true situation.

Wilde Oil was a speculative company, risking huge sums of money on distant investments in countries which were – sometimes, and perhaps – less than stable. Many of its drilling projects were sound, but some were not, or they might be marginal – destined to recover only a portion of the company's substantial investments. Returns on these investments, in the risky energy sector, depended on many factors, some of which were technical. But there were other, unforeseen or unmeasurable aspects of Wilde Oil's widespread investments which fluctuated and were unpredictable – technical, moral, political, human, or even ... meteorological.

Following his retirement from the State Department in Washington – as an Ambassador and Under Secretary of State, Highsmith had been recruited by a wealthy college classmate, and a major stock-holder, to become President of Wilde Oil, Inc., the fourth-ranking American oil and gas-producing company, based in Houston and named for its founder, Colonel Hammersmith Wilde. The compensation offered was considerable, and the perks were difficult to resist – residences in Houston and New York, a vacation home on the Caribbean island of St. Barts, travel in a company plane, and virtually unlimited stock options. He took the offer and left Washington behind, just as the Republican Party, with which he was affiliated, lost the Presidency. And he did not look back.

Like so many other senior officials, he was delighted to escape from Washington before being ignominiously replaced as the Under Secretary of State by someone from the "other" political party. He and his wife moved – seemingly happy but with some underlying uneasiness – to Houston. It was the first time they had lived in a city which was not a national capital during Pen Highsmith's long diplomatic career.

And at first his new position was like a vacation – in some hot and humid foreign capital. He presided meetings, met with people, went on speaking tours around the USA or abroad, addressed civic groups, entertained key share-holders, etc. As a former senior diplomat, he could do this sort of work in his sleep.

But – little by little – problems started to appear – both professional and personal. Or perhaps he gradually discovered – or was handed – some problems that he had not known about but had to deal with. One way or another, his work gradually became more serious and challenging. In some, even most, cases these problems were international – one of the reasons why he had been recruited by the Chairman of the company's Board of Directors. Some Board members liked to remind him of this when he was not keen to accept responsibility for dealing with the latest mess – an oil spill problem, a bribery investigation, or a hasty withdrawal of company personnel after a violent coup d'etat in some distant, under-developed hell-hole.

Pen was used to dealing with such a continuing stream of complex "issues" from his days in Washington, and he normally just took the difficult decisions that were required – without focusing too much on the multiple effects of his decisions.

It was only when this latest problem, this frankly troubling new situation, "crossed his desk" that he thought of Joey Torino. This new "issue" involved the Russians, a complicated low-key civil conflict, ancient suspicions and animosities, and a ruthless, relentless enemy, hidden in the mountains – in Afghanistan. And of course it involved monumental investments by the Wilde Oil company – investments which might be put at risk, under certain circumstances, in some situations, and assuming a few possible sets of key developments. There were clear risks, and even potential dangers, which had to be dealt with and surmounted, in a country, in a region, which was complicated and potentially dangerous. So he reached out to Joey Torino.

It was the complexity of this latest problem – in a rugged, distant land – which led him to think of Joey – the low-key, silent but efficient, problem-resolver whose talents he had come to appreciate when he was at the State Department. And the more he thought about it, the more he was convinced that Joey could help him to deal with the latest problem the company had dropped in his lap.

4.

It was late in the afternoon, Houston time, when Joey called Highsmith back. "Mr. Undersecretary? Mr. President?" Joey said, "I'm not quite sure what to call you in your new job." It was already dark in the forests of Maine, and Joey was comfortably installed in front of his fireplace, where a blazing stack of cut logs was slowly warming the room.

"Hello Joey! I'm really delighted to talk to you after all this time. I hope all is well in your world! I sometimes recall with great nostalgia our work together at the State Department, and I hear that you are now happily retired in Maine! Sounds wonderful! I really envy you! Here it is just hot and humid all the time!" He paused, half expecting Joey to say something friendly and responsive, but Torino remained silent, waiting for Highsmith to open the discussion, since he was the one who had initiated the call. It was his way, as Highsmith knew.

"Yes, well, I suppose you are wondering why I'm calling you – out of the blue, so to speak."

"Yes," said Torino, "I was wondering that." He was looking out the window, through the trees, as the last rays of sunset gradually dimmed in the night sky. Darkness was closing down through the Maine forest, and the flames were just now spreading among the logs he had arranged in the fireplace to take the chill out of the air.

"Well," continued Highsmith, "You know how highly I value your ability to deal with problem situations. That is just a fact! So I was wondering whether you might be able to help me with a problem

I face, here in my new life. As you might know I'm working with an oil company here – named Wilde Oil – I suppose you know the company, or at least its gas stations."

"I've seen the signs."

"Well, we need someone with your skills, and I thought of you! I always appreciated your work in the Department – especially that last episode in Russia, in the Caucasus mountains. You did a great job there! You deserved a medal! But I know you preferred to retire and leave the Department altogether, and I respected that."

Highsmith could sense that Joey was not very interested – in virtually anything he might say, or propose. He was a very independent person, and was happy to be out of all the – complications – he had dealt with before opting for early retirement and disappearing up in Maine. But Highsmith was determined to pursue the matter he had called about. When he decided on a course of action, Pen Highsmith was difficult to discourage.

"You could name your price, Joey," he said. "This is the oil business, not the State Department. You might be surprised by the salaries in this line of work." He paused, waiting for some indication of Joey's possible response. When Joey said nothing – that was his style – Highsmith pursued the matter: "We need someone who can deal with a problem in the field, Joey, and I thought of you. Quite simply, you are the best field man I know, and I also know you can be trusted in difficult – sensitive – situations."

There was a pause, and then Joey responded: "Why don't you just tell me what you need, Pen, and then I can give you my response. It would save us both some time. But just remember that

I am very happy with my life here, and I don't really need – or want – a change. I'm sitting by the fire in my house, here in the woods, in Maine, after a great afternoon hike. This is the life I always wanted, and, well, I have it now."

Highsmith thought quickly, and decided to tell Torino the whole story. He was counting on Joey's instinct to step up to a challenge – the more difficult, the more he might be tempted to accept.

"It's a difficult situation, Joey. We are deeply invested in Central Asia, and everything depends on our ability to work in Afghanistan. We need you to help us there."

"Me? In Afghanistan? What could I do in Afghanistan?"

"We want you to go there – as soon as possible – to, well, sort things out."

5. Houston

As soon as Joey stepped out of the plane, he realized that he was in another world – he had arrived in Houston. The temperature was soaring and the humidity hit him like a soft wall. Crowds of determined travelers pushed ahead without much concern for others, and the oppressive air was only slightly relieved by air conditioning. Fans whirred everywhere, slowly rotating to disperse the heat, and even outside terraces were air conditioned. He could only regret the cool, quiet days at his house in Maine.

A car was waiting for him at the exit doors, with a driver waving a sign marked "Wilde Oil," as Joey emerged from the terminal. The driver seemed to recognize him, and Joey nodded in acknowledgement. He sat next to the driver and was immediately driven away through the busy traffic.

"Welcome to Houston!" said the driver with a huge smile. He was a friendly Mexican-American who took pride in his ability to thread his way rapidly among the dense lanes of cars, busses, trucks and trailers. He continued an amiable stream of commentary as Torino fell asleep.

It took an hour to get to the Wilde Oil office building, in an expensive Houston suburb. It was an attractive small sky-scraper of 15 stories, set in its own park by the side of an artificial pond with a fountain rising near the center. The park was filled with shade trees against the local heat, and there were walking paths winding thru it. In the distance Joey could see tennis courts and at least one basketball area. The company encouraged physical fitness for its employees.

The air-conditioned car had permitted him to cool down, and he had slept for about a half hour during the ride. He noted a discreet "Wilde Oil" sign on the lawn as the car pulled up to the main entrance – a huge glassed-in area with no people visible anywhere. Joey was impressed by the expensive, studied calm of this company headquarters – Wilde Oil was an icon of the energy business, famous for its audacity and its risky, but very profitable, investments around the world. As he stepped out of the car he almost staggered in the humid heat, and hesitated as he recovered his breath to move up the expansive steps, through the automatic glass doors and into the vast, empty, air-conditioned lobby.

"Mr. Torino?" came a voice from the other side of the lobby, and Joey nodded in response. "I am Conchita Rivera, Mr. Highsmith's Assistant. I hope you had a pleasant flight. From Boston, I think?" Joey nodded and grunted in response, and followed this young woman toward an elevator, which opened automatically as they approached.

"Have you been to our offices before?" she asked as the elevator doors closed. She seemed to be examining Torino, sizing him up, and her question was a part of this evaluation. Torino understood this, and limited his response accordingly; he disliked being subjected to judgements of any kind.

"No," he replied in a flat voice, which had the effect of terminating the conversation. The two rode in silence to the 12th floor, apparently the last regular floor in the building, but with some sort of roof-top level listed on the elevator's control panel. The doors opened to another vast lobby area, and Conchita Rivera led Joey thru a corridor to the open door of a comfortable reception room. An office door opened as they entered the reception area, and Pendleton Highsmith – former Ambassador and former Under Secretary of State – stood in the doorway to greet his visitor.

"Joey!" he said with exuberant pleasure. "How great to see you! Welcome to Houston! Welcome to Wilde Oil!" Highsmith looked exactly the same as he had when he was the Undersecretary of State, but his entire personality seemed to have changed. He smiled broadly, gesticulated with his hands, and spoke as though an entire audience was listening. He seized Joey's hand and shook it warmly, as Joey marveled at the transformation of the discreet senior government official he remembered from their meetings in Washington.

Highsmith already had his arm across Joey's shoulders and was warmly easing him through the door of his office. Joey could not help having a flashback to his last meeting with Highsmith, at the State Department in Washington. Highsmith had been aloof and disdainful, asking Joey to undertake a difficult and dangerous mission to regain his reputation, tarnished because of a bar fight in Moscow. Torino had been recalled from his posting at the Embassy there, and Highsmith had offered him a dangerous mission to redeem himself. This former senior diplomat had clearly gone through some sort of transformation between his bureaucratic Washington identity and this new persona as a Houston oil baron.

Everything about Pendleton Highsmith had changed – his voice and tan, his facial expressions, his personal style, and of course his clothes. Highsmith would never have worn a light-colored suit to his office in the State Department – in Washington's Foggy Bottom – but here it seemed quite normal among these vast office spaces and freezing air conditioning systems. Even Joey, with his dour, closed-mouth style and generally cold attitude toward virtually everyone, could not help but relax – just a bit – as he tried to focus on learning what was expected of him. He needed to know exactly why Pendleton Highsmith, former Ambassador and former Under Secretary of State, had pressed him to come to Texas, and to help this world-wide energy company with its problems in Afghanistan.

They sat in deeply-cushioned chairs opposite a huge fireplace which was clearly seldom used. After a few moments a waiter brought the drinks they had ordered, along with a bowl of prepared shrimp, fresh from the Gulf of Mexico. Highsmith was clearly enjoying Joey's surprise at seeing his new life-style, his new persona.

"You know," he said when the waiter had left them alone, "I was a bit reluctant to leave Washington when I retired. But, well, this is the oil business, and they can really make it worth your while! It takes some time – but not too long! – to, um, adjust! But when you get used to it, well, it can be very ... comfortable!" He laughed and gazed out the windows toward the distant skyline of central Houston. "Everything has its place in life, you know!"

"Yes, well, I understand your point," said Torino. "But what, exactly, do you want me to do? You said it was important, and that I was the only person you knew who could do it. That's why I came down here. I know I owe you for your help in closing down that business in Russia. So I came. But now I need to understand the problem. To see if I can really help – or – well – or not."

Torino spoke in his soft, slow manner, his voice with its somehow menacing quality, which never seemed to change. Highsmith offered him some shrimp, but Joey declined.

"We have a project in Afghanistan," Highsmith began, pausing to inhale, and exhale, slowly – a kind of exaggerated sigh. "A pipeline. A very long pipeline – from Central Asia to the Indian Ocean. And we need to build it across Afghanistan." He paused to gauge Torino's reaction, but the man sat – immobile and expressionless – waiting for the story to continue.

"There have been some cost overruns," Highsmith continued, "but that is really nothing, in our business – there are always overruns! This is the oil business! You'd be amazed by some of the cost overruns!" He paused. "But now we are being targeted by the local guerillas, and that is a more serious problem! Already five of our employees have been killed! I know that does not sound so huge – after all, this is Afghanistan! But we have shareholders, you understand? And they don't like to see the share price undercut! They don't like problems! They are worried that the whole project might just crash!" He looked Joey in the eye.

"So ... we have to find a solution. We are open to any reasonable solution! But we need to find one soon. Fast! Otherwise we must withdraw, and that would be a big loss for us, after all we have invested in this project."

Joey was surprised by the somewhat emotional tone in Highsmith's voice. It was just a flicker, but Joey could feel it. He recalled the surpassing calm and self-control for which Pen Highsmith had been famous in the State Department. That had been another world, one where the USA dominated, while this was just

... business. Joey knew that no one dominated in Afghanistan – not even the US – and that the risks of doing business there were ... elevated. That could indeed make someone ... nervous, he thought. Even someone like Pendleton Highsmith.

"What is it you want me to do?" asked Joey. "I've been to the region – some time ago – but I don't know the languages, and I'm pretty out-of-date on the situation there." He knew he "owed" Highsmith for helping him to exit the Russian operation without some sort of nasty inquiry, and he was ready to pay off that debt ... up to a point. But he wanted to understand exactly what was expected – and what might be possible – in the complex situation on the ground. Afghanistan was, well, complicated ... to say the least. And there were ... risks.

Highsmith walked to his desk and returned with a rolled-up map, which he spread on the broad coffee-table. He pointed out some of the major points of reference – Kabul, Mazar-e-Sharif, Kandahar, Multan, the Hindu Kush mountain range, and the surrounding geography of the region, including Russia, Iran, Pakistan, China and India. He pointed to the route options for the pipeline, which were different from the possibilities considered for earlier, similar projects. Those had circled along the Western border of the country, whereas this new route would cross more directly from North to South, coming close to the Capital, Kabul. Highsmith noted that one intention was to supply natural gas directly to the Afghan capital – which, he argued, made the project more interesting for the Afghan government. The government would benefit directly from the availability of the gas, and from electricity generated in Kabul.

The cost factors between the possible routes would be similar – on the scale of such a project – but the political advantages of supplying oil and gas to the capital would be considerable. The planned route would also bring oil directly to the center of Pakistan, and would include a pipeline extension to India. This could supply energy directly to key areas, and have a huge economic – and political – impact across the region.

Even though Joey was not an expert on pipelines, he could see the potential interest in this project – not only in bringing energy to the region, but also in promoting common interests and thus – possibly – a more stable, peaceful political situation. But that was in the future; for the moment, there were many problems and very few promising prospects.

When Highsmith had finished his presentation, he waited for Joey to comment. After a few minutes of silence, Joey said, "Looks like a good project to me. But what exactly do you want me to do?"

"Well," said Highsmith, "we want you to go there."

"Yes," said Joey, "I assumed that much. But what do you want me to do there? What are your objectives for my role? What am I supposed to try to do?"

Highsmith paused, seeking the right phraseology. "We want you to explain our plan, present it to the different factions, explain how they will benefit from it, and convince them to accept it – to approve it."

Joey responded immediately: "Why can't you do that? I don't know anything about this business, about pipelines, about oil and gas."

"We want you to do it because we think you will be credible for them, whereas we are certainly not," said Highsmith. "There isn't that much to know, and our experts can explain any technical matters in simple terms. But we need you to convince the Taliban leaders, and we think you will be able to do this, which for sure we are not. We think you can convince them that this will be good for them, for their families, for their children – even for the country.

"We will give you all the support you need, but we want you to be out front, to be the person who talks to them, as a leader for us in this situation. These are people who judge everyone they meet. They judge a person on the basis of their strengths, the confidence they inspire. They are tough, and they only respect people they think are as tough as they are. They only believe people who they think they can trust. We think they will listen to you."

Joey thought about this, wondering what was hidden beneath the surface – what were the real challenges he might face if he accepted this new mission. He knew that Afghanistan was a complicated, dangerous environment, where many foreign efforts had failed because of the determination of the local people to force their departure. "What about the Taliban," Joey asked? "You haven't even mentioned the Taliban! Anyone who follows what is going on in the world knows that you are up against the Taliban out there."

The conversation continued, with Joey asking a broad range of questions, and Highsmith giving him frank, no-nonsense answers. The situation of the pipeline project was not very attractive; on the contrary, it was pretty grim, even dangerous. But Joey also knew that he owed something to Pendleton Highsmith, who had given him the possibility of an honorable early retirement from the State Department, after he was sent home from the embassy in Moscow because of a fist fight in a Russian tavern. Joey knew he owed Highsmith for that gesture, and he was always inclined to pay off his debts.

"Joey," said Highsmith after a pause, "let's go get a drink and something to eat. Houston has some great restaurants, believe it or not – Tex-Mex or anything else you might like. We can talk over some good food! And the temperature even goes down a bit in the evening, so eating outside is almost, well, pleasant." He stood up with a smile. "Let's get a Texan dinner!"

6.

"I did say "almost," didn't I?" Highsmith and Torino were sitting on an outside terrace, under artificial lighting and out-door air conditioning, which Joey had never seen before. He was used to the weather in Maine, and also of course in Moscow – but not to the hot, humid night air of Houston in the summer. Pen Highsmith joked about it, which amused Joey because his style was so completely different from the serious senior civil servant he had known in Washington. This was Pen's retirement persona – part of his new personality as a Houston oil executive.

Joey ordered local fish – fresh from the Gulf of Mexico – a specialty which he always enjoyed with a couple of beers. Highsmith chose filet mignon with a dry Manhattan. Their discussion grew less formal.

"You seem to be enjoying your new life-style, Pen," said Joey.

"I love it," replied Highsmith, thinking to himself that he could not help but love it, with the outrageous salary he was receiving, and the multiple benefits which accompanied it. This year alone his combined income would equal more than ten years of his salary in the State Department. No wonder it was ever more difficult for the Foreign Service to recruit the "best of the best" young people – to enter a career which was, after all, filled with difficult challenges, personal hardships, disruptions, isolation and periods of pure physical danger.

And he was prepared to offer generous compensation to Joey, too – this was the oil business, after all, not the US Government! But he would approach that matter very carefully, because he knew that Joey was scornful of such considerations, and had a very low opinion of people with financial ambitions. He would wait before discussing money.

"But let me tell you something of our Afghan project. We want to build two pipelines – along the same route. One for oil and the other for natural gas. They will go from Central Asia south, across Afghanistan and Pakistan to India and the sea. And they will offer cheap oil and gas for the entire Indian Ocean region, one of the most dynamic future growth areas in the world. It will be one of the biggest projects of its kind – ever. And it will be friendly to the environment, too. We have built that into the project. And it will lift millions of people out of poverty!"

"But there is a very challenging aspect to this project – as there always is, with any worthwhile project. In this case the challenge is called "Afghanistan." Highsmith took a sip of his cocktail. "That is why we need you!"

"I know very little about Afghanistan," said Joey. "I've only been there once."

Pen Highsmith leaned forward toward Joey, as though to say something confidential. "You and I both know that's not true, Joey. You were there some years ago, before you came into the State Department, when you were in Special Ops. Don't forget, I've seen your file – the whole file, not just the unclassified part! You know more about that area than most of our so-called experts do! Many people out there know you from that period. And – most important – you have the temperament for this challenge. This will be a piece of cake for you!" He paused: "Well, maybe not exactly a "piece of cake," but anyway something that you can do better than anyone I can think of." He chuckled, just imagining Joey dealing with the Afghans he would encounter.

Highsmith speared two shrimp, and dunked them in the reddish sauce by the side of the huge bowl. He wiped his forehead with a handkerchief while he bit into one of the shrimp with gusto. He watched for Joey's reactions, but there were none. "The man is super-cool," he thought to himself, "He never reacts visibly to anything! That's why we need him – he is perfect for this challenge"

"That was a long time ago," said Joey. "I'm older now, more mature. My judgement is a lot sounder now than it was then, and my muscles are a lot stiffer. Anyway, why would I want to do it? I live in Maine, and I like it there. I like walking in the woods. I like being left alone."

"Joey," Highsmith replied, "This is the oil business. It's not like the US Government! We can pay you what you deserve!"

But Highsmith knew more than Joey did – he had done his research, his homework. "Also, Page is there," he added softly, watching Joey's eyes. "She is running a clinic for children in Mazar-e-Sharif. It is her clinic – she is the Director." There was hardly a shadow of reaction – Joey never showed his emotions. But there was something, Highsmith thought. Some little flicker ... and he noted it. It would be useful.

He changed the subject, started to talk about Houston, football, the beaches along the Gulf Coast, Washington. Joey grunted, responded from time to time, talked a bit about his life in Maine. He was more responsive than Highsmith had expected, and the dinner was delicious.

Highsmith left the subject of Afghanistan alone, and they talked about other things – the State Department, their past lives as American diplomats, their adventures overseas. These two very different individuals had shared many experiences over the years. They were not exactly friends ... but they were longtime colleagues, and they knew each other better than either one of them would admit.

It was midnight before they finished their dinner – two very different older men with some common past life episodes, and considerable mutual respect.

Highsmith dropped Joey off at his hotel – a high-rise luxury icon, of which there were quite a few in this city. He told Joey he would send a car to pick him up in the morning. They could have a further discussion, and then Joey could decide whether he wanted to join up ... or head back to Maine.

7.

Joey awoke with a start, in the totally dark hotel room. He saw from the dimly-illuminated clock on his night table that it was 3 AM. Instinctively, he froze and did not move. Someone else was there, in the dark, nearby. He sensed a presence and prepared to move. He counted to three, and then sprang – across the bed to the entrance to the room, where he knew there was a light-switch.

He flicked the switch, but it did not work. He grabbed the door-knob and pulled the door open, just as something hard crashed against his head. He stumbled and fell before regaining his balance, while a man slammed against him in the dark, throwing him to the floor. His head hit the night-table by the bed just as the man jumped over him and ran out the door.

Joey was stunned for an instant, but quickly recovered and leaped to the door to look out and down the corridor, but the man was gone, surely down the emergency stairway. He turned on another light in his room and called the front desk.

Within minutes a hotel security officer knocked on Joey's door. He listened to the story and called the main security office to report. A hotel detective and two other security agents arrived, searching the room and taking down Joey's story. They moved Joey to another room and stationed a guard outside his door, while they looked for any evidence or fingerprints.

In the dark outer rim of the hotel parking area a figure quietly slid into the passenger seat of a non-descript car, and was driven away. The car did not turn on its lights.

***

Joey did not sleep again, but lay awake, reviewing this incident and what it might mean. Could this be connected to his meeting and dinner with Pen Highsmith? And if so, how, and why? What connection could there be between Wilde Oil and their project in Afghanistan, and this incident? What was the intruder's intent – to rob? To scare? To kill?

The Houston police were also interested in these same questions. They were waiting to see Joey when he descended to the hotel lobby to look for the breakfast room.

"Mr. Torino?" The man displayed his police identification card. "I'm Detective Juan Osperone, and this is my colleague, Detective Patrick Mahoney. We are looking into the incident of early this morning. Do you have a few minutes?" Torino sat down with the two police inspectors, and asked if they would like a cup of coffee. They accepted and he waved for a waiter, who brought coffee and some small breakfast pastries from the buffet.

"Mr. Torino, we have looked up your background, and our first question to you, as you might expect, is about the purpose of your visit to Houston. What is your business here, and could that business have something to do with this incident?" The detective paused, then continued. "Frankly, it is very unusual to see this sort of an incident in a nice hotel in Houston at three AM in the morning. We see a certain number of hotel thefts here, like any big city, but nothing like this. So our first thought is that it may have something to do with you – your business here, and possibly also your business in general. You seem to have been involved in a number of international ... episodes." He drank some coffee and waited for Joey to respond.

"I only arrived in Houston yesterday," said Joey. "And I don't really have any business in Houston. I live in Maine. I was here to see an old colleague of mine, who is now working with Wilde Oil. His name is Highsmith. You can check with him if you want – he's the President of Wilde Oil. Maybe this guy who was in my room was just a robber, looking for something to rob."

"Yes, that might be the case," said the detective reflectively. "But – frankly – we don't think so." He sipped his coffee again. "That just does not happen here in Houston, at three AM, in one of the city's best hotels." He looked steadily at Joey.

"We think what happened was related to you, to your work, whatever that may be. Or to your past work." He sipped some coffee. "We know about Wilde Oil, about their project relating to Afghanistan. We follow the activities of the major oil companies which are based here, and we are well aware that their projects may provoke protests, or opposition. Here in the US or, well, elsewhere. That seems to us to be more likely than some sort of attempted robbery ... or whatever it was ... in the middle of the night."

The two police officers looked steadily at Joey, waiting to see if he would react, or if he could add something that might be relevant. But Joey had nothing to add, and remained silent. Finally he said that they might want to talk to the people at Wilde Oil. Maybe someone had followed him from his meeting there in the afternoon, thinking he might have something worth robbing. Or

35

maybe the incident had to do with Wilde Oil's work, or their competitors.

The police officers nodded, but were clearly skeptical. They said they would do some research, make some inquiries, and asked when Joey planned to leave Houston. He told them that he would probably leave shortly – today or tomorrow.

The lead officer asked that Joey call them – if anything came up which might be relevant to this incident – at the number on the cards they left on the table.

He added that the Houston police would "keep an eye" on Joey while he was in town, and the two officers left.

Joey had a full hotel breakfast, with scrambled eggs, toast, orange juice and coffee, alone.

8.

"There is something I don't understand," said Joey to Highsmith over lunch. "What, exactly, do you expect of me?" He was back at the Wilde Oil Building, talking again with Highsmith, this time sitting under an awning in the roof-top dining area reserved for senior executives of the company. It was a sunny day and the temperature was already reaching the uncomfortable level, with the usual humidity which made it even worse. Discreet fans kept the area comfortable.

Highsmith was pursuing his objective of the previous day – trying to convince Joey to join the company, to undertake a special mission in Afghanistan, to help the consortium of companies that Wilde Oil had organized to push ahead with their planned pipeline project across Afghanistan. It was a vast project, which envisioned twin pipelines for oil and natural gas, to bring these natural resources from wells in Central Asia to markets in Pakistan, India and beyond. But it had been plagued with security problems from the outset, scaring off some investors and putting the whole project in a more difficult category.

As Highsmith explained, the project had provoked opposition from several groups in the region, and his company, which had organized the investing consortium, was managing a delicate balance. It was trying to convince opposition groups, of which there were many in the country, to accept and even support the pipeline, while containing the rising number of local attacks on the construction work which was now underway, and was advancing slowly across the broad empty spaces along the pipeline route.

There was opposition to the project everywhere – from the Taliban and many other local groups along the pipeline route, to armed opposition forces in the mountains, to political activists wherever the project was pushing forward, and from environmental groups all over the developed world. The Wilde Oil company, which was composed largely of geologists and petroleum engineers – a few of whom had risen to leadership positions – plus its thousands of loyal shareholders – was not equipped to deal with, or even respond to, this opposition, and needed help.

The idea was that Joey would be a sort of "point man" who would visit the regions where opposition was strongest, meet with local leaders, and try to convince them of the benefits which would be gained from the pipeline, for the tribes, the towns, and the peoples who lived along the route. There would be many benefits – jobs, investment in local projects, and energy from local use of the gas to generate electricity or to be burned as a natural fuel for household heat and cooking. New infrastructure would be built as part of the project, such as roads, bridges, schools and hospitals. And there would be an important increase in available jobs for both men and women.

To carry out this assignment Joey would have a team of specialists, plus backup and financial support. Joey would oversee these efforts, ensure their security, and would be expected to personally keep in contact with the many local warlords along the route. He would be expected to gain their respect, and to maintain cordial contacts with them. He would be the company's ambassador to the Afghan warlords! It was a vast and complex challenge, and Highsmith was convinced that Joey was the man to undertake it. He knew Joey's abilities, and was determined to recruit him.

9. New Orleans

The sun was setting in New Orleans, but it was as hot and humid as it had been since dawn. Crowds of tourists were pushing through the streets – with every race, nationality and gender represented in the throngs of casually-dressed visitors. Music – New Orleans jazz, and melancholy blues – was playing loudly from bars and open spaces, with singers using microphones to make themselves heard over the pervasive noise – from the crowds, from the singers, from the jazz.

A man waited in a doorway, watching the passing crowds with visible indifference. He was casually dressed and wore a baseball cap that cast a shadow across his face. He was not a tourist, and did not show any interest in the music which played loudly from doorways and spilled into the side-streets. He watched the faces of the passers-by, looking for the person he was to meet. It was difficult in this crowd, but he was patient, and this was his assignment.

Twice he seemed to recognize someone, but then relaxed when he realized he was mistaken. He seemed somehow foreign, but in this place everyone was foreign – the city was jammed with tourists. From a nearby doorway came the traditional strains of New Orleans jazz – just what these tourists had come to hear, to experience – and the crowds would slow as they walked by, peering into the dark interior and smiling at the familiar songs, played in the local style.

The man took a cigarette from a package he drew from a pocket. He was not nervous, nor was he a regular smoker – he was supposed to take a few puffs from a cigarette to confirm to his contact that everything was okay, that they could meet without a problem. He lit it with a pocket lighter, and puffed a bit nervously; he was not really used to cigarettes.

A dark man wearing a baseball cap walked past him, alone, and a few minutes later passed again, catching the eye of the smoker, who dropped his cigarette, snuffed it out with his foot, and lazily followed the baseball cap. He ambled almost aimlessly, looking about like all the other tourists, as he made his way through the crowd, the music, the jugglers, the laughing couples and costumed locals.

Soon the baseball cap turned a corner into a narrow alley; the smoker followed. A few streets later they entered a small park and sat on a bench, both men scanning the park warily to ensure they were not being watched.

"Salam," said the man who had been waiting in the crowded street.

"Salam aleikum. Please report."

"There is nothing to report. My mission was interrupted. The man woke up."

"What do you mean, he woke up?"

"Just that. He woke up before I could search his things, and pushed me against the wall. He is very strong. I was lucky to get out. No time to search his things."

"We know this man. He is alert and clever. We have dealt with him before. He will not be easy for us."

"What do you want me to do?"

"You must watch him – from a distance. Report where he goes, what his mission is. He is an enemy … . And he is dangerous."

"I will do as you say."

"Call me every two days, on our changing phones. If he travels, you must follow him, or tell me where he goes so I can alert our friends."

"Who is this man?"

"His name is Torino. That is all you need to know."

After a few minutes, one of the two men rose and walked away through the trees. The other sat for twenty minutes by himself, then rose and walked in another direction.

The noise from the crowds was distant in this park, and hardly disturbed the chirping pigeons.

10. Kabul

Joey's plane from Houston arrived in Istanbul at noon. He had a brief stopover, and took the next flight for Dubai, where he spent the night in a hotel near the airport. The next morning he flew from Dubai to Kabul. He was not followed, but it was easy for trackers to learn his destination, and when he passed through customs in Kabul he was followed, as he assumed he would be. He was a careful man and was used to dealing with hostile activities. From the moment he had discovered someone in his hotel room in Houston he had assumed that he would be the subject of hostile surveillance.

In Kabul he was met by a company car – one thing he knew about the oil business was that they were always able to cover expenses, and they assumed that their key officials would prefer to live comfortably. The driver took him to the East-West Hotel, where a comfortable room had been reserved for him. From the moment he stepped off the plane he was alert to possible watchers, and he was not disappointed; he was sure the company car had been followed to the hotel.

11. Foggy Bottom – The State Department

"It's Ambassador Highsmith on line two," said the secretary.

Ambassador Rudolphus looked at the phone and paused a minute before picking it up. What was her predecessor calling about this time, she thought? Could it be about the Chinese pipeline argument? Or the Philippine drilling episode? It seemed like he was calling every day! Actually, he did not call every day, but he had indeed called several times since Elaine Rudolphus had replaced him, following his retirement.

But she was always ready to help him, thinking of her own future and the options she might have for a lucrative onward career following her departure from the Government. Administrations were always changing in Washington, and it was best to have some options available when the time came to leave. She considered Pen Highsmith, her predecessor in her current position, to be a potentially valuable asset for possible post-State Department employment options.

"Hello Pen," she almost shouted into the phone. "How are things in Houston? Warm? I saw the weather report this morning, and it looks like you guys are having even more of a heat wave than we are!" She tapped her long nails on the desk-top, an old habit, while she quickly ran thru, mentally, the issues Highsmith might be calling about. There were several – an oil drilling problem in Central Asia, a grand-daughter trying to get into Harvard, some advice he had wanted on a possible investment option ... .

"Hello Madam Undersecretary! Hello Elaine," came Pendleton Highsmith's booming voice over the phone. "Wonderful to hear your voice." He always started with some implied compliment, and only got to the point after some time had passed. It was impossible to find a short-cut thru this routine, she thought, so she just listened, grunting or laughing occasionally to ensure that he knew she was still there. One had to listen, she thought, to be sure that one laughed at the right moment, when the other person had actually said something he thought was funny. The worst error in any conversation was to laugh at the wrong time!

At a certain point she realized that Highsmith had finished his friendly greetings, and was actually talking seriously about something which concerned him. She tuned in more carefully, but could not immediately grasp what the subject was. There were so many subjects these days, she reflected, briefly, then realized that he was referring to something in Afghanistan, and the whole story of his oil company and their proposed pipeline project came into her focus. So he was calling about his pipeline project, in Afghanistan!

"…. and you cannot imagine how complicated it has become," he was saying. "These people make the Russians look simple!" And he laughed again.

"So why don't you just invite them over," said the Undersecretary, on the spur of the moment. "It's always better to meet people face-to-face, you know! Get to know each other! Build trust! You know how to do that better than anyone, Pen!"

"You mean invite them here?" Highsmith asked. "To Texas?"

"Well, yes! Why not? Have they ever been there? I don't suppose so. Just imagine how impressed they will be with all your, uh —

whatever it is you have, there in Texas – oil wells, I suppose. Show them your oil wells!"

Highsmith was silent for a moment, considering this idea. "Well, maybe, we'll see. But for the moment I just wanted to let you know that we have sent Joey over there to see what he can do. Just so you know. You could tell the Embassy."

"Joe who?" asked the Undersecretary.

"Joey Torino," said Highsmith. "You remember him – went up into the mountains, in the Caucasus. A couple of years ago. Looking for that young diplomat of yours, who got lost. Or whatever ... I never was too clear on the details. Anyway, I have hired him – Joey – to go to Afghanistan for us. To see what he can do there."

"Well, that sounds excellent, Pen, really excellent! I have made a note of it."

"In case there might be any fuss about it," said Highsmith. "You never know. Things are getting a bit tighter there, so you never know."

"Right. Well, thanks for informing us." She made a note on her daily schedule, which was open on her desk: "Talk to Emerson." Emerson Todd was the Assistant Secretary of State for South Asia. "And thanks for calling. I hope everything is fine in Houston!"

After some final goodbyes, she hung up the phone, wondering what that was all about, and pressed the buzzer on her desk, signaling to her secretary that she was ready for her next appointment.

12. Herat

The old man left his slippers by the side of the entrance, as he always did. He washed his hands and feet at the flowing fountain, and humbly entered the holy building. He never sought a prominent place, but found a modest corner where he could pray and meditate alone. It was cold, with the north wind sweeping through the building's open doorways and its many windows, high in the ancient walls.

He chose an open space and knelt. Facing in the direction of Mecca, he prostrated himself on his shabby rug, reciting the ancient verses, asking for forgiveness and redemption. He bowed his head multiple times to outwardly reflect his humble request for Allah's forgiveness. As he mumbled the familiar phrases tears ran from his eyes. He was a believer, and followed this same ritual every day at this hour, on his way home from his job as an entrance guard. Every building in the city had a guard at the main gate. It was necessary to ensure some level of security. Bombings or street attacks were frequent.

When he had completed his daily ritual, he rose and turned toward the vast entrance area of the Great Mosque, carrying his rolled-up carpet. After a few steps he was joined by another man, of a similar age, and they walked together in silence. Outside they recovered their sandals and walked away from the Mosque together.

"Salam, brother Muhammed," said the other man, "Peace be upon you." Muhammed answered with the ritual response, and added, "What news do you have?"

The two men walked slowly across the vast open square together, as pigeons flew in every direction. The sun was setting behind the ancient buildings of the city. The muezzin started his chanting from the highest minaret of the mosque. Across the square people stopped, and many knelt, facing in the direction of Mecca. It was the solemn moment of sunset, as shadows stretched across the open area in front of the mosque. Everywhere people stopped and faced toward the sacred city. The two men mumbled their usual prayers, and after a few minutes continued walking.

"I bring you news," said the other man. The older man responded with a nod of his head, and the other man continued. "The American infidels will send a new representative, who they think will be more able to talk and reason with our people. He will try to talk to us, to convince us that their project is acceptable to Allah. We do not know this man, but our brothers say he is very single-minded, and very strong. They say he is very determined and that he knows our ways."

The two men were walking slowly across the great open square before the ancient mosque. Pigeons rose in clusters and flew off in front of them as they advanced thru the cold evening air. It was getting dark now, and there were few lights in the broad square; it was the ancient tradition.

The old man thought with a slow – a kind of burning – look in his eyes. After a few minutes he responded: "I will meet this man, if that is what he wants. I want to know what these people are seeking in our land. Then we will see." He paused. "We will meet him ... in Kandahar."

He walked away in a different direction, leaving the younger man alone in the darkening square. He stood in quiet reflection for a few minutes, watching his elder slowly limping toward one of the many dark street openings which led into the surrounding city. When the old man had disappeared into the shadows, the younger one turned and walked rapidly off in another direction.

As he walked he covered his face with his headcloth and bowed his head against the shuddering wind. It was a wintry evening, and the muezzin began his last chant, echoing from the minarets across the square, the city, and the darkened country fields. It was the same somber ritual throughout the vast Moslem world, from the North African deserts to the Middle East and the Caspian Sea, to the cold, mountainous regions of Central Asia.

Soon the square began to empty as the crowded mosque completed its evening prayers and worshippers left to return to their modest homes. The lights near the mosque were dimmed as the evening faded into darkness. And shortly only the muffled sounds of the city echoed quietly through the narrow streets, as the moonless night settled across the silent, sleeping country.

13. Kabul

Joey was awoken at dawn by the chanting of the muezzin. It was a powerful, amplified voice from a nearby minaret, and there were other, more distant voices from all the mosques across the city of Kabul – the ancient daily ritual of the Moslem world.

He opened the curtains and the window of his room to hear these multiple chants better, especially the deep, ringing voice from the nearest mosque, with its flat resonances and abrupt, breathless endings. He was not a Moslem, but he always found this daily ritual moving and humbling – it made him feel strangely at home in this distant part of the world.

He made his way down to the breakfast room, which was filled with foreigners, poured himself a cup of coffee and found a seat at a vacant table. There was a broad mix of languages and national appearances across the room, but these men – the people at these tables were almost all men – looked strangely similar. This was despite the clear differences in the way they dressed, their haircuts, and their personal styles. There were Americans and Europeans of course, but also Asians – from Pakistan, India, China and Japan. And there were some whose nationalities – even their geographic origins – were not so obvious, plus a few who were definitely suspicious-looking.

But Joey was used to such multi-national places, and could guess the national origin of most people within a few minutes. He had spent much of his life in countries with other cultures, among people whose languages he did not fully understand.

The man he was expecting to meet was not there, at least not yet. A waiter brought a menu, which Joey studied while he looked around more carefully. He ordered a soft-boiled egg and toast.

The crowded breakfast room emptied slowly, and soon the waiters had cleared half of the tables. A man entered the room alone, looked around, and came directly toward Joey's table. "Mr. Torino?" he asked quietly, standing directly opposite Joey, who nodded and gave a slight hand motion signaling that he should sit down. "I am so very sorry to be late. There was a bomb near my house, and the traffic is very confused. I hope your travel was good." Joey nodded and said that his trip had been fine.

The man gave him a business card showing his name as "Mohamed Abdul Azeem, Businessman," and said he was called Azeem. "I am working with the Wilde Oil office here, and I will assist you in any way I can. We are very happy that you have arrived so safely, and we will do our best to be sure you have everything you need." Joey said he was happy to be in Kabul and looking forward to meeting the Wilde Oil team.

After a few minutes Azeem suggested that they go in his car to the Wilde Oil offices, where the staff would be pleased to welcome Joey, and to provide a briefing on the current status of their pipeline project.

Joey and Azeem drove together across the city, thru streets crowded with people, cars, bicycles, wagons, children, mules and other domestic animals. There were street vendors everywhere, and tiny shops lined the streets, with their patrons shouting to announce the goods they had available for sale.

Finally the car pulled up to a tall, un-marked iron-work gate, with several armed guards both inside and outside the closed entrance. Azeem brought down his window and shouted to the guards, who opened the gate and let his car enter, drawing the stares of all the people in the street. Inside was a large courtyard in front of an ornate small office building which had seen better days. Azeem parked in front of the unmarked main entrance, and Joey got out to look around.

"So this is your headquarters here in Kabul?" he asked Azeem.

"Yes, is very nice, no? Was embassy of Cuba, but now they change."

Azeem motioned, suggesting that Joey enter, just as the main door was opened from inside and Joey stepped into an elaborate entrance hall, with a high ceiling, a dark staircase, and a gloomy overall feeling. The Wilde Oil company logo was displayed on the wall opposite the stairway, along with a large photo of Emerson Wilde, the founder of the company, taken about 1900, with his long sideburns and white hair – the only visible embellishment in the vast entrance area.

A man in shirtsleeves came rapidly down the stairs, smiling and holding his hand out to greet the visitor. "Hello, hello, hello! Welcome to Kabul! You must be Mr. Toroni! Great to have you here! At Wilde Oil H-Q Afghanistan!" He vigorously shook Joey's extended hand. "We have been looking forward to meeting you! Heard a lot about you! All good, of course!" He tried a couple of artificial laughs, but quickly moved on.

"How was your trip? Long, I'll bet! Always is. Especially from Houston! How was it in Houston? We're all from Houston, here! Can't wait to go back!"

"That's Torino," said Joey. "I was only there for a couple of days. It was hot."

"Oh! Forgot to introduce myself. I'm Max – Max Anders. I'm the Project Manager here. For the pipeline project. I'm really glad you've come on board," he said, with feeling, still shaking Joey's hand. "We can really use your advice, your contribution. It's a challenging situation, I'm sure they've told you, in Houston." He raised his eyebrows and gave a tentative smile, sizing Joey up.

But Joey, as usual, was difficult to judge. He said little, coolly looking around at the entrance space, with its company logo, high ceiling and dark stairway. Joey tended to sense a place, just as he sensed the woods, in Maine, before judging what it might hold, what surprises might be waiting.

"Well, I can't really say I'm glad to be here," said Joey. "But Mr. Highsmith asked me to come, to give him my views on your - uh - situation. He's a former colleague, so I agreed to look things over. I won't be here very long – just want to look around a bit." He paused. "And I apologize in advance if I take up some of your time. I'll try to keep that to a minimum."

"We are at your disposal," said Anders. "I thought we could give you a little briefing this morning, and then visit a work-site this afternoon, to give you a sort of overview of what we are doing – the state of play. Then tomorrow we can meet some of the people who are involved with us." Joey gave a slight nod, and the

Project Manager motioned toward the stairs. "Our conference room is up one. Sorry, we don't have elevators here!"

"This place used to be an embassy – I forget which country. Somebody here will remember. I'm not too good on history!" At the top of the stairs they entered a large space which had been converted into a modern conference room, with bright neon lights overhead, a screen for projecting slides, and a large office table, surrounded by executive-style chairs. Several men and one woman were already there, waiting, and stood up to greet the visitor. Joey walked around the table, shaking hands with these people, the senior staff of the Wilde Oil team in Afghanistan – the site of the company's most complicated and ambitious project – its largest investment, world-wide.

When Joey had greeted everyone, they sat down, and Anders, the Project Manager, introduced Joey, as an "experienced international advisor," and then asked the others to introduce themselves, one-by-one around the long table.

The local team started into the briefing, using charts and maps to show the route of their planned pipeline, mixed with photos of towns and cities near the route, which would benefit from the project, either through the availability of new jobs related to the pipeline, or because of the supply of natural gas and the electric power which the pipeline would ultimately generate. There were also charts displaying the numbers of jobs the project would offer locally, the numbers of homes which would have access to electricity, the company's local aid program, which was directed to help the towns and villages near the route of the pipeline, along with a time-line diagram displaying expected dates for the numerous steps in the construction process.

Joey asked questions as the briefing proceeded – on some technical points, about the attitudes of the local population toward the project, and about potential opposition groups and local acceptance or hostility. The discussion was animated and professional, but also candid – the many problems were highlighted and discussed, openly and professionally. These were experienced pipeline construction specialists or petroleum engineers, who had successfully carried out similar projects in other difficult parts of the world.

But Joey noted an undertone of caution – these experts were practical people, oil and natural gas specialists with broad international experience who focused on the engineering challenges of their work. And it was also clear that, with long years in the energy business, in many locations around the world, they had learned to expect the unexpected. They understood that there were elements in this project which were not technical, and which were therefor beyond their ability to plan for, to analyze, and to take fully into account. They were engineers, and they knew that the project was going to be subject to factors which they had not included in their planning, could not predict or control, and which would ultimately be determining for their work.

There was a coffee break in the briefing, and Joey took a big cup – black, no sugar – and walked to a window which looked out toward the street. From this distance he could see crowds of people passing – in traditional robes and western suits, or sometimes a combination of the two. There were women who were completely covered, with only their eyes showing, between a black shawl which covered the head down to the eyebrows and a black veil which rested on the bridge of the nose and hung down to the neck, with a long, shapeless black robe hanging down to the feet. But there were also some who were only partially covered, and a few who wore Western clothing.

The men also wore clothes which ranged from traditional to Western, with most outfits falling somewhere in between. About half the men wore traditional beards, while others wore only a mustache, or a mustache plus a small beard, or even just the beginning of a beard – the result of not having shaved for several days. And there were a number of people who were clearly Westerners, seemingly at home in this crowded street.

The general appearance of these people was a mix of Western and traditional dress, and of the continuing separation between competing religious and cultural currents. The country was a true meeting-ground, where there was a broad and public face-off between East and West, between history and the modern world.

Joey recalled his previous period in Kabul – years earlier, when he was an aspiring geologist on a research project, the profession he had given up to join the American diplomatic service. The place had changed considerably, but he could recognize the basic elements – the city, the habits of the people, the clothing they wore, elements of the limited vocabulary he had mastered at that time, the mix of local and Western elements. He felt a certain nostalgia, and sympathy for the people he had come to know, the hard life they led and their demanding personal discipline.

"Ready to get involved with our project?" asked one of the leaders of the local staff, who had approached Joey at the window. "It's not everyone's favorite assignment."

"Yes," said Joey, "I can imagine that." He turned to face the questioner, and realized the man's face was familiar. "Haven't we met before?" he asked.

"Two years ago, very briefly, in Moscow. I was with the Embassy then. I sat in on one of your meetings there." He held out his hand, "Josh Mills," he said, introducing himself. I'm supposed to be the political advisor in this Wilde Oil team, but understanding the politics in this place is a real challenge, so I can't really say that I have a clear understanding of everything that's going on. But we're all very pleased to see you here. We need some help keeping this project moving. It's not in good shape."

Joey shook hands with this man, sizing him up and thinking he might be a useful colleague. He was surely aware of Joey's somewhat unorthodox way of dealing with problems, which could be helpful.

"I recall our meeting – in Moscow, as you say. When we had a few problems with the Russians. How did you wind up here? Aren't you with the Government anymore?"

"No. I got fed up and thought that if I was going to do risky work, I might as well get paid for risky work. So here I am, working for Wilde Oil! It's not bad, and the pay is much better!" He smiled and gave a kind of shrug of his shoulders.

14.

The Project Manager started to organize the "site visit" he had announced, which would be carried out in two armored jeeps, with a security escort. The four people who would go included Joey, Max Anders, Josh Mills and the company's local security chief. They would be split between the two armored jeeps, and would have a security escort. This was the routine of life in Kabul, and in the surrounding countryside.

Joey was escorted to the courtyard, where the party assembled in armored jeeps marked discreetly with the company logo. Joey was placed in the first car, with Anders and Mills, plus an armed security guard in the front passenger seat. When they were ready the gate was opened, pedestrians were halted, and the convoy drove out into the street, where they were surrounded by four armed Afghan police officers on motorcycles.

They drove quickly, with the police escort officers pressing the crowds to open a pathway for the jeeps, and soon they had left the suburbs of Kabul and were driving fast through the arid countryside and up into the nearby mountains. There were few buildings, and only scattered vehicles, with numerous Afghans walking by the side of the road.

After only twenty minutes the convoy started up some foothills toward the mountains which surround the capital. The straight road became a continuously rising set of curves, doubling back and rounding steep turnings through the foot hills, driving toward the distant snow-capped peaks. The stream of people walking along the roadside dwindled until there were almost none.

They passed a peak, followed a steep turn, and there, below them, was a broad depression in the mountains which extended well beyond the local area and out of sight through the nearby landscape. Ahead they could see vehicles, machinery and workers, and a vast construction line stretching off to the north. Nearby was a kind of tent city, with smoke rising through smokestacks, and numerous vehicles and mobile machinery, in use or parked. It was a vast, living construction site, where the huge sections of pipe, each one a meter in diameter, were being welded together and gradually lowered into the deep trench, in one long tube.

Further away it was possible to see bulldozers slowly covering the pipe, two meters below the surrounding land surface. And off into the distance was the line of freshly-bulldozed earth, where the pipe had already been buried two meters under the surface of the land. It was a vast operation, focused on the newest length of tubing, the welding and burying of each newly-joined section of steel pipe as it was attached, inspected, buried in the trench, and became part of the monumental pipeline, stretching off to the North, to Central Asia.

Joey had never seen such a huge construction site, even more striking to see here because it was isolated among these barren mountains, far from any city or village, and was visibly growing as it pushed forward slowly across this empty region. He could not help but be impressed by the vast project, which was clearly monumental in its conception and its dimensions. As he knew from the briefings he had received in Houston, this pipeline would eventually stretch more than a thousand kilometers, from Central Asia to the Indian Ocean.

The vehicles stopped on a promontory and Joey stepped out to listen to a short briefing on the work they were seeing below. The group gathered while the specifics of the project were explained for Joey's benefit. He asked a few questions as he took it all in – the terrain, the isolation of the project, surrounded by mountains, its monumental scale and its visionary objectives, and the numerous workers participating in the pipe-laying activity. And he reflected on what he could imagine must be the reactions of the isolated people who had inhabited this region for hundreds of years – and considered it their own – to this strange intrusion into the region which was their homeland.

The convoy descended slowly down a steep mountain road to the worksite, where they got a closer look at the deep trench which was being dug across the landscape, and the huge joining, welding and lowering operations that were being carried out as the project moved ahead. It was a colossal undertaking, and Joey, the eternal skeptic, could not help but be impressed. The workers were a mix of Afghans, Pakistanis, Uzbeks and Tajiks, and other nationalities from the region. The supervisors were also an international mix – oil industry men who had worked in multiple places around the world. For them the ground was just that, and they were not concerned with who owned it, nor the history of this region; it was just rock, sand and earth, in a remote and uninhabited area, where they were laying down another long pipeline.

15.

By the time the convoy started back toward Kabul, it was late, and the sun was setting over distant mountains to the West. The day disappeared quickly; suddenly night had fallen and darkness engulfed the landscape. Headlights were turned on, and the vehicles had to drive more slowly on these simple roads.

At several points they were stopped by police barricades, where the vehicles were inspected and each person had to show their identification. But the last stretch was a semi-modern highway, and they were able to accelerate as they approached Kabul, despite the people walking, alone or in groups, away from the city toward their villages in the surrounding hills. It was a colorful procession of both men and women, carrying large packages balanced on their heads, thru the intense darkness and under a night sky crowded with stars.

The two project leaders, Max Anders and Josh Mills, invited Joey to a late dinner in a small restaurant where they were regular clients. This was the moment for more informal discussion, for a frank presentation of the situation of their project, and of their concerns, stimulated by a couple of glasses of imported beer.

"Well," said Joey, "I'm really impressed! It is a huge project, and seems well organized. Frankly I did not expect to see such a huge project being carried out in such an organized and determined way." His two hosts remained silent, clearly wanting to make some comment, but hesitant to do so. Joey felt this, and wanted to hear their candid thoughts and feelings.

"But what I really want to hear is what you have on your minds," he said. "I know there are problems, and concerns. That's why your President, Mr. Highsmith, sent me here. I'm an independent voice – an outsider. And I want to know what you really think. I deliberately came here alone, and now there are just the three of us, sitting around this table, so I'd like to hear your frank thoughts, your real opinions. What are the problems here, as you see them?"

There was still a long silence, with the two managers focused on their drinks. Finally, Max Anders, the project manager, started to speak, hesitantly. "There is something in the air here," he said. "I cannot put my finger on it, but it is there, and it is only a matter of time before we will face it – whatever "it" is." He took a sip from his drink. "And when it starts it will overwhelm us all."

He gave Joey a hard look. "You are an outsider," he said. "Of course we know you by reputation. You have surely seen difficult situations, violent episodes. We have not. We are engineers, technicians, welders, bulldozer operators. But we are not fighters. And most of us have families, not here of course, but waiting for us in Texas or somewhere else. We work here because we need the money, for our families. The energy industry is the only thing we know, and we are lucky to have work. And our work is here." He stopped, took a long drink from his glass, and looked down at the table.

The other man, Josh Mills, picked up where Anders had left off. "I will be more specific, if you don't mind. Sooner or later," he said, "the Taliban will attack us. We know this. But we do not know when, or where, or how. We know they are watching us do our work, waiting for what they think is the right moment, before they attack. And meanwhile we are just working, waiting. It is very difficult for us.

"They do not understand our position, our feelings – the people in Houston," he continued. "And anyway, they are heavily invested, and can do nothing but continue the work, continue the project, while we are out here in the field. We are the ones who are exposed, and when the time comes, we will be the targets. Sooner or later we know we will be attacked." He looked at his drink, nervously turning it as he spoke.

Joey listened in silence. He had been well aware, even before coming here, that this was the situation. It could not be otherwise. He had seen it himself, in similar circumstances. This was why Highsmith had recruited him and sent him to this distant place, to understand the situation and to identify possible solutions. But listening to these men talk, describing the situation of their project, he could not help sharing their anxiety, their sense of frustration and despair. What could be done in this situation? They were on a collision course with the Taliban – building a modern structure which challenged their historic rights, in their own lands.

Joey understood the situation well: sooner or later the people here would move against the Wilde Oil project – they were people whose leaders hung obstinately to the past, who wanted nothing to do with the modern world outside their borders, and who would never accept a foreign project that would intrude into their own lands, and upset their traditional world, their simple society, their way of living. Afghanistan was their country, and Joey himself felt a broad sympathy for these people, clinging to their traditional lives in the face of the modern, and foreign, challenges that were intruding. He was wondering what could be the objectives of his mission in this situation? What he could do ... what should he do ... here in Afghanistan, in carrying out the mandate he had been given.

Torino walked alone the short distance back to his hotel, thru the empty night streets of Kabul, against all the established rules for foreigners. He wanted to feel the city, to take its pulse at midnight, to understand it, and also ... to make his presence known.

16. Mazar-e-Sharif

Page Wheatley opened her office early, as she did every morning. There was so much work to be done that she always needed the extra time. She lived in the clinic, which saved a lot of time – it would have been impossible to live somewhere else and do her work effectively.

Today there would be at least three cremations, and one burial – a typical ratio – there were never burials if the child had no known relatives. Unfortunately most of the children in "her" clinic had none – they were either abandoned or their parents could not be found. That was the situation in "her" city, where she had found this clinic, in need of a manager. It was in Mazar-e-Sharif – near the northern border of the country, deep in Central Asia.

It was the violent on-going terrorism, the ruthless, sporadic fighting, and the uncertainty of all aspects of life which produced this continuing tragedy. The situation in Afghanistan had been the same for years, and would surely continue for many more. The few clinics like this one, which was only for children, were scattered around the country, and they were all very busy. There were not enough places to care for all the children who were alone and needed help.

She spent the early morning bringing the paperwork up-to-date. Deaths had to be certified and recorded, and new arrivals identified – when this was possible.

Often small children could not easily identify themselves, and then the clinic's registration office had to conduct some research

– with medical offices, schools and mosques near the place where the child had been found, in their effort to identify them.

But many children could never be fully identified, or it was determined by the local authorities that their immediate family had been killed, officially making them – at least tentatively – orphans. Page hated that determination, and worked hard to avoid it in "her" clinic. In her three years in Afghanistan she had registered "only" thirty-six orphans, with many other children returned to their nearest relatives. Page considered that her biggest achievement, her sad achievement.

Some orphans had been adopted, but twenty-two remained at the clinic – some because of the on-going treatment they needed, and the others simply as "homeless" children. This was the saddest and most tragic result of the war, which had continued sporadically for decades. No one knew when it would end, or how it would end.

Yes, it was a "sporadic" war – if seen from a distance. But seen "up close" it was often simply sudden, violent, and disastrous for the people involved, and many of the victims were children. Some of these small victims were long-term patients at Page's clinic – learning to overcome handicaps, with or without family support, while at the same time learning to read and write. Learning to live, sometimes handicapped and alone.

There was a knock on her office door, which was open. She looked up to see her assistant and friend, Aiea. She smiled, and the teenager came into her office, shyly, lowering the scarf which had covered her face. Page motioned for the girl to sit down at the desk, opposite her, which she did, and Page realized that she had something she wanted to say. "What is it Aiea? Do you want to tell me something?"

"There is an American who has arrived in Kabul," said the girl. "It is my friends there who have told me."

"There are Americans arriving in Kabul every day," said Page. "Too many Americans, if you ask me. How can Afghanistan be itself with so many Americans coming here?"

The girl was not deterred by this comment; she knew her boss well. And she had heard the stories about her past career, her involvement in an adventurous undertaking in the Caucasus mountains, and her decision to come to Afghanistan with a private organization to run the center for children, here in Mazar-e-Sharif. "I think you know this American," she said.

Page looked up at Aiea, surprised and curious, wondering what she had to say, what she meant, what she knew. She was well aware that the local people she dealt with every day had learned about her background, the story of her involvement in that episode in the Caucasus mountains. The Afghans were always curious about Westerners who came to work in their country, and there had been a lot of international press interest in that past episode – the strange disappearance of an American diplomat in the Caucasus mountains, and the efforts to locate him. Page now wondered what the girl had to tell her.

"It is him," said Aiea. "Who?" said Page. "What are you talking about?" She was annoyed. What gossip had this young girl heard, what did she know, what was she saying?

"It is the man called Torino. He has come to Afghanistan. He is in Kabul." Page felt her face going red with embarrassment, in front of this young girl who worked for her. How would she even know this name? No one here had ever referred to her connection with that old story, that adventure when she was stationed in Moscow. And what did it mean that Joey Torino might be in Kabul – here in Afghanistan! She had come here to get away from all that – the stories in the press, the speculation, the gossip. How would this young girl know about all that? Could it be that the stories from that long-ago episode had followed her here? All the way to Afghanistan?

Aiea was unhappy now – she had thought her boss would be interested in this news, would like to know that this man had arrived in Afghanistan. But now she saw that this was unpleasant news for Page, and that made her unhappy too.

She tried to change the subject, to talk about the work they would do today, their normal routine. She shrugged off Page's questions, said she knew nothing about the matter, that it was just a local story. And she made the first possible excuse to leave the office – to do some other work which was urgent and needed doing.

When she was alone, Page reflected on what the girl had said. Joey, in Afghanistan? What did this mean, and why would he be here? She had thought that he was at his house in Maine, and probably would never leave it. She knew that he valued his privacy and was determined to stay away from Washington, from overseas adventures, and from the kind of episodes he had been involved in when she had first met him – in Moscow and then in the Caucasus mountains. Why would Joey Torino be in Afghanistan?

17. Kabul

Joey met again with the project leaders the following morning, in the main conference room at the Wilde Oil office building in the center of Kabul. This was to be a briefing on the potential threats to the pipeline project, and the measures which had been put in place to counter these threats – the subject which was of most interest for Joey, since it was the basic reason that Highsmith had recruited him and sent him to Afghanistan.

The company had several advisors and contact men who were responsible for overall project security, and another set of specialists who were advisors on the local political situation – the persons who were important, or less important, in the different regions, cities, towns and settlements which were on the planned route of the pipeline, or near it. Most of this group were Afghans, who were from the districts or towns near the pipeline route, and had been recruited because of their knowledge of these places and regions – the local areas which would be most affected by the construction project, and by the on-going presence of the pipeline. They advised on which leading personalities in their regions might be helpful and influential in explaining the company's plans to the local people.

Joey greeted and shook hands with all these men – they were all men – looking them straight in the eyes and touching his heart when they were introduced, and offering a greeting in Dari or Pashtu. From his earlier time in the region, he knew enough words in these languages to be able to handle such situations, and his use of familiar phrases brought smiles and nods of appreciation from these Afghan employees of the Wilde Oil company.

Today the briefing and discussion was about the local areas which the pipeline would pass thru as it crossed Afghanistan, and the ways in which Wilde Oil had tried to create positive relations with each of the villages and tribes along the pipeline route. In each case there were local issues and considerations – key personalities, traditions, places and areas which were important for grazing animals or planting crops. These had to be respected to the extent possible, and any damage done had to be repaired. There were many locally-focused efforts to win the understanding of the population, including explaining the benefits of the project, which would ultimately provide electric power in these remote regions, to be used for lighting and heat.

The Wilde Oil company was trying to find ways to offer these – and other – benefits directly to the people who lived along the pipeline route, as an incentive for them to view the project favorably. Many local men, and some women, were also hired and trained for the broad range of jobs which surrounded the project, and some of these jobs would continue after the pipeline was complete.

But the people along the pipeline route were basically mountain people, living in small, remote villages, and they were suspicious of outsiders – especially foreigners. They had little understanding of the benefits they might gain from this monumental project, and were suspicious and afraid of its intrusion into their lives, their families, their traditions. There was a huge gap of understanding, and Wilde Oil had little experience in such matters. Also, there were a few determined groups and nascent organizations which were fiercely opposed to the pipeline project, and were determined to stop it.

There was a detailed briefing for Joey on the different cultures, nationalities and languages in the areas the company was working in, or would work in, as the pipeline project advanced. This was followed by a description of the Wilde Oil programs to assist the communities along the pipeline route – schooling projects and educational opportunities, medical and housing assistance, job skills training and general assistance in housing and agricultural efforts. The presenters recalled that Afghanistan is mountainous and arid; that agriculture and maintenance of livestock are both difficult in the dry and dusty terrain. And they also explained the delicate subject of education – for all children, but especially for girls, which was opposed as a matter of principle by many Afghan groups.

Of course some improvements were possible, but traditions were strong and outsiders were viewed with great suspicion; this made schooling and training difficult. The ageless dictates were followed: boys were taught to read the Koran – to memorize it – and girls were prepared for early marriage and motherhood, in village structures which were tightly bound by tradition. This timeless way of life was slowly evolving, but the evolution was mainly in the cities; outside the urban areas the age-old customs were still followed – and were strongly enforced by the structures of the villages and families.

Joey knew most of this, but it was always useful to be up-dated.
He had spent time here before, and knew the social structures and the traditions of the Afghan people. He even spoke some Dari, which was at least understood in most of the country.
More importantly, he needed to understand where these new colleagues of his stood in relation to the local customs and society. One of the basic guidelines for foreigners in any country, Joey

believed, is to understand and respect the local customs and traditions. This was the most basic, normal rule. So he wanted to understand what the Wilde Oil team was doing, and how it was handling these delicate issues.

The meeting turned to more specific information – the current state of the company's pipeline project, and the growing hostility to it in some areas of the country. The sources of the opposition were multiple, and were based on the suspicions of those who favored rigid adherence to local traditions. There was a sweeping resistance to foreigners seeking to alter or supplant local habits and customs, or encouraging – even imposing – another way of life. Those who favored a more modern way of life for the country were in a minority – at least outside of the main cities. A majority of the population favored the maintenance of, or at least respect for, Afghan traditions, and resisted changes which were viewed as western, and foreign.

Toward the end of the morning the meeting adjourned, and several of the senior management team invited Joey to lunch. The restaurant was only one street away, so the group decided to walk. They emerged through the gated entrance to the building together, and struggled against the usual thick crowd of passing Afghans which seemed determined to block their way.

Without warning, what seemed like a scream sounded from across the street, and the crowd tried to push back, with at least two people losing their balance and falling roughly to the pavement. There was a flash and a thunderous explosion, seemingly on the other side of the street from the Wilde Oil offices.

People began to run in all directions, away from the explosion, with a few standing in place and straining to see what had happened. There were shouts, and police officers in uniform came running from several nearby posts, some with their automatic pistols drawn. A siren could be heard, coming closer. Two people lay by the side of the street, in front of a doorway, where smoke was rising from the pavement.

Joey ran to the site of the explosion, but was pushed away by a policeman. A man's body lay on the ground, his clothes partly burned, with blood everywhere – spattered on a nearby wall, over his face, and in a puddle under his knees, already draining into the gutter.

Joey did not know what the Afghan authorities would call this event, but to him it was clear. It was a suicide bombing in front of the Wilde Oil headquarters in Kabul – a bloody protest against the company's only activity in the country: the pipeline it was building across Afghanistan. And it was clearly intended as a warning – that there would be more bloodshed, as long as the pipeline construction continued.

18. Herat

The Old Man was late, and was hurrying across the open area in front of the Great Mosque, as a few other late-comers were washing themselves before entering. The Old Man washed his hands and feet at the fountain, according to the custom, and another man pushed in from behind to stand close to him. He was very tall, and leaned forward so that he could speak in a whisper into the Old Man's ear.

"It has been done," he said, "Exactly as planned, inshallah!" He slipped away as quickly as he had appeared, and vanished around a dark corner of the sacred building. The Old Man did not even have time to greet him, nor to thank him for this good news. He was left watching the man's back – moving quickly away toward the shadows, then disappearing close to a dark wall, where the lights of the open square could not reach, and he did not reappear.

The old man said a prayer of thanks to Allah, inside the mosque, prostrated on his rug amid the Imam's rhythmic chanting of the service. He was thinking of what he would say, when he met this new man from the American oil company, who had arrived in Kabul. He was thinking of the meeting which he planned to have with this man ... in Kandahar.

He would travel to Kandahar for this meeting, which would be in the private rooms of the Great Mosque there. He knew that this man had been sent to his country by the people who were building the pipeline. He had been sent to try to convince them to accept the pipeline.

But there was no question of such acceptance. The pipeline was an evil intrusion into their country, defacing the landscape and intruding into the natural world, and the lives of the people. This was not a work of Allah – it was something which came from human greed and disrespect for the country, for the mountains and the earth which had been given to the people, for them to use and protect, to keep in its natural state – forever. These foreign people had no right to desecrate the land of the Afghans. The old man repeated this thought in his mind, again and again.

He would talk to this man. It was said that the man knew the people of this country, that he understood their habits and their laws. Then let him also respect those laws. That is what he would tell this man. Respect the laws of the almighty – that is what he would say. That was the law, as safeguarded by Allah. If this man knew the country, the people, the laws of the Afghans, he would understand.

This is what he would say to this man ... in Kandahar.

19. Kabul

As evening settled across the streets and alleyways, Joey walked alone into the principal mosque of the city. He had washed and left his shoes outside, as the rituals demanded.
Inside he looked around until he found a young man in a white robe, replacing candles in the wall lamps.

"Salam," he began, and the young man responded with a slight bow.

"Salam aleikum. May peace be upon you."

"I am a stranger here," said Joey. "I need to see the Imam." The young man looked at Joey intently, not saying a word. Then he leaned his tray of candles against a column, nodded slightly, and turned, walking slowly away across the open area behind the prostrate worshipers.

The young man opened a small door and motioned silently to Joey, who followed him into a cramped passageway. They mounted some stairs, to another doorway, where the young man knocked softly.

After a few minutes, the door opened halfway, and an older man, with a rich white beard, stood waiting. The young man said something softly, and the Imam nodded. He backed away from the door, motioning to Joey to enter. Joey followed in silence, into a modest living area, with a table and a few chairs. The Imam motioned to Joey to take a chair, and Joey sat at the table, with the Imam across from him.

The young man positioned himself behind the Imam, who spoke a few sentences, which the young man translated: "The Holy Imam wishes you peace and long life. He asks what is the subject you would like to discuss with him?"

Joey nodded and placed his hand over his heart, to show his gratitude for these words, and for being welcomed into the holy place. He spoke slowly and quietly. "I thank the Imam for his welcome, and for taking time from his duties to listen to me. I seek his advice on a matter which is important to us all. I am here to find peace, to ensure peace. It is the company which is building the pipeline which has sent me here, to your country, to ensure peace. That is what I am seeking. But I need the Imam's advice on how to do this. There must be no more bloodshed in your country, inshallah."

The young man translated Joey's words, and Joey continued: "If it may be useful, I would like to meet, face-to-face, with your leader, the person you trust the most, to talk to him about our work and how it can help Afghanistan, and your people. I know this will help us to understand each other. I would value such a discussion."

The young man translated again, while the older man closed his eyes, listening patiently, without facial expression. Soon the young man finished his translation, and waited to translate the Old Man's response. He said nothing for a few moments. Then he opened his eyes and pronounced a few short phrases. The young man waited for more words, before translating. But there were none, so he turned to Joey and said: "Our leader will meet with you ... in Kandahar."

The old man closed his eyes in prayer. The meeting was over.
Joey understood. He started to stand up, but added an afterthought: "In Kandahar then, inshallah." He gave a slight bow to indicate a farewell, and the young man rose to escort him from the building. The old man's eyes were closed; he was immobile, deep in prayer.

The sky outside was black, with no moon, as the sun set beyond the walls. From all over the city, one could hear the voices from the minarets, the call to prayer. Here and there men were prostrate, their heads bowing toward Mecca. People were hurrying home as the streets emptied, and soon the only lights were in windows, behind heavy curtains. This day was over.

Alone, Joey walked to his hotel through the dark streets.

20. Washington

The Under Secretary came back late from her lunch at the French Embassy, thinking of the dishes they had served. It was always such a delight to have lunch with the French. They took it so seriously! The food, the décor, the wine, the flowers in silver vases, the discussion – everything!

How different it was to be American, she thought. Only the discussion has any importance. I wonder why, she asked herself? Was anything of any importance discussed during this particular luncheon? Certainly not. But the whole affair was taken so seriously – it was a kind of ... religious service! While at the same time most Americans were buying a hot-dog.

When she got back to her office, her secretary pounced with a list of phone calls she should return, and a few messages, which she left on the desk as the Under Secretary disappeared for a few minutes into her private bathroom. When she came out she slumped down behind her desk and poured herself a cup of black coffee, from a thermos which her secretary always prepared for her when she was coming back from a luncheon at the French Embassy. This was a standing instruction.

As she slowly drank her coffee, the Under Secretary stared at her appointment calendar. There was a notation on it: "Talk to Emerson," it read, and it was in her own hand-writing. "Talk to Emerson," she thought, "Yes, okay, but what about?" She could not recall making the notation, nor what had been the point of it. She could not talk to Emerson without recalling what she wanted to say. She buzzed her secretary: "Do you recall what I need to talk to Emerson about?" she asked. "No," said her Secretary, thinking, "maybe it was about Israel?"

The Under Secretary thought for a moment – she had nothing to tell Emerson about Israel!
So she turned her attention to other matters.

21. Kandahar

The old man held the black scarf which fell from his turban across the lower part of his face, against the pervasive dust. He had travelled a great distance, and he was tired, but it was not a time to rest. The car he was in held a number of people – it had been converted to add an additional row of seats – and the windows were partially open to the swirling dust.

As they approached the city there were the usual streams of people along the side of the road, some – usually women – with large packages on their heads, balancing the produce they had to sell at the market, as they walked with singular determination, faces covered, sometimes with small children following behind, or even wrapped in slings and hanging from the shoulder.

The driver knew where the old man was going, and that would be his first stop. The other passengers would likely get out there too, and walk to their destinations in the city. It was already warm, though the sun was still low in the East, just above the mountains. Later it would be hot and windy, with sand blowing through the air. It was always like this, he thought, here in Kandahar. Even in winter it was dusty and windy, though the air became icy and there were few places to shelter.

But this was their place on earth, allotted by Allah for these people – his people, thought the old man – as his eyes roamed across the scene at the center of the city. He had not been here for more than a year, though it was the center for his group, his "followers" as some would say.

Of course he did not claim to have "followers" – he was a simple man, always dressed in black, with his long beard and shroud, wrapped across his face so that only his eyes were visible – his piercing eyes, which made others avert their looks.
It was his eyes which ensured his leadership.

He entered the mosque through a small door in a narrow alley. Inside there were other men, but they all backed away from his imposing small figure when he came through the doorway, in his black robes. The men backed away, heads bowing, mumbling various respectful greetings. He was expected.

A younger man opened a door for him, and he went into a meeting area, where a group of men was waiting for him. They were all dressed the same way, in the same robes, bearded and with black turbans. No one smiled and no one spoke. They all lowered their faces in small bows of respect as the revered leader moved to the place which had been reserved for him. They all turned as he moved among them, mumbling words from the Koran. Their eyes were fixed on him as they waited to hear his words, his message, his instructions.

He stopped in front of a raised area, and sat on a backless wooden bench at the front of the large room, a small older figure facing the crowded group of men. It was a little-used corner of the Mosque, and today only these men were using it. The rest of the interior was empty at this time of day – later it would fill, following the chant of the muezzin.

The meeting began with a prayer. All the men sat down, on their knees, facing in the direction of Mecca, and prostrated themselves as a muezzin chanted some lines from the Koran.

Then there was a moment of silence.

The first person to speak was the old man, who had just arrived following his all-night trip. "Allah be praised," he said, and the group repeated his words in a vast echo which filled the space around them. "I have come to speak my heart," he said, "to my brothers." The group fell into a respectful silence.

"A man has come to our country," the leader began, "A man who can be useful to us. We must convince him that the Westerners should leave our country, that their work here is the devil's work, that we follow the way of Allah, and that the outsiders must leave us to follow our own way. They must leave us alone, and leave our country, our land."

There was a murmur of agreement through the men in the gathering. The speaker continued. "If we can convince him, he can be useful to us, and can help us to reach our objectives. He can help us to bring the Westerners to leave."

"How do you know this?" asked a voice from the crowd of men.
"Yes," said another, "Why is a single man so important?"
"What can he do?" "Who is he?"

"We know this man from the past. He has helped us, some years ago. And now he is sent by the makers of the long trench. If we convince him, he will speak for us. We must use this moment, this opportunity which has been given to us by Allah."

There was a murmuring among the large group of men. "What are you proposing, lutfan?"

"This man will come here, to Kandahar. We must talk to him, convince him, engage with him, so that he will help us. He can explain to his countrymen – so that they will leave us alone, inshallah." There was a murmuring among the group of men.
"If he explains our views, in his own country, it will help us. It will bring our views directly to the leaders, inshallah."

There was more murmuring, as the men discussed the matter among themselves. After some minutes had passed, one of the older men rose. "We will see this man, and will hear what he says. Then we will discuss among ourselves, inshallah."

A boy brought tea in a samovar, which he placed on a counter against the wall. He took a glass of tea to the old man. Some of the men started to leave. A cold wind swept through the open door, stirring the dust. The old man sat, motionless and silent, as the dust swirled around him.

22. Mazar-e-Sharif

Page struggled with the phone, which never seemed to do what you wanted it to do – it always had its own mind. The first number she had called, several times, did not respond. That was the number at his house in Maine. This time she was calling the gas station-general store, where he had his car serviced regularly, and did most of his grocery shopping.

"Hello, is that the supermarket?" she asked.

"Yes, can I help you?"

"I'm calling to ask if you have seen Mr. Torino recently? This is his friend, Page." The line was crackling and it was not easy to hear.

"I asked around the store," said the voice at the other end, after a moment of silence. "We haven't seen him here for a couple of weeks. But that's not unusual – he sometimes doesn't come in for two or three weeks. He travels, and he goes hiking sometimes."

"Okay, thanks. Sorry to bother you. I'll try his house again tomorrow." She hung up the phone, knowing that her first instinct had been correct. He was not there – at his house in Maine.

So it was surely him – the man who had appeared here in Afghanistan. But why would he be here? She knew that the former Under Secretary of State, Pendleton Highsmith, was now the head of the company which was building the pipeline across Afghanistan, and she knew that Highsmith had valued Joey's quiet way of closing down that unpleasant problem in Russia – with no publicity and no complaints. She had been involved in that matter herself, and had seen how Joey had made that problem – the whole problem – just go away.

It seemed clear to Page: Highsmith had convinced Joey to help the Wilde Oil pipeline project to succeed, and had sent him to Afghanistan for that purpose. But she also understood that Joey would be the one taking the risks, and also the one who would take the blame, if the multi-million-dollar Wilde Oil project had to be cancelled, with the huge financial losses that would entail. And the odds of such a project being completed in unwelcoming Afghanistan were, well, quite small. The Taliban were already opposing it, and were sabotaging the construction whenever, and wherever, that was possible.

The probable outcome was that the project would not be completed, and Joey had been brought in to try to save it. And if it failed, Joey would be set up to take the blame for that, to be the scapegoat when it happened. The company had made him a target, and had put him up front, facing the Taliban in what would surely become a dangerous situation – especially for Joey Torino.

Page, with her intelligence and intuition, her knowledge of the situation and the players, and her instinctive ability to deal with hostile situations, was not about to let that happen.

23. Kabul

Joey arranged for a Wilde Oil company plane to take him to Kandahar. They took off from Kabul at 7 AM, and circled before landing at the Kandahar airport at 8:20 AM. The plane taxied to the main terminal building, which was modern and clean, but seemed empty.

When they arrived, and Joey was leaving the aircraft, the pilot told him, in a hushed voice: "I will come back at 6:00 o'clock, and I'll wait for one hour. They won't let me stay longer than that."

Joey understood perfectly well: apart from this one possibility of a return flight, he was on his own. It was not clear how he would get back to Kabul if he missed that plane, but he would deal with that issue if and when it arose.

As had been arranged, a car was waiting for him at the deserted airport – there were no other flights arriving or departing from this facility – at least not today – and the only car was clearly there for him. He checked with the driver and then took his place in the passenger seat next to him. The driver looked at him and said "I am Alu. Where we go?"

"Well," said Joey, "let's go to the center of the city, so I can walk around."

"Not good you walk in Kandahar," said Alu flatly. "We drive around, maybe OK. You not walk. Not good."

"Drive into the center of the city," said Joey. "Then we will see."

87

They drove. At first there were few cars, and few people, but this gradually changed as they approached the ancient walls of the old city. Soon there were crowds, walking, and people jammed into vehicles of all kinds – busses, trucks and a few cars. Every vehicle was full of Afghans – men, women, children, jammed into every space in every car or truck, just as in Kabul. Most of the cars, trucks and people were carrying heavy loads – on top of the cars, and on the heads of the people who were walking. This was the ordinary, every-day life of the cities of Afghanistan.

The roadway was difficult, with pot-holes and swarms of vehicles, moving in both directions among the crowds. They passed roadside merchants selling their wares, and vendors offering items for sale, food, or snacks – sitting or standing, shouting about their offerings. At times it was difficult to advance, and the car slowed to the same speed as the many pedestrians.

Soon they reached the ancient walls of the old city, and Joey signaled to the driver to stop, just inside the wall, where there was an open area for departing busses. "You wait here," he said, "I will walk to the center. I know the city. I will be back, later. Don't move from here." He walked away, leaving the driver bewildered and wondering what would happen to his passenger.

But Joey did know the city; he knew it well, and he walked quickly through the crowds toward the center. His movements showed he knew where he was going, and this helped him to blend into the crowds of locals – going to work, or to school, to pray, or to shop in the ancient city center.

He moved with the crowd, at its pace and in the same direction, observing, listening, understanding. He knew this way of life, this mood, this daily program – and although he was clearly a foreigner, he blended in with the crowd, became almost a part of it.

Soon he came to the great mosque near the center of the city, the place where he knew he would find the man – or the men – he had come to see. It faced the large square, with its minarets towering above, imposing and reserved. It was the center – of the open square, of the city, and of the surrounding countryside. And it was the center of devotion, of thought, of life itself, in this ancient place.

Joey knew all the rituals, and, as always, he carefully respected them – he knew he was being watched. He washed carefully, hung his hat on a hook, changed his shoes for cloth sandals, put on a prayer cap he had brought for the purpose, and slowly entered the mosque. The men around him ignored him, and he chose a place among the many worshipers; it was the hour for mid-day prayers.

Above, the deep voice of the muezzin sounded from the minarets of the mosque, chanting the traditional words, with his pained verses echoing through the building and across the square outside. Joey participated in the ritual, along with the other men crowded into the mosque, and felt the strange sense of calm which he often drew from this ceremony.

As he was slowly moving, with the crowd, toward the open doors, a young man pressed close to his side. "Salam aleikum, Mister Joey," said the man in a low voice. "We are most honored to see you here." The man touched his forehead and his heart, in a gesture of respect and greeting. "Please come with me." Joey replied with a similar greeting, and the young man led him to the back of the mosque and through a small inner doorway.

The corridor beyond the door was totally dark, and Joey followed the man carefully, as the passageway curved to the left, and then to the right. Joey imagined that they must be circling the base of one of the ancient minarets which towered over this, the central mosque of the city.

Another door was opened, and Joey found himself in a meeting room, with chairs and sofas arranged in a circle, and light filtering in from a small window, high in an outer wall. One chair was empty – the rest were filled by stern-faced mullahs in black robes and turbans. All of them focused on Joey, turning their heads as he entered the room. They all stood up, and one – he looked like the oldest – advanced toward Joey, giving a slight bow as he expressed his ritual salaam, touching his forehead and heart, and giving another bow – ever so slight. Joey did the same, along with all the other mullahs in the room.

The elder mullah gestured toward the empty chair, and Joey stood in front of that chair until they all sat down together. There was a silence until the elder mullah launched a chanting prayer, with the other mullahs moving their heads and lips in the rhythm of the chant, their eyes closed. After a few moments, the room grew silent, and the young man who had escorted Joey to this part of the mosque took his place next to the elder, waiting to interpret his remarks.

"Mister Joey," said the chief mullah, through his interpreter, "we wish to welcome you to our humble home, our small city, and our poor country." The elder waited for the translation, then continued. "We know of you, and we know that you understand our country, and our ways." There was some nodding in agreement among the other mullahs. "We have hoped to be able to speak directly with you, and you have given us this possibility. We are grateful for this." Again, there was some nodding agreement among the group of mullahs.

Joey responded with the same humility, pausing frequently for the interpreter to translate his words into the Pashto language spoken here. He thanked these mullahs for meeting with him, for awaiting his arrival, and praised their knowledge, their judgement, and their ability to transform words into real deeds. He beseeched Allah for some modest wisdom and vision, to make the most of this opportunity to discuss – himself a modest and insignificant visitor – with these wise mullahs who are in their home, and who represent the will of God in this part of His earthly realm.

Joey paused to allow the interpreter to complete these remarks, and to indicate that these words were just his polite way of opening his comments. When the interpreter had finished, and turned to look toward Joey, waiting for some further words to translate, Joey continued to wait, in silence, for a perceptible moment. Some of the Mullahs raised their heads to look at him, wondering why he had paused, and what he would say next.

"I come to you to ask for your wisdom," he said, "So that your people and your country will benefit the most from the world as it is, and as it can be. We know that Allah has offered this world to mankind, the humble and the unworthy, and that mankind has never been able to respond to the gifts of Allah in a way which matched these gifts. And yet Allah the almighty continues to offer his gifts to us, his humble and unworthy servants."

Joey looked around the room. The mullahs were listening carefully. But he could see, and feel, their skepticism. This logic was not theirs; they knew of this line of argumentation, had heard it and considered it. But they did not believe this logic – it was contrary to their view of the world, and Joey was not going to somehow change their ancient way of viewing life, and the cosmos, in a short discussion in the private meeting room of a mosque in Kandahar.

Joey knew all this, and he also knew that he had to make this presentation, in a sincere and meaningful voice, to open the way, and to make some sort of discussion possible. He paused, signaling that he was awaiting a general response.

This response was given by the elder mullah, in exactly the terms which Joey had anticipated. His tone was polite, but his statement offered no flexibility. Although it was not mentioned, everyone in the room understood that the discussion was about the pipeline project – the arguments which Joey had presented were about the practical benefits which such pipelines – for oil and for natural gas – would bring to the peoples along the route, and for the country which would be the host for such a pipeline.

Joey knew all these arguments – both positive and negative; the broad concepts and also the specific details – the case which could be made both for, and also against the project. And he was also well aware of the futility of making such arguments to these mullahs. He knew that their ideas were founded in their solid faith, in the wisdom of their beliefs, and that nothing he could say or do would change all that. Not in its broad concepts, nor in any of its details – nothing would change the fierce opposition of these mullahs to the pipeline project. They viewed it simply as an intrusion – something from outside, which was not a part of their world, or their relationship with Allah. It was an unwelcome intrusion, an unacceptable initiative by outsiders, who had no place in their country, in their world.

When it was once again his turn to speak Joey asked questions – local questions. He asked about the number of children born during the year, about the results of the last harvest in the region, about the health of the people of the city, and the numbers of faithful coming to the city's mosques for prayer. And he congratulated these elders for the vigor and responsibility which they brought to their work in the city and the surrounding lands.

Tea was offered, along with sweets, and Joey took some of both. The conversation turned to the city, its problems, its historic past, and its future. Joey remained in the room for two hours, before making a gesture to leave. He thanked the leading mullah for his hospitality and for the useful discussion, rose, and slowly began edging his way, as politely as possible, toward the door. He knew this discussion was futile; he had expected exactly that.

24.

Joey ambled through the narrow streets of old Kandahar, enjoying the feel of the place. It was a city which he knew, and he savored its scents and sounds in the mid-day calm. No one approached him, and he seemed a part of the local scene. Some of the streets were so narrow that two persons could not pass, but there were few people visible, and the old city was silent in the mid-day heat.

He emerged into an open square, with sparse traffic and public buildings on all sides, and started walking around it, along a concrete sidewalk. There was almost no one in the square, the fountains at the center were not working, and a hot silence hovered in the air. He sat on a bench near the dry basin of the non-functioning water fountains.

After a few minutes, a car pulled up next to him, with two men in the front seat. "Meestair Torrinno? We are friends." The two men wore the omni-present white shalwar kameez. They were bearded, and smiled at Joey in a friendly way. "We can have coffee, talk. We have interest in your work. We know your name."

Joey stood, approached the car, and appraised the two men. They were young and clean, smiling and a little timid. He asked them some questions, about the square they were in, the main sights to see in the city. They spoke few words of English and often fell back on their own language, trying to express themselves. Joey asked who they represented, were they in an organization?

"We are from this city, our city, here in Kandahar," said the boy nearest him. "We are the young Talebs!" He smiled with pride:

"We are Talebs!" Both boys smiled. "It is our leader who wants to ..." he searched for the word ... "invite you. For to talk. Please," and he gestured to the car. "We can drive. After, we take you to car. We know where is your car." He smiled proudly.

"Who is your leader?" Joey asked. "Does he have a name?"

"Our leader is great man here. He has send us to find you, and" ... he searched for the word, "ask you ... "

"In-vite!" interrupted the other boy, the driver. They both laughed. "Yes! Not to ask! To in-vite!" They smiled broadly. "In-vite! You come?"

"How could I possibly say no?" said Joey, and got into the back seat of the car. The two boys laughed, exchanged some words, and the car drove off. "Just get me to my plane on time, please!"

The boys smiled and laughed as they drove away from the square.

25. Houston

In Houston, Pendleton Highsmith, the President and CEO of Wilde Oil, had received some puzzling information: Joey Torino, who he had hired to get the Afghanistan pipeline project back on solid ground, had disappeared. The company's senior people in Kabul had reported that Joey had taken a company plane to fly to Kandahar, where he had been left this morning, Kabul time. The plane was supposed to pick him up and bring him back to Kabul in the evening, but the situation was still very worrying.

Highsmith put in a call to the company office in Kabul, where he reached Max Anders.

"What's this I hear about Joey Torino? Has he really gone off to Kandahar by himself?"

"Well, you know him better than any of us know him," said Anders. "He made his own arrangements and commandeered one of our planes to fly him to Kandahar. He told the pilot he would come back this evening, but we have not heard from him all day."

"What is he doing? Did he say anything to anyone?"

"No. The simple answer is that he didn't say anything to anyone, just took the plane. Our air crew will be there to pick him up, as they agreed, and I hope he will turn up. We don't have anyone permanently in Kandahar right now. He's very independent! He didn't tell anyone what he was planning, so all we can do is hope he is okay, and that he turns up as planned."

"This is very worrying," said Pen Highsmith, thinking that he was the one who had hired Joey, so if anything happened ... the Wilde Oil Board would blame him. "Keep me informed of any ... developments." He ended the conversation and hung up the phone, now very concerned. He knew that Joey Torino was, well – creative – but he had not expected him to just wander off and disappear ... in Afghanistan!

26. Kandahar

Joey and his two young escorts drove into the courtyard of a shabby building on the outskirts of Kandahar, passing two armed guards who opened the gate for the car. The young men got out and escorted Joey into a somber building across the dusty courtyard area, where multiple cars were parked. Inside, they climbed a narrow staircase and knocked on a heavy wooden door. A guard with a sub-machine gun opened the door, studied Joey for a moment, and then waved the group inside what appeared to be a business office, with desks, telephones and computer screens.

Joey was shown into a comfortable living room with windows on the courtyard, where he was asked to sit down, along with his two escorts. After a few minutes, a tea tray was brought in by another guard, who poured a glass of tea for Joey and offered him some biscuits. After more waiting there were noises in the entryway outside the door, which burst open with the noisy arrival of the leader of this group, a prominent opposition figure called Kabil Malek. The man was well-known throughout Afghanistan, and was said to be unpredictable, ruthless, and ambitious – an Afghan nationalist with a large following, based in Kandahar but well-known throughout the country.

Malek pushed into the room with a loud voice, as he shouted some orders back out the door toward the men who were following him, then closed the door to keep them out. He hung a belt with a holstered pistol on the coat rack by the door, then turned toward Joey.

"Welcome Meester Joey, Meester Torino," he said. "We all know your name, and we are happy to see you here. You are most welcome in Kandahar!" He sat down heavily at the other end of the sofa where Joey was sitting, and looked intently at him.

"I am also very pleased to meet you," said Joey, shaking this warlord's hand, which was decorated with several gem-stone rings. Joey's host gestured to one of the armed men who had come into the room with him, and they set about preparing to serve tea. A huge tea samovar sat on a table near the window, and a tray was prepared with short tea glasses and a teapot. Soon they were both served with tea and Afghan sweets, and settled back into the comfortable sofa.

"I have been admiring your city," said Joey. "This morning I met with some of your religious leaders."

"I know," said Kabil Malek, "I know everything that happens in this city – or in this part of the country, for that matter. My people keep me informed." He drank some of his tea.

"But those mullahs," said Malek, "they can do nothing for you. They will do nothing. It is the people who decide here, and the people know what they want. And what they do not want." He looked at Joey with a direct and steady gaze. "And the people do not want your pipeline," he said. "Whatever it takes, however long is needed, we will prevent this pipeline. That is what the Afghan people want, and that is what we will do." He finished his tea and handed the glass to one of the men standing near him. It was immediately re-filled and handed back to him.

"We know about you, Mister Joey," he said, "and we know that you have reputation to get what you want. This will not happen here. You will understand this. Not here!"

Joey looked steadily at his host, taking the measure of his determination and his strength, weighing these elements against the other factors in the situation facing him.

For Joey such a judgement was always based, firstly and most importantly – not on what could be done or not – but rather on what was the right way to resolve the situation he faced, or the wrong way. Not what could be done, but rather what should be done – or not.

He also knew these people, the people of this rugged country, and he understood the determination of many to maintain their lives as they were, with their own ways of doing things, just as they had always been.

Malek offered Joey tea, or something else to drink, and said he would be happy to take his guest on a tour of the city, or the surrounding area. Joey declined, saying that he had to start thinking about getting back to the airport. He explained his arrangement with the pilot of the plane, and his need to return to Kabul. He said he had been honored to meet Malek, about whom he had heard a great deal.

Malek was playing the welcoming host, and suggested that Joey stay for a few days – he would arrange for transportation back to Kabul whenever Joey decided he wanted to leave. But Joey said he had commitments in Kabul and could not stay. He had come for his meeting with the mullahs, and his colleagues would be wondering where he was. He said he hoped to visit Kandahar again, and that he would be honored to meet Malek again when he returned.

Malek was understanding, and said his driver would take Joey back to the city, to the place where the Wilde Oil driver was waiting for him. As they said goodbye, at the entrance to the house, standing in the courtyard, Malek made a final suggestion. "If you ever need to see me," he said, "all you need to do is to tell them at the mosque." He stumbled to find the words. "Any one of the boys who serve at the central mosque, here in Kandahar! – or in Kabul! Anyplace in Afghanistan! Just tell them, any one of them, that you want to meet with me, and it will be arranged. We need to understand, need to find an understanding. You must find a way. It is necessary! Or there will be – not good things will happen."

He opened the palms of his hands and tilted his head to one side, looking Joey in the eye. "I know you are strong man," he added. "I know about you! We do not want to be your enemies. We want to be your friends!" He repeated the hand gesture, and opened his arms wide. "Inshallah!"

Joey offered his hand, and Malek shook it warmly. And then Joey got into the car and was driven away, toward the city center, where his own driver was still waiting for his return. He was taken to the airport and left as planned on the Wilde Oil company plane, back to Kabul.

27. Houston

Joey called Highsmith in Houston. He was unavailable but his secretary noted a time on his calendar when he would call back, and two hours later he was on the line.

"Hello Joey!" shouted Highsmith, not realizing immediately that he had a good connection and could speak normally. "How are things going? Anything new? What can you tell me?" Highsmith was always excited by very long distance phone calls.

"Well," said Joey, "I would say that you've got some problems here." He paused, and Highsmith immediately shouted back.

"Problems? What problems? We want you to work out any problems, so things can move ahead as planned."

"Nothing's going to move ahead, Pen, unless you decide on an entirely different program. The pipeline is just unwelcome here!" Joey believed in getting to the bottom line right away, and this was the bottom line. There was a silence at the Houston end of the call.

"You tell us what we have to do," said Highsmith, "and we will do it. Or at least we will try to do it. We can't just change course. Give me some ideas, some alternatives, some things we can do. We're a big company! We can do a lot of things!"

"Well, you wanted my frank advice, so I am giving it to you. The best thing to do is to get out now. Period." He paused, to let Highsmith speak, but there was just silence at the Houston end of the call. "If you don't want to get out, you can try to convince some of these people, but I'm telling you in advance: that is not going to work. This is a traditional place, Pen. They don't change their ways from one day to the next. They will fight you. And ultimately they will win, because it is their country. You want to fight for your pipeline? How long? For five years? Ten years? Twenty-five?"

He paused, waiting for a response from the Texas end of the call, but there was only silence. "Are you there, Pen? Are you getting this message?"

"I hear what you are saying, Joey," said Highsmith. "But we are businessmen, and we have a lot invested in this project. We need to find a way forward, not a way back! There are a lot of things we can do for these people. We have thought about this. We can build roads, dams, schools, even mosques! You name it. Whatever they want!"

Joey thought for a moment. "You don't understand," he said. "They don't want anything you can give them. They just want to be left alone." He reflected again, then added: "Of course you could organize some programs – development, schools, agriculture, transportation. But the traditionals will still resist – maybe even more! They just don't want any outsiders here – any outside influences, any development programs."

Highsmith thought for a moment. "We can invite them here," he said, thinking out-loud. It was an idea which had been discussed in the company. "We will show them what we can do, what we have done, with pipelines." He elaborated his idea: "We can show them some of our structures, some of our underground pipes. They will see how we do this – how we build and use a pipeline.

And we can show them the benefits. Gas in the furnaces, gas in the kitchens, oil for the cars."

Joey listened to Highsmith's ideas, thinking as he did so that, after all, the man was not as dumb as he had always thought. But also reflecting that these modern ideas were exactly what the traditional elements in Afghanistan did not want. These potential benefits were what they were resisting, exactly what they feared.

"Talk to them," said Highsmith. "Invite them to come. A delegation, whoever they choose. Say six people, six to ten leaders – respected leaders. We will show them around, give them a short course in pipelines! They will love it! Then they can go home and convince their friends!" He said he would get it organized, and Joey should contact the appropriate person – or persons – to pass on the invitation. Joey was apprehensive, but listened carefully. In the end he said he was willing to try this idea, to see if it might be accepted.

28. Kabul

Joey asked the telephone operator at the Wilde Oil headquarters in Kabul to get Kabil Malek on the phone in Kandahar. The operator was a local man with many contacts, and was experienced in finding someone's telephone number, virtually anywhere in Afghanistan – a rare and highly-prized skill. And Malek was a well-known figure in his city. The operator called Joey back after a few minutes and said he had the number and would place the call. After about 20 minutes he called back and asked Joey to stay on the line; Malek was going to take the phone.

"Hello Meester Joey!" said Malek, booming into the phone. "You have call me? I am here, in Kandahar! We are looking for your return to our city, where we will give you nice dinner."

"Hello Kabil," said Joey, "I hope all is well in your city, your family, and in your life, inshallah. I am in Kabul, in our office here, but I am calling you with an interesting idea – an opportunity for you, as the leader of your movement, as an Afghan leader."

"Yes," said Malek in his booming voice, "I am leader. This is true. But I cannot do everything, you know! I am leader, but I am not – what is it you say in your country – dictator! I cannot dictate, ha ha ha!" And he roared with laughter.

"No," said Joey, "I am not asking for you to dictate! I am inviting you to visit my country! As the guest of our company – of the Wilde Oil Company. It is a very big company, you will see. You will be our guest ... in America, in ... Texas!"

There was a silence at the other end of the line, then Joey could hear Malek discussing, in Afghan, with other people.

"You want me VISIT?" said Malek, coming back on the line. "You want me come to America? I never been. I go to Mecca once – only place I travel. I never go to America."

Joey realized that Malek was carrying on two conversations at the same time. He was talking with someone else, in Afghan, and then responding to Joey's comments. The other conversation seemed to be with a person in the same room, and Joey could hear parts of that conversation – along with laughter and various noises – in the background.

"Listen," said Joey. "This is something you should do." He spoke in his slow way, stressing the words. "Believe me, this is something you should do. No others from your country have done this. You will be the first. And you will become an expert on the oil business. It is very important. For you, for your people, for everyone." He listened, but there was no sound on the phone – as though someone had covered the speaker.

"Meester Joey," said Malek, "I want understand what you say. You want I go to your country? To see your oil company?"

"Yes," said Joey. "As our guest. You and a group – six people, for example. We will show you what the oil business is, what we do, how we do it, in our own country. We will show you our oil wells, and our pipelines! You can go with your friends – maybe one or two friends, business associates. For a one-week visit, for example, or even a few days. You will see everything."

"I never go to USA. I hear much about. I hear about Texas. I see movies. Is great country! You want me to go to USA?"

"Yes, our company invites you. We will take you, as our guest. We will have dinners, visits to oil wells, oil fields, pipelines, big American cities. You will fly on our plane – our company has its own planes. You will take some friends with you – one or two friends. Then we will bring you back to your country. You will be famous here. Everyone will know you have done this, for the good of your own country." Joey stopped in order to measure the effect of his words. He heard a heated discussion going on in Afghan, away from the phone, then some minutes of silence.

"Meestair Joey," said Malek. "I discuss this idea with my friends here. I call you back." He waited for Joey to respond.

"Okay," said Joey, and he gave Malek his telephone number in Kabul. "I will wait for your call. Then we can meet to discuss your visit."

Joey hung up the phone, wondering where all this would lead.

29. Kabul

Joey called Pen Highsmith in Texas. "Pen, I hope you know what you're getting into here. I passed on your invitation. They are discussing it – or whatever they do. My contact will call me back. Do you have a plan for this operation? If so, what is it?"

"Don't worry, Joey!" said Highsmith over the phone from his office in the Wilde Oil Building, in Texas. "It is called hospitality! Generous American hospitality! Texas hospitality – the biggest of all! It always works!"

Highsmith hung up the phone and buzzed his assistant. "Get me Lewis!" he almost shouted. "And Suzette what's-her-name! I think it's Suzette – anyway, you know who I mean. And, uh, Mrs. Lewis and her assistant. Also someone from PR – a press person – one of the smart ones please! Plus the pipeline folks! In the conference room as soon as possible!" He hung up the phone and began walking around the room, deep in thought.

He picked up and buzzed the intercom again. "And Security," he said! "Whoever's there! The top person who's there!"

Ten minutes later his assistant called on the intercom. "Everyone's waiting for you in the conference room," she said.

"Okay. I'll be there in two minutes!" He went into his private bathroom and looked at himself in the mirror, pushed back his white hair, and marched swiftly across the corridor to his conference room, where all the people he had invited had assembled and were waiting to learn what this sudden meeting was all about.

Highsmith entered the room with a broad smile on his face, and took his place at the head of the conference table. He nodded to the more senior people, giving the impression that he had important good news to announce.

"Thank you all for coming, on such short notice, and I apologize if I interrupted your work!" He smiled again, looking from left to right. "But I wanted you all to know immediately, because this will require some advance preparations, and we will all need to put everything in order quickly." He paused, for effect. "I have invited the Taliban to Texas!"

"I have invited them to send their representatives here, as our guests. We will show them around. We will show them what the oil and gas business is all about, here in Texas!" The people at the table were momentarily stunned, not knowing what this announcement meant, nor how they should react to it.

"I want you all to think about this, and how we should prepare. We do not yet know exactly when this visit will take place, nor how long it will last, nor how many visitors will come. But it may happen soon, and we need to plan ahead: what should they see, what do they need to learn, how can we impress them with our seriousness and expertise. What will be the benefits we can bring to their country, to their people! All of that, and much more. This is our opportunity – to bring our project in their country to a successful conclusion! It will make history, and this visit will be the foundation!"

Highsmith looked around the room, at his colleagues assembled at the table, eager to see how impressed they were. But what he saw instead was a mixture of questioning and concerned faces, as these specialists began to think how they would fit into this project as it moved ahead – in Houston, and also, half-way around the world, in Afghanistan.

30. Kabul

Joey asked to meet with the senior staff of the Wilde Oil office in Kabul, and they assembled in the conference room, somewhat apprehensively. When everyone was seated, the company's leader for the Afghan project opened the meeting saying that Joey had spoken to Mr. Highsmith, and had some news for the team in Afghanistan. He nodded to Joey to give him the floor.

"I just spoke to Mr. Highsmith on the phone," said Joey. "As you know, he is the person who asked me to come here to support your operations. I told him that I had met with some of the Taliban leaders in Kandahar, and, as you would expect, I gave him my impression that they were strongly opposed to our pipeline project. I was confirming what all of you have been reporting on this subject." He looked around the table, and saw several heads nodding in agreement. "His reaction was that we needed to give them more information, so that they will understand the project better – the fact that the pipeline will be underground, out of sight, and will not affect the on-going use of the land. I explained all the reasons why the locals here are opposed to the project." Joey paused, looking around the conference table. Everyone was anxious to hear the results of his discussion with the leader of the company, the person most committed to the pipeline project.

"To my surprise," said Joey, "he wants to invite the Taliban leadership to visit the company – in Houston." Around the table there was astonishment and disbelief. These specialists were looking at each other with skeptical expressions on their faces. "He wants to send a company plane to pick them up here, and take them directly to Houston, to show them some of our pipelines there, so they will understand the project better."

Joey paused to let his colleagues digest this news, this idea, to understand it and to be able to react with comments or questions. "His idea," he continued, "is to gather a representative group of about five or six leaders, and to fly them to Texas in a company plane, then show them some of our pipelines across the USA, so they will understand what a pipeline here will look like, plus what it can mean for them – power for heat and light, in their villages and towns. He thinks this will help to convince the leaders that it will be a good thing for the people here."

Joey paused again, and waited for reactions. There was a moment of silence, then one of the engineers spoke up: "He doesn't know these folks. They don't care about the pipeline! They just don't want us around. They want to be left alone." There was some nodding agreement with this point, around the conference table.

Another voice said, "It's even worse than that. They see the pipeline as a threat, to their way of life, to everything!"

Once again, there was nodding agreement around the table. "They don't care what it looks like, or how it works, or what good it may bring." The speaker paused, then continued: "It's the outside world they're afraid of, coming in and destroying their way of life."

Joey responded that he had made these points, and would do so again. He wanted to inform everyone of this idea, this plan, which they were all going to have to develop. The hope was that at least some of these visitors would see the benefits of the planned pipeline, what it could bring for the Afghan people. That was the hope.

He said he would continue to keep everyone informed. For the moment, this information was only for them – no one should mention it to anyone outside of the people in the room. Everyone nodded in agreement; they did not want this plan to become local gossip. They did not know that the invitation for a Taliban delegation to visit Houston was already being discussed ... in Kandahar.

31. Mazar-e-Sharif

Page finally learned – from a friend who worked in the US citizens' office at the Embassy in Kabul – that Joey was visiting the Wilde Oil office there, temporarily. She tried to call, and left a message for Joey. She knew his abilities, and also his tendency to get involved in difficult situations. And she was also aware of his long-standing relationship with Pendleton Highsmith, who was now the President of the company which was building pipelines across Afghanistan. The foreigners working in Afghanistan knew of the complex challenges that project was facing, so it was not surprising to Page that Highsmith had somehow recruited Joey to help him with this effort.

She called the Wilde Oil Office in Kabul; Joey was not available so she left her number with a message asking that he call her back in Mazar-e-Sharif. But the day passed with no response. She knew the US Consul in Mazar, and walked to his nearby office. It was a small operation, surrounded by serious security installations, but she was well-known there and was immediately admitted to see the Consul. He was a young American diplomat in his first independent overseas assignment – a bit nervous but staying on top of things. The principal focus of the Consulate was its own security, and that was also the main preoccupation of the Consul. He was always pleased to see Page, who was one of the very small number of Americans present in Mazar.

"Well, hello Page!" he said in his friendly style. "To what do I owe the honor of this visit?" he jumped up from his desk to greet her, and offered her a comfortable chair in his large office. "How about a cup of coffee?" The Consul was very proud of the coffee machine which he had installed just outside his office, since the personnel of this small American presence in the city were not permitted to go to coffee shops, for security reasons. The machine had been specially imported from India for installation in the consulate.

Page sat down and explained that she understood that Joey Torino, a US citizen, was in Kabul, and she was trying to reach him. She asked if the Consul knew why he would be in the country. He did not, but offered to call and ask his friend, the Consul in Kabul, if he knew anything. He dialed on the direct line he had to the Embassy, and was connected to the Consul.

"Hello Jerry!" he shouted. The connection was very weak. "I'm trying to find an American citizen named Torino. You have any idea what he is doing in Kabul?" He listened, putting his hand over the speaker, smiling and nodding to Page. "Okay, we'll try to reach him later." He hung up the phone. "He's in Kabul," said the Consul, "but not at the Embassy. He's working for Wilde Oil – the company that's building pipelines here."

"Working for the company?" said Page. "How can he be working for them? He retired, to Maine! Don't tell me that Highsmith convinced him to come to Afghanistan!" She was thinking rapidly, and imagined Joey, using his usual unorthodox methods to develop relations with the Taliban, to help the Wilde Oil pipeline! But, she thought, they do not realize how dangerous that can be!

32. Kandahar

In Kandahar the Wilde Oil invitation for a visit to Houston was already being discussed in the meeting room of the central Mosque, where Joey had visited a couple of days before. The same group of mullahs was gathered there, quietly exchanging views on this new proposal from the foreigners. It was viewed as another deliberate effort to tempt influential Afghans to support the pipeline construction. Some Afghans were already growing wealthier because of the American pipeline project, which was clearly a devious temptation.

The earth was being disturbed by huge machines, which cut into the very soil of their country. This was never intended by the creator of the world, and had no place in their homeland. It was disrespectful toward the way the country had been formed, toward its rocks and rivers and mountains. Nothing was exempted from the cutting and digging and pushing of the bulldozers, across the mountain ranges and sweeping valleys of their country. This destructive work would change the very face of their lands.

And the effect of this pipeline would be to bring foreign culture, and the temptations of the modern world, into the heart of their country. This was why they had all vowed to oppose it by any possible means. Now they had to find ways to counter this new temptation; they all agreed that they had to oppose the idea of a visit to America, and step up their efforts to block construction of the pipeline. As was said in the ancient Afghan proverb, "Even the sheep must fight his enemy."

There was much nodding in agreement with the words which had been spoken, and the group grew larger as the discussion continued in the crowded meeting room of the mosque.

33. Mazar-e-Sharif

"What are you doing with that oil company?" said Page when she finally got Joey on the telephone line from Mazar-e-Sharif. "That whole project means nothing but trouble. You know this."

"I owe Highsmith," Joey replied. "That's something YOU know." There was a silence between them, on the phone line between Kabul and Mazar. They had not spoken for almost two years, had not exchanged letters, had no news of each other.

Finally, Joey added, "Anyway, it probably won't happen. The chances of getting a group of Afghans to travel to Texas to look at a pipeline is pretty remote. Even sounds dumb."

"I don't think so," said Page. "In a place like this there are always a few people who will do anything to call attention to themselves, even if they know they will regret it later." She paused, wanting to hear Joey speak. That was the way she would be able to understand what he really thought. His voice always told her what he wanted to say.

"Anyway, it is now in the frying pan, so we will have to see what the results will be."

"It could be dangerous," said Page, flatly. "It WILL be dangerous! You know this better than anyone." She was worried, but she was also angry. How could he let himself get involved in this matter? The pipeline project was already becoming the central issue in a sort of guerrilla war, with bombings, kidnappings and assassinations practically every day, somewhere in Afghanistan. "When will your guided tour leave for Texas, anyway?"

"Probably about a week from now."

"A week! How can you get organized so quickly? How can THEY get organized so quickly?" She was grasping for any possibility which might delay or prevent the planned trip. "I will come to Kabul!"

"No! Don't come! I don't want to go thru everything again." There was a silence between them. "I will go on this trip, and after that I will go back to Maine. You won't have to see me again."

"Have to see you? What does that mean?"

She was almost in tears, and then she was in tears. "I will come as soon as I can. It may take me a couple of days. I will see you then. Remember!" and she hung up the phone, not knowing what else to say.

She stepped shakily out of the Consulate's phone room, said a hasty goodbye to the Consul, who was mystified by her emotional exit, and walked unsteadily the few steps to the exit door, putting up her black burka, and masking her face before she stepped into the courtyard to leave. It was a short walk back to her office, but she had to be sure to cover up so that she would blend into the pressing crowds. She had to look like a woman of the town, a woman of Mazar-e-Sharif.

In the street the shadows were long; it was nearing the end of the day. The muezzins would start their chanting shortly. She did not like to be walking in the street when the sun set. It was not popular for women to be out after dark, especially alone. She kept her face covered, awkwardly, as she disappeared into the crowded street.

34. Kabul

Joey slowly hung up the phone, overcome by the past, and the way it had suddenly intruded into the present. He had tried to forget – but had been unsuccessful. He realized that now. The past was still with him, even here, halfway around the world, in the middle of Asia. He wondered whether he would ever escape all that had passed – the tearful goodbye, and the somber days and nights, weeks and months, he had spent alone, in his empty house, in Maine.

Joey had always thought he was a natural "loner" – a man who could live happily by himself. And he had spent a lot of time learning to become such a man. But after all that had passed he knew that he was not a loner, could not be happy by himself. That was a lesson – the basic lesson of human life – that he had learned. And maybe, after all, he had learned it too late.

His phone rang, and he picked it up quickly. It was one of his colleagues from the Wilde Oil office. "It seems like the home office has lined everything up for the trip to Texas," he said. "All we need to do is recruit some guests to go on this trip, and tell Houston when to send the plane."

"Well, that's the hard part," said Joey. "I'm still waiting for a response. Maybe I'll call again tomorrow."

"I think that's a good idea. Your pal Highsmith has everyone in Houston fired up about this, and if the whole project comes crashing down there will be a lot of bad blood! Everywhere!"

"Yeah, I know," said Joey, and hung up the phone. He was not in a mood to discuss the trip to Houston.

He called the company pilot, and said he would need to fly to Kandahar early the following morning. The pilot knew that Joey was working directly for the President of the company, so he immediately took steps to be ready to leave, with his co-pilot. It was a local flight, so arrangements were not a problem; there were very few flights to Kandahar. Take-off was fixed for 8:00 AM. Joey also arranged for a car to take him to the airport, and one to meet his flight when he arrived in Kandahar.

Then he climbed into bed and fell into a fitful sleep.

35. Kandahar

The car was waiting for Joey when his plane arrived in Kandahar, with the same driver as on his previous visit. "Where we go today, Meester Joey?" asked his driver. Joey was sitting next to him.

"Same place as the last time." Said Joey. "You drop me off, and then wait."

Out the window he saw again the timeless life blood of the city, the endless procession of people, coming from the country with their products to sell or trade, in fragile, overloaded wagons or walking, with outsized bundles on their heads. Men in long white jellabahs, and women in burkas, their faces covered, with packages weighing them down and small children trailing or hanging on to their mother's robes. Eternal Afghanistan, as Joey thought, walking, carrying, trading. Men, women, children, in the dusty air of the roadway leading, slowly, to Kandahar.

When the driver had parked the car, near the gateway to the old city, Joey started off on foot with the dust swirling in the wind. He held a handkerchief to his face against the dust; he knew the way to the mosque. When he arrived before the open doorways he left his shoes and washed his hands and face, like the other men entering. Soon he was greeted by a young man who indicated that Joey should follow him. They walked quickly to the doorway in the back of the main assembly area, and Joey found himself, again, in the dark passageways of the building, finally arriving at the doorway to the meeting room. The young man knocked softly on the door, and opened it slowly, motioning to Joey to enter. Joey stepped into a room filled with Mullahs in dark robes, with grey beards and turbaned heads. They were squatting on crowded carpets, all facing toward the door, where Joey had just entered.

The Mullahs in this room were stern-faced and silent. One, alone in the front row, motioned to Joey – first with his hand touching his forehead and his heart as he said the ritual "Salam," and then with a gesture indicating the place, facing the full group, where Joey should take his seat. Joey took the place indicated, squatting like the others and placing his hand over his heart, the eternal gesture of peaceful greeting.

A young mullah offered a brief prayer, in the flat tones and abrupt words of the Adhan, as sung from the minaret. Then there was a silence, as all the mullahs present looked intently at Joey.

"I come in peace," said Joey, "and respect, inshallah." All the eyes in the large room were focused intently on his. "I am a stranger here, a visitor from a distant land, in your country, your home. And I thank you all for your wisdom, for bringing your wisdom to our discussion here today." He paused and moved his head slowly, looking at each of the mullahs, meeting their eyes, so that he would have looked eye-to-eye with as many of them as possible. They expected this, were waiting for him to look each of them directly in the eye. He knew the ritual.

Slowly, in very simple terms, he explained the pipeline project which Wilde Oil was developing, and the benefits it would bring to the country. Light and heat for cold nights and cold seasons, to warm the homes of the people, to show the way through the streets after dark, to make it possible to read the Koran at night. The mullahs watched him carefully, listened respectfully, without emotion and without hostility. At the end of his presentation Joey put his hand over his heart, indicating that he had finished, that he was open to discussion.

But there was no response. The Mullahs had listened politely, but they had no questions. Joey added a few points – for clarification and also to show that he was open to discussion. But the Mullahs remained silent and stony-faced. Finally, the leader in the group said that he spoke for everyone present: they had listened, and they would discuss and consider the matter among themselves. This was their duty, inshallah.

The mullah who had escorted Joey to the meeting room stood up, indicating that he was ready to escort him out, and Joey rose, placed his hand over his heart to indicate his appreciation, and followed his escort out of the room. The meeting was over.

"You did good," said the escorting Mullah quietly as they crossed the main hall of the Mosque. Joey looked up and caught his eye. "It is not you. It is the, how you say, "pipe-line." It is too much strange for us. We do not understand it. We are simple people. We fear what we do not know." The Mullah stopped near the main entrance to the Mosque, and Joey looked him in the eye.

"Come with me, and your friends, to America," said Joey. "I will take you on our airplane. I will show you pipelines in our country. You will see what they are, what they can do." He looked the young Mullah in the eye, and smiled.

"I ? Go?" asked the Mullah.

"Yes, you! You can see for yourself. Then you can come back and tell your friends what you have seen. They may not trust me; why should they? But they will believe you. We will fly to America, and I can show you."

"I?" the young Mullah asked again. "I? Fly? To America?" He was astonished by the idea, did not believe it.

"Yes," said Joey. "I have an airplane. I will take you, and some others from here. Other Afghans. We will fly to America, and I will show you a pipeline in our country. I will show you how it works, what it does. You will see for yourself!"

The young man was silent, lost in thought. Then he said: "I will try, inshallah!" He turned back toward the central area of the Mosque, walking quickly, and disappeared out a back door. Joey continued out into the sunlight in the broad square, where he recovered his shoes and walked on, toward another part of the city.

36. Mazar-e-Sharif

Page took a window seat near the front of the crowded bus, dressed exactly as the other women who were pushing into the dilapidated vehicle. Many of the passengers were women, and Page, in her shawl, robe and face-covering, fit into the group without any problem. It was an all-day bus-ride to Kabul.

When all the seats were filled, the driver closed the door and the well-used bus, with a full load of suitcases and carrying-bags on the roof, started slowly on its way, through the heavy morning traffic toward the outskirts of the city. It was a sunny day, cool and breezy, with most of the passengers on the bus chattering away. But Page remained silent, looking out the window at the crowds streaming into the city as they did every day; she was uneasy about this trip – not even certain what she hoped to do, and wondering herself what her objectives were.

The bus maneuvered through the crowds until the driver managed to slip onto the main highway leaving the city, where it accelerated a bit. Luckily the heavier crowds at this time in the morning were pouring into the city of Mazar-e-Sharif, one of the biggest towns in the north, near the border with Tajikistan, Uzbekistan, and Turkmenistan, in the very heart of Central Asia. The main road to the South was relatively empty, making it possible for the bus to move faster than Page had expected.

She had done some research before leaving Mazar, and had learned more about Joey's mission here. She already knew that the hostility to the oil and gas pipelines which were planned across Afghanistan was growing, and that the "experts" on such matters were not at all sure they could be completed. She had already known that Pen Highsmith was now the President of Wilde Oil, the company which was building the pipelines. Highsmith had been the senior official who assigned Joey to the rescue effort in the Caucasus, and who had also covered up for him when the mission had become dangerous and controversial. That was when Page had met Joey – in the high mountains of the Caucasus.

But things had changed, and Page left to follow her own career, which had led her to this job, as the head of an orphanage and clinic for children in Mazar-e-Sharif, treating these small victims of the war, and trying to find homes for them. She was immersed in her work here, convinced that, without her modest clinic, these children would be lost. It was the most important work she had ever done, and she was devoted to it.

And now, out of nowhere, Joey had re-appeared! In the middle of Afghanistan, working with the oil company which was building a huge pipeline across the country! How could this happen? And the situation was even worse, because surely the Afghans who were opposed to foreign influence in their country would fight against the pipeline. Already the opposition to the project was gaining in force and visibility, and many leaders were afraid to support it. And now, in this country, where a vicious conflict was spreading and becoming more dangerous every day, Joey had re-appeared, and was now at the center of a complicated and dangerous effort, trying to put together the very project which had become the focus of opposition to the growing foreign presence in the country.

Once again Joey had put himself in a dangerous position, at the very center of a bloody war and widespread opposition to foreign intrusion. Page could not help thinking this situation through, again and again, as the bus bumped and swayed its way along the highway toward Kabul.

37. Kandahar

Joey was early for his other appointment in Kandahar, and deliberately slowed down as he walked across the city. There were new buildings and even new areas developing in the midst of the traditional over-crowded urban spaces and the branches of the local river, which passed directly through the city. Joey walked along the river bank, and was followed by chattering boys, fascinated to see a stranger in their city.

Eventually he came to the heavily guarded home of his acquaintance, Kabil Malek. As he approached, across a wide square, he was already in the sights of the guards, and they shouted to ensure that he was aware of this. He shouted back that he had an appointment with Malek, but there was some confusion as to who he was and whether he was an enemy or a friend. Eventually one of the guards came forward from the building entrance to have a face-to-face meeting with Joey, close up. Joey showed his passport, which helped to convince the guard, who waved a signal to his colleagues and walked with Joey to the entrance gate. Joey was escorted to a waiting room, where he sat on a sofa and ... waited.

Forty-five minutes later Kabil Malek arrived at the main entrance to the compound in his chauffeur-driven limousine, with his body-guards. Malek slammed his way into the room where Joey was waiting, and embraced him like a long-lost brother. He was wearing a long white shalwar kameez and his kufi prayer cap, and had evidently just come from praying at a mosque. "Joey, Joey," he shouted. "I am so happy to see you again!" He pulled Joey to the center of the room and brought him to an upright sitting position, on the sofa, with the two of them smiling for his personal photographer.

Joey moved to pull away from Malek, trying to look serious while keeping an up-right position on the sofa. Without a break, servants were passing out pastries and tea, all at the same time, with Malek continuing to announce – over the phone – his meeting with "my friend Meester Torino, from USA America, who is here to visit me, to see our great country."

After a few minutes of photo-shooting, Malek clapped his hands and dismissed most of the people who were in the room. All but Joey and Malek remained, along with one of Malek's more senior staff people, who spoke English. Malek continued to use his own mediocre English, with his staff person translating words when Malek could not find the right expression.

When most of the people in the room had left, Malek became more serious. "Joey," he said with emotion, "I am so happy to see you! I am now planning for visit to your country! It will be great occasion! I will bring my loyal followers, my assistants, my staff. They all want to see America!" He smiled and refreshed Joey's drink, which was straight Coca-Cola.

"Well," said Joey, "in fact that is what I came to see you about, to pin down a date to fly to Texas. And some other questions." He paused. "I went to see the mullahs at the Mosque today – I have also invited them to send a representative, and I am waiting for them to tell me who they will send. And I need to know who you will bring with you, as your personal ... party. Maybe one or two people."

Malek beamed his broad smile, relishing the news. "We go when you want," he said, "when you want! Ha ha ha! I am ready! Will be great event! We will go to America! Together!!"

Joey was there to pin down the dates for the visit, and he pushed ahead. The Wilde Oil people in Houston needed to know the dates, in order to make concrete arrangements. Joey suggested: "We can leave next Monday from Kabul," picking a date out of the air. "For a visit. As soon as possible." This was what the Wilde Oil team in Houston had suggested.

Malek became serious, and consulted his assistant, looking at a pocket calendar. They exchanged remarks, with Malek clearly over-ruling his assistant. "Is Okay!" he said. "Monday! We say "gola"! Is very good! We go next Monday!"

They drank a toast for the trip, and Joey asked Malek to give him a list of the persons he would like to take with him – so that they could be checked. He said everyone traveling would need to have a valid passport and a US Visa, but added that the Wilde Oil staff in Kabul would help with all that – it would all be organized.

38. The Road From Mazar-e-Sharif to Kabul

The bus suddenly slowed to a crawl; there was a huge line-up of cars stretched out on the road in front of them. Page strained to see what was happening, but could not see farther than the truck they were following. The Afghans on the bus remained silent – it was not unusual for traffic to be stopped – it could be the result of an accident, or a car bomb. Drivers opened their doors and leaned out. Some shouted questions to the cars ahead of them. And soon answers came back, but they were confusing – it was an accident, a flat tire, a hole in the road.

Suddenly, up ahead, people were running back to their trucks, or cars, and the whole line of vehicles started creeping forward. In front of them there was dust rising, with occasional shouts. And then there was the sound of guns – short bursts of machine-gun fire – but it was impossible to see where these noises were coming from.

Then Page saw men running among the cars, wearing the black shalwar kameez of the Taliban and carrying machine guns. They were firing their weapons into the air, and briefly looking into each car as they ran along the stalled vehicles. When they approached the bus, they opened the door, jumped in, and walked the full length of the passenger compartment, then jumped back down to the road. They were looking for someone!

The men with machine guns were soon just outside Page's bus. The driver opened the door, and the men in black climbed into the bus, their machine guns aimed forward, ready to fire. They moved back thru the bus, looking at the passengers, who were all Afghans, mostly women. They scrutinized each passenger quickly, staring at the faces under the veiled coverings. When they were next to Page's row, they scrutinized the woman sitting next to her, then turned their intense gaze toward Page, covered with a black headscarf and a black face mask.

"My daughter." Said the woman sitting next to Page, in Afghani dialect. The man continued to stare at Page for a few seconds, then moved on to the next row. Page and the woman exchanged looks in silence, over their veils, as the men worked their way to the back of the bus, then rushed to the main door and jumped down, running on to the vehicles behind them. No one spoke. The driver closed the door of the bus, and the traffic started to move again, slowly, creeping along.

Page looked at the woman next to her, but said nothing. The woman took her hand, and squeezed it in silence. No one spoke until the traffic was moving normally again, along the road, moving toward Kabul. They were running late; the driver was in a hurry to get to his destination. The event was normal for these people, a minor inconvenience. Most of them would not even mention it when they arrived in Kabul, when they met their relatives, when they entered their family homes, when they relaxed for their evening meal.

Page kept hold of the woman's hand until they got out of the bus, and the two walked together briefly, away from the terminal area. Page mustered her Afghan vocabulary: "How can I thank you?" she asked.

"I did nothing," said the woman. "We never met." And she disappeared into the crowd around the bus terminal, in the center of Kabul.

The crowds were pushing and walking rapidly; it was evening. From the Mosques the muezzins were beginning their haunting flat chants. The faithful were putting down their prayer rugs, and kneeling in the direction of Mecca. There were echoes along the narrow streets as Page hurried toward the orphanage, covering her face. She knew she had to get there before they closed their gates for the evening.

39. Houston

The Houston evening was warm, and the humidity was at its maximum. A man leaned on the back of a bench in a green area between two broad streets, smoking a cigarette. He was watching the entrance to this small park, waiting for the person he was supposed to meet. Soon an older man entered the park and sat on the grass, under a tree. The smoker waited a few minutes and then started in the other direction, intending to walk around the path and approach the old man from the opposite end of the park. There were almost no other people in this small park - just a couple in an animated discussion at the other end of the lawn.

The smoker ambled slowly, enjoying his cigarette in the evening air, and sat on the grass near the old man, leaning against the tree. "Salam," he said, and the old man responded with "Salam aleikum."

"I have been waiting," said the smoker, but the old man simply made a gesture with his hand, which meant "That is not important." He turned and looked at the smoker. "We have work to do, he said. There will be a visit, here. That will be our opportunity, and our challenge."

"A visit? What kind of visit?"

"A visit from our country," said the old man. "It will be our opportunity, and we must make the most of it. I have asked our brothers to come here, to help us. They will come. This will be our moment, inshallah!"

The two walked to a nearby bench, where they sat and talked in low tones. They paid no attention to a delivery van, which drove through the square and parked in a street on the other side. It carried the logo of a dry-cleaner which was located in a nearby shopping center. The driver of the van walked away and disappeared around a corner.

The driver stopped in a shadowy doorway and spoke into the palm of his hand. "They're talking," he said. "We're getting it."

40. Kabul

Joey travelled back to Kabul on the Wilde Oil plane, arriving after dark. A Wilde Oil car drove him to his hotel, where he found a message from Max Anders, asking him to call back at his apartment – the message indicated that it was urgent. Joey called back.

"We're trying to organize this excursion to Houston," said Anders, "but it ain't exactly what you would call easy." He paused for Joey to speak, hoping to get some indication of his mood, or of some new information which might clarify things. He had no idea who Joey was seeing, which Afghans he was organizing for the trip to Houston, or how the company would handle this new project.

It was not exactly a Wilde Oil tradition to invite locals who might have some interest in a project to visit company headquarters in Houston, and there were already multiple hesitations about this project, in both Houston and the company staff in Kabul. They knew it had been approved by the Wilde Oil President, and the Board of Directors, but they were also aware of the character and the attitudes of the Afghans toward the project, and they were uneasy about the idea of a visit to Houston.

"I know," said Joey. "Maybe we should meet with the staff tomorrow, at least the people who are directly concerned, and go over the plans. I can brief them on where things stand."

"Well, that would be a good idea," said Anders. "Everyone is anxious to know." He paused. "Have you recruited some Afghans to visit the company in Houston? Who are they?"

"Well," said Joey, "I'm not exactly sure. I think it will include one or two mullahs, and maybe a couple of war-lords."

"Mullahs? War-lords? You're not sure?"

"No. I'm kind-of ... waiting for responses." Joey paused. "I'm guessing we'll have a mixed group, maybe five or six people." He paused again. "War-lords and mullahs."

Anders knew that Joey was not someone who talked a lot, but he was frustrated in this situation, waiting for information on what would be a difficult and sensitive operation under any circumstances – pretty far outside the company's normal comfort zone.

"Well," said Anders, "Please keep us posted. We'll have to give the pilots a few days' notice before they leave Houston, and it will take them another couple of days to get over here for pickup. And we'll need to get the visitors some visas before they fly." He paused, and Joey said nothing. "It would probably also be a good idea to meet with the travelers before they go, to go over their program, tell them what we plan to show them, get their own ideas, that sort of thing." Joey remained silent. "Well, anyway, please keep us posted."

"Yes," said Joey, "good points." They hung up. Anders was wondering how this project would turn out.

***

Page made it to the children's hospital before the staff closed the gates for the night. She had called before coming, and the night nurse took her to the room she had asked them to reserve for her. It was a regular hospital room, but was empty; the staff knew Page and were always helpful. She did not know where Joey was staying, and the Wilde Oil offices were closed for the night.

41. Kandahar

The Embassy in Kabul expedited visas for the group of six Afghans who were invited to visit Houston as guests of the Wilde Oil company, and within a week the arrangements had been made for the trip. Joey had stayed in a hotel in Kandahar, meeting every day with the visiting group to discuss their preferred program for their time in Houston, and to supervise a hastily-organized orientation program for them. This was designed to prepare them for what they would experience on this trip – none of them had ever traveled outside of Afghanistan, except for two who had made the pilgrimage to Mecca, and one who had visited Pakistan. Joey sat in on all the sessions of this hastily-organized program, intervening with his own comments when he thought it necessary.

The group became more congenial as they sat through this program. At first they resented it, but gradually understood that it was useful for them because life in America was so dramatically different from their own lives in Afghanistan. The program focused on elements which were common to both societies – family, education, work, society, leisure, daily activities.

At the end of the week the group was more focused, discussing some elements of the program among themselves, raising questions, and sometimes expressing disbelief in what they were being told. Joey tried to answer their questions and to draw out those lingering suspicions which would not go away.

At the end of the week Joey thought they were ready, and they were keen to travel. The program had been pinned down and the company plane had arrived to take them over the North Pole to Texas. On the last evening in Kandahar, Joey walked out of the hotel's entrance to take a walk and breath some fresh air. As he left the building a familiar voice spoke his name. "Joey!" He turned and looked around. It was Page.

She was in a black burka, with her face covered, but he knew immediately that it was her. And he froze as their eyes met.

"What are you doing here?" he asked, disturbed and concerned for her safety.

"I came to find you. I must talk to you. You have to listen to me!"

"I cannot. I leave tomorrow morning."

"Leave?"

"For Houston. We are travelling to Houston. With a group of Afghans. We have invited them to visit our installations in Houston. We will fly tomorrow, over the North Pole, to Houston," he explained quietly.

Page was dumfounded and could hardly speak. "You ... you cannot! It will be dangerous. I know ... "and her voice trailed off. She grew silent, not knowing what to say, here in the street. People were already looking at them. Veiled women did not speak to Western men in the street! It was forbidden!

"I need to talk to you, privately," she said, quietly. "It is urgent." But the hotel doorman was already looking at them, concerned about the hotel's reputation. It was against the law for men and women to talk in the street, at the entrance to a hotel. Hotels were obliged to ensure that there were no such meetings in the street, at the hotel's entrance – especially with foreigners.

"I am staying at the school," she said, quietly. Come there, so we can talk. You must!" and she walked off, with the doorway guard watching her closely, and Joey standing in front of the hotel entrance, not knowing what to do.

42.

Dark night had settled over Kandahar, with heavy clouds and no moon. The streets were unlit and empty; even the floodlights on the great mosques had been turned off; it was after midnight. Joey, wearing a dark djellaba and a pakol hat, walked briskly through the narrow alleyways; he knew the way to the school where Page had said she was staying. He also knew that the gates would be closed at this hour, and the doors locked, but he was determined to find a way into the building. He covered his face with his patu shawl as he approached the building, with its high walls and padlocked gates.

The walls posed no problem for Joey – he leaped up and grasped an iron stake, pulling himself up and over in a single swinging effort, and lowering himself quietly on the other side. Inside the walls he swiftly moved around the building, trying to open doors and looking for windows which might have been left ajar. He found one which had been left slightly open, and tried opening it further with his knife. It moved, and he was able to push it up just enough to slide through. He pulled it closed again when he was inside.

He looked around – he was in a classroom, with mid-sized desks and chairs for students. He went to the teacher's desk and pried open the top drawer. It was filled with papers, which he leafed through until he found a school handbook, which contained a diagram of the school showing the classrooms and other facilities, labeled in Afghan. And on this diagram he found a corridor marked as teachers' quarters – just what he was looking for!

Joey quietly tore the diagram out, put the book back in the teacher's drawer, and moved to the door of the classroom. Consulting the diagram under his tiny flashlight, he moved silently down the dark corridor and up an open stairway, then down another corridor to a closed door, which he opened and moved through. On the other side the corridor became smaller, with single doors on either side. Joey could see from the diagram that this was the teacher's living quarters area, where he was guessing that Page must be staying, as a visitor. He could not know which door was hers, but she would surely be expecting him to come. He took a risk, opening and closing the hall door with a clear sound, then waited.

Down the corridor a dim light came on in one of the rooms, showing through the crack under the door. Joey moved quickly to this door, and brushed softly against it with his hand. The light went out, the door was opened a crack, and a tiny flashlight illuminated his face for just an instant, then was turned off. The door opened and Joey stepped into the room, with the door silently closing behind him. Page gave him a silent embrace, holding him closely and touching the back of his neck. Neither one of them spoke in the darkness.

43. Herat

Back in Herat, the old man hurried toward the mosque in the center of the city. He was dressed entirely in black, but there were dust spots on his robes from his travels. He had just arrived back from Kandahar. He passed the central mosque and turned into a small alley, then followed it, twisting and turning through the old buildings, becoming an archway which led to a small courtyard, and stepping into the building through a low entrance. Inside he knocked and waited until the door was opened.

"Salam," he said to the young man who had opened the door. "Is he in?" The young man motioned slightly with his hand, indicating a door at the rear of the room. The old man moved forward, knocked once, and opened the door. Inside the interior room there were several men sitting around a table, with papers scattered across the tabletop. An older man at the table rose in silence, bowing slightly and touching his forehead and his heart. The newly arrived man made the same gestures, murmuring "Salam aleikum." The others at the table rose and did the same. A chair was brought for the new arrival, who sat at the table.

"We must act quickly," said the new arrival. The infidels will take a group of brothers to America on a flying plane. They will be shown a working pipeline there, and will be told of its benefits. Some of them may be convinced by this gesture that the pipeline is a good thing, that it will not harm our country or our people, that it is not contrary to the teachings of Allah. We know these ideas are false, but it will not help our cause if some of our brothers start to believe these Americans."

The men looked at their newly-arrived colleague. "But our brothers cannot believe these infidels!" said one of the men at the table. "They will not be fooled by such a false story!"

The men at the table looked at each other, silently. "We must be strong," said another, "and show what we can do."

"What can we do in such a distant place? We do not know their ways!" said another.

An older man stood and held out his right hand, flat and palm-down. The rest of the group fell into silence, looking at the older man from under their thick black and grey eyebrows.

The older man spoke softly, almost inaudibly. He was short and wore a full grey beard. He steadied himself with his hands, trembling slightly, their knuckles closed and white against the tabletop. His voice was almost a whisper.

"Now is our time. We must show our strength. We must destroy the home of the demon which is threatening us. Our action must be decisive and clear. It must make these foreigners tremble. They must tremble!" He stood for an instant longer, and then sat down.

The other men nodded enthusiastically as they all started talking at once. The older man whispered into the ear of the young boy, who rushed out of the room. The meeting was over; the order had been given.

44. Kabul

There was a colorful send-off for the group of Afghans traveling from Kabul to Houston on the Wilde Oil company plane. A large group of family members and other close associates came to the airport to bid them farewell. There was also another group – composed of Americans and international officials – from the Wilde Oil staff and the American Embassy, to see off the group which was going on this important trip.

All those concerned with the vast pipeline project understood the importance of this venture – if this group of Afghans returned from America to Afghanistan with favorable impressions, the news would circulate broadly and would give a boost to the pipeline project; if they came back with negative views, it would feed the already-growing opposition to the project.

Page was there too. She had decided to stay in Kabul until Joey left on this venture, and then to return to her work, in Mazar-e-Sharif. She had warned Joey of the rumors she had heard, that the Wilde Oil excursion to Houston would be a target for the opponents of the pipeline project. She was concerned because Joey, as usual, showed no anxiety – he never worried about anything – and she knew this. But she was also well aware that this travelling party of Afghans, who were guests of the Wilde Oil company, would be a tempting public target for those who wanted to shock and signal to these Americans that the pipeline would become a nightmare for them.

A band from the American school in Kabul came to play traditional American music, as a send-off for the traveling party, and this gave the departure the atmosphere of a grand occasion, a celebration of American-Afghan friendship – as the Wilde Oil staff was portraying the venture. The trip would indeed be a landmark for the company, and for the relationship between the two countries. Only a few well-informed people in the crowd which assembled for the send-off were aware of the rumors which were circulating that the visiting group might well become a target for those who wanted to send a warning to the Americans ... and to any Afghans who were friendly toward them.

The American Ambassador was there, and wished the group an enjoyable and worthwhile trip. He foresaw the usefulness of these well-respected Afghans learning more about America, and especially about pipelines, which would help Afghans in general to understand the scope and importance of the pipeline project.

A senior representative of the Afghan Government (no one seemed to know exactly who he was – just that he was a "senior representative") echoed the same sentiments before quickly departing from the airport with an escort of armed police on motorcycles. The gleaming Wilde Oil executive jet taxied to the runway in stately fashion, and quickly rose into the clouds, flying northwest to Moscow, before continuing on, over the North Pole, to Houston.

Page, dressed in her Afghan robe and face-covering, took a taxi from the school to the bus depot, and boarded the next bus, back to Mazar-e-Sharif and her clinic, deeply concerned and wondering whether she would ever see Joey again.

45. Houston

"We have an appointment," said the big man – he was over six feet tall, with broad shoulders and a massive head of dark hair. He was showing his FBI identity card to the receptionist in the expansive entrance to the Wilde Oil headquarters building in Houston. The other man held back and was silent, simply showing his photo identity card by opening his wallet. "With Mr. Highsmith," the big man added.

The receptionist called the office of the President, and read the name on the identity card. She hung up the phone and gestured toward the elevators. "Tenth floor," she said. "His secretary will meet you there." The two visitors signed the register and took the entry passes which the receptionist handed them, attaching them to their lapels as they walked to the elevator doors.

The visitors' elevator went straight to the top floor and opened on another huge reception area, where Highsmith's assistant was waiting for them. She took them straight to the door of Highsmith's office, opened it, and announced the visitors. Highsmith came around his desk to greet his visitors and gestured toward some comfortable easy-chairs, where they sat down.

"We understand you have some visitors arriving," said the big man, "from Afghanistan."

"Yes," said Highsmith, "we have been working closely with Washington on this visit. I assume you have been informed about it. We will be taking good care of them and I can assure you they will not cause any problems. We will escort them everywhere they go, and they will virtually always be on our own property.

We will show them some oil wells, pipelines, offshore platforms – that sort of thing. Our own installations."

He paused. "I hope there are no problems – they are already enroute. In our company plane. Must be refueling in Moscow right about now!" He offered his visitors a drink; there was a tray with glasses and a pitcher of iced tea on the coffee table. "We have been keeping the authorities informed."

"Yes," said the big man. "We have received your notification, and the program for the visit. And we have taken the usual precautionary measures. Even more than the usual precautions!" He took a sip of iced tea. "But there is a new element, and we thought you should be aware of it. It is not very clear, so we cannot do much with it right now, but we are looking into it. And we thought you should know."

"A new element?"

"In the security area, basically," said the big man.

Highsmith picked up the phone on the coffee table. "Send Carlos up," he said into the speaker, then returned his attention to his visitors. "What exactly do you mean by 'a new element?' he asked"

The big man paused before responding. "As you can imagine, we keep track of a certain number of people. People we consider to be 'of interest' – for one reason or another. And from time to time we learn things, or hear things, which may – or may not ..." There was a knock on the door, which then opened. Highsmith's secretary stood aside to let another man enter. It was Carlos Espero, the Chief of Security for the Wilde Oil Corporation. He was a small man, wearing glasses, and was almost completely bald.

"Good morning," he said as he entered the room. "Your assistant asked me to join your meeting." He handed his card to each of the visitors, who gave him their own cards.

"Yes," said Highsmith. "This is Mr. Espero, our chief of security," he said, introducing his associate. The men shook hands. "It seems that our visitors from Afghanistan have already come to the attention of certain ... elements," he said to Espero. He motioned to his visitors to continue their presentation.

"Well, as I was saying, we track certain people, and just yesterday we obtained some information. We are not certain – not one hundred percent certain – that it relates to your visitors, but we think it may. That is our working assumption. So we thought it best to inform you, to alert you. And of course to let you know that we are following this matter, and are prepared to work with you to ensure that, uh, nothing unpleasant happens. For your visitors, I mean."

The discussion showed that the FBI had no specific information – just the clear indication that "foreign elements," as they referred to them, had been tracking plans for the Afghan visit to Wilde Oil headquarters in Houston, and had been trying to find a way to use that visit for some sort of violent attack, to show that Afghans were opposed to the Wilde Oil plan to build an oil pipeline across their country, and to generate opposition to it – in the US as well as Afghanistan.

To do this they were apparently planning a spectacular attack, which would shock the public in both the US and Afghanistan. It would be a major attack, designed to kill people, and to make headlines in both countries. The attackers apparently hoped this would arouse public opposition to the project – and would lead Wilde Oil to cancel the project.

The visitors made it clear that the FBI did not have conclusive information, and that they did not know key elements – including the time and place of the planned attack – but said their agency judged that the company should be informed, so it could take its own precautions. The FBI would follow this matter closely, and wanted to cooperate with Wilde Oil's security team, to block this planned attack, to avoid a catastrophe, and – hopefully – to identify and arrest the people involved.

After some further discussion Espero took the FBI visitors to the security offices, where the company had its own 24-hour company-wide coordination and information center, following any security or safety problems which might relate to their broad-ranging installations. Wilde Oil had active oil wells, drilling operations, offshore rigs and pipelines across the continent, and in numerous countries around the world, and its security division watched over all of this vast international program. The company had considerable experience, expertise, and a substantial security program to protect itself against accidents, natural occurrences and hostile incidents – throughout the world, and especially in the United States.

Espero's staff assembled his colleagues – the Wilde Oil Security staff – and they gave the two FBI agents a full briefing on the program for the Afghan visitors, the security measures they had already put in place, and the sensitive points they were aware of. The company gave these agents a full printed program, plus briefing materials on the installations to be visited, including a short trip, on company helicopters, to an off-shore oil-drilling rig in the Gulf of Mexico. The FBI had also alerted the Houston and Texas State police, and both the company and the FBI agreed to maintain contact throughout the visit of the Afghan group.

These were normal precautions, but these security professionals knew very well that it was almost impossible to defend against surprise attacks, especially since so many of the company's facilities were out in the open, with little or no protection against deliberate, planned destructive attacks, and much of the visitors' program would be in public areas in and around Houston. In such circumstances it would clearly be difficult to ensure full security.

46. Enroute to Houston

After refueling and take-off from Moscow, the passengers settled down in the comfortable accommodations of the Wilde Oil executive jet. Some were sleeping, others were watching movies – an unheard-of luxury for Afghans. The selection of available films had been severely edited, and alcohol was not being offered on this flight.

Joey sat in the seat nearest to the pilot's cabin, and frequently walked through the rows of passengers to see that everyone was comfortably installed and at ease. These were not people who were used to travelling long distances, and some had never flown at all, so it was a time to ease their concerns and help them to relax, hopefully to sleep on this very long flight.

At the back of the passenger compartment, where the plane's galley was located, he found Ali, the young Afghan interpreter, having a late-night snack. He was a lively, friendly young man, who had never traveled outside his country, and had never flown in an airplane, before this trip. He was wide-eyed and amazed by almost everything he saw.

"This is great trip, Mr. Joey!" he said. "I am so excited I cannot sleep!"

"I can understand that," said Joey, "Reminds me of the first time I ever traveled in a plane. You'll get used to it." He smiled at the young man, and took a small sandwich from a tray on the snack bar.

"But you have traveled all around the world, Mr. Joey. I know! Everyone says this." Joey took a bite of his sandwich. "They say that you know everything, that you are very wise. They say that you only speak when necessary, and this shows your wisdom." He stopped and reflected. "I will watch you, listen to you. I will learn from you," he said, nodding his head. "I will do this."

"Not too much, I hope," said Joey. "No one knows everything. Certainly not me! Not anyone."

The young man looked at him intently. "Where did you learn to live?" he said, "How did you learn about life?"

Joey could not respond quickly to such a question; he thought for a moment. "You are always learning about life," he said. "Life is all around you, and you learn from it all the time." He looked the young man in the eye. "For everyone life is different," he said, "but for everyone the lessons are the same." He smiled and finished off his small sandwich, turning to return to his seat.

Ali watched Joey walk away toward the front of the plane. He mouthed the words Joey had just used: "For everyone life is different, but for everyone the lessons are the same." He repeated it, several times. The young man was memorizing it – a small bit of Joey's wisdom, which he intended to keep.

47. Houston

"How do you know they will come here?" the younger man asked the older one.

"It is what we have been told."

"Do we have an exact time?"

"No, just 'in the afternoon.' "

"That makes it difficult."

"Yes."

There was a silence between them.

"I could string a wire along the curb ... "

"It would be seen there. There will be security guards, experts."

"Or thru the long grass ..."

"That would be better."

"The grass is long, overgrown, all along there."

"They would have to walk along there, I think."

"Probably. But there are bushes. I can use the bushes. For cover." The man looked around. "I could wait, over there ... "

"It is a good plan. We will do this. When it is dark. You have everything you need?"

"Yes."

"Then it is decided!"

"Inshallah!"

48. Houston

"Where did you get the band?" asked Joey. He had descended the stairs from the Wilde Oil plane. The Houston heat was oppressive. There was a marching band playing American tunes, and a string of limousines waiting for the passengers to descend from the aircraft.

"It's from a local junior college. There are lots of them here! And they love to play at events! Not bad, eh?" Highsmith himself had come out to the airport to greet the arriving group, to make them welcome in Houston. The company's "Event Organizer" was standing with him, very proud of the band's performance. She had been a producer of musical comedies on Broadway, in New York, but, well, things had been slow and the pay was better in Houston. She loved organizing events.

Joey introduced the Afghans to Highsmith, one-by-one, as they descended from the aircraft. There was a lot of bowing and gesturing, as the band played familiar Sousa marches. The sun was strong and the humidity was oppressive. Each Afghan spoke to Highsmith for a few minutes, with the company interpreter translating into English. Highsmith, with his white hair, broad smile and elegant outfit, was perfectly suited to this role. The Afghans were arranged in the limousines and the whole line of cars, including a police escort, drove off toward their hotel.

A dinner had been arranged at the home of one of the Vice Presidents of Wilde Oil. His family were away and the absence of women simplified the whole scenario. There were, of course, no women in the Afghan group. There was one mullah, from Kabul, who was included because the company wanted to invite people from every influential group in Afghan society. He was unpretentious and participated in the group without any special treatment, but he was given a special place by the others.

The group was impressed by the size and luxury of the Vice President's home. They had never seen a house as big as this one, with all its luxurious features. Outside, there was a swimming pool, and the gardens of this private home were as big as some of the parks in Kabul. It was difficult to explain to these Afghans that this house was much bigger and more luxurious than most American homes; they somehow concluded that it was a typical American family home.

Joey stood at the fireplace in the living room, as an older Afghan visitor examined the family photos on the mantel, with the young Afghan interpreter at his side. He pointed to a picture of the host's wife, with their four children, all standing in front of the pool. The old man puzzled over the photo, as Joey indicated the different family members. "The Russians told us," said the Afghan visitor, "that Americans did not have families, that it was not in their culture." Joey was too stunned to respond.

The evening concluded early, after the long flight, and the group set out for their hotel in the Bigg Oil bus. Enroute, they stopped at a well-known viewing spot, with a view of the Houston skyline. Almost all of the group got out of the bus to take in the spectacular view. It was then that the bomb exploded.

The bomb was almost, but not quite, directly under the main bus — it was a few feet away. But it was a sizeable bomb, and destroyed the bus. Everyone except the driver had left the bus before the explosion, substantially reducing the number of casualties. The driver – a (possibly illegal) Mexican-American immigrant – was the only person to be killed. He was the only person who had stayed in the bus.

In the confusion which followed, several people suffered minor wounds – from broken glass or from awkward falls. The press, which was following the whole unlikely visit to Bigg Oil in Houston by a VIP group from Afghanistan, made the explosion front-page news, which drew headlines around the world. And in Afghanistan it seemed to be both a warning and, for many people, a foreseeable consequence, of working with the Americans.

There was some talk of cancelling the rest of the Afghan visit to Houston, but this was rejected unanimously by the participants, who thought such a course of action would amount to yielding to terrorism. And so the program of the visit was maintained, and continued as planned, with dramatically heightened security.

49. Mazar-e-Sharif

When she heard of the attack on the Bigg Oil bus in Houston, Page was afraid for Joey's safety, and tried to call him in Texas. But it was never possible for her to connect with him. The phone lines were difficult, and he was constantly moving around the city, or unavailable. She left messages for him, but he did not call back.

She noticed a marked increase in hostility toward Americans in the aftermath of the Houston bus bombing – there were even some attacks on her children's clinic, which was international but was seen by many Afghans as an American institution. But these were nothing more than anti-American slogans scrawled on the outer wall of the orphanage – a daily happening.

She was frantic with concern about Joey's safety, but there was little she could do about it. She knew that Joey was indifferent to the dangers surrounding his work, and that he became annoyed when they were called to his attention. He always downplayed, and brushed off any such dangers.

She knew a young woman who worked at Bigg Oil headquarters in Houston, and finally connected with her by phone. "I'm trying to reach Joey," she said, but her friend could not find out where he was staying. She said she would keep trying to pass the message to Joey – if she could find him. Joey had a talent for avoiding contacts when he was preoccupied with his responsibilities, and information about the visitors' program was now being kept private.

The whole Afghan visit had suddenly been hidden away, for security reasons. The entire visiting delegation had been moved to other quarters, and it was impossible to connect with them without some sort of senior-level approval, which she knew would simply annoy Joey without bringing any result. Finally, unable to make a connection, she called the Wilde Oil office in Kabul and asked that a message be passed to Joey asking him to call her in Mazar-e-Sharif.

News of the attack on the Afghan visit to Houston had become the main subject of TV and radio reports, and ordinary conversations, in Afghanistan, especially in the main cities, where it was the principal political issue, focusing public attention on the desirability – or undesirability – of the Wilde Oil pipeline across the country, and its looming dangers.

Every day the international media reported on the activities of the Afghan group which was visiting Houston – one day they were examining an existing gas pipeline across America, which would be a model for the pipeline the Wilde Oil company planned to build across Afghanistan, and another day there were photos of the Afghan visitors being flown by helicopter to a Wilde Oil drilling platform, fifty miles out in the Gulf of Mexico.
But Page could not reach Joey.

50. Kandahar

A man in a black robe knocked on the door of a plain house in a narrow street at the edge of Kandahar. After a few moments the door was opened and he was admitted. He joined a group of men in a small room, with dim light coming in through a half-covered window high in one wall. They were sitting on the carpets which covered the floor, leaning against the walls, and were mostly silent. Only a few of the men spoke at all, and there were long silences between their comments. When they spoke it was in short phrases – often not even full sentences. The speakers were the leaders, and the others would follow the decisions that were taken.

"The best time for us is now," said one. He wore a black scarf, wound loosely over his head and falling over his shoulders. When he left the house it would cover most of his face, but here, in this meeting, his face was uncovered. His eyes were diluted and unfocused; he was blind – or partially blind; no one knew, exactly. There was some nodding of heads, and some of the men mumbled "inshallah."

"We must attack the foreign pipe," said the man with the black scarf, in his faint and grating voice. "Directly." Once again heads nodded amid murmured responses. "We have the material for this."

"We watch from the mountains," said another man, who uncovered the lower half of his face to speak, "we can act at any time."

"We have what is needed for this, inshallah!" said another, gesturing with his hands. "We have very much." He paused. "Our brothers know how to do this. It can be done in the darkness, at night. It can be done very quickly!"

"Then we are agreed," said the leader. There was a low murmur through the group, and some slight nodding of heads. "These nights we will do this, inshallah!"

A boy brought a samovar forward, and placed it on a low stand. A tray with an assortment of cups and short glasses was slipped onto the carpet among them. They all drank tea, with some small dark pastries.

Shortly they began to leave, one by one, in silence, with their faces covered against the blowing wind. Each time the door opened, there was the blowing wind. And again, the wind, in the darkness. The blowing wind.

51. The Gulf of Mexico

The Wilde Oil helicopter circled above the drilling platform, far out in the Gulf of Mexico, the helicopter itself slanting sharply on its side, to give the passengers a dramatic view straight down at the huge installation, complete with a helicopter landing area and a tall central drilling rig. The passengers, uncomfortably holding on to their seat handles and safety belts, gazed downward through the windows on the side of the helicopter as it circled the huge platform, then leveled itself and slowly descended to the raised landing area.

The passengers were breathless with anxiety and stupefaction. They had never seen such a structure; they had never flown in a helicopter; they had never seen the sea.

They had travelled, at high speed, from the Texas shoreline twenty miles out into the Gulf, to visit a Wilde Oil drilling rig. It was like a small town on a platform, raised on skeletal steel towers above the broad ocean, with white-capped waves crashing against its angled I-beams and vertical pipes, at water level, far below. The Afghans were astonished and anxious as the helicopter slowly touched down on the small platform at the top of the complex steel structure.

A strong cross-wind was blowing as they climbed down from the helicopter and stepped onto the landing deck, and those who wore robes had to hold on to them carefully. They were uneasy about getting out of the helicopter, but Joey helped them to step down as the crew attached the helicopter to the deck; it would stay there until they were ready to leave.

Joey knew that this visit to an off-shore oil well pumping station would be the highlight of the trip. These men had never seen the ocean up close, and a visit by helicopter to a platform so far out in the endless, white-capped sea was a unique and daunting experience, even for very experienced oilmen. It was impossible to see land in any direction.

The noise, from the helicopter and from the wind, was deafening on the landing platform, as Joey helped his Afghan delegation to step down from the passenger compartment. They were greeted amidst the brisk wind and deafening noise of the helicopter's engines, still churning to steady the craft, as deck-hands attached it to the landing deck.

The Afghans were visibly astonished to find themselves in such a place – on the towering platform, buffeted by a strong ocean wind, far above the white-capped waves of the Gulf of Mexico, stretching to the horizon in all directions. Most of them had never in their lives seen the sea, and could hardly believe what they were experiencing.

They descended the steel stairway with great caution, and were able to enter the main meeting area on the deck below. They were talking rapidly among themselves, all smiling and shaking their heads in astonishment at this experience. They fully understood the physical challenges – and all the other routine dangers – of their visit to this far edge of the working world, and were trying to digest the importance of this activity – what it was for, and why it was thought to be so necessary that people would routinely risk their lives to work here, on this very fragile structure built above the white-capped ocean.

And part of the briefing they received was the map of pipelines – from each of the hundreds of offshore oil-wells they had seen from the helicopter – to the shore, and then onward in every direction, transporting oil and natural gas across the land, to cities and refineries, to fuel the vast energy needs of the country.

After an hour of briefings, snacks and some basic sight-seeing around the drilling platform, the Wilde Oil helicopter flew the group back to Houston, the amazed Afghans chatting excitedly, non-stop, among themselves.

52. The Panjshir, Afghanistan

There were just two young men, dressed in black robes which covered their heads and faces. They ran in short spurts across the dusty landscape, carrying what looked like heavy suitcases, strapped to their backs. It was a cold night, with a strong wind from the north, but the terrain was flat and empty.

There was no moon, and the wind blew the dry sand in resounding gusts. When they reached the barbed-wire fence around the pumping station they sat on the ground, their backs against the outer fence, to catch their breath and study the challenge they now faced.

They assumed the outer fence would not be electrified – that was too dangerous – but the inner fence surely was. They would cut an opening in the outer fence, and disable the electricity to get thru the inner fence. The explosives they carried were for the pump. They knew their craft well, had used explosives in numerous attacks against the foreigners, and they worked together in silence.

The strong wind and the blowing sand were nothing to them – they had grown up in these hills, among these flat sandy plains, with their endless shivering winds. In any case they did not care about such matters; they had been raised to fight the foreigners, to defend their lands from such intruders. And what they knew best was how to attach the bombs, the wires, the detonators. This was their special skill, and they did it in silence, in the dark, with their own desert wind blowing about them. It was their wind.

When they were finished they looked at each other and nodded. It had been arranged correctly. They spun out the wire from the roller they carried, and moved away from the pumping station in the dark, spewing out the wire as they moved, crouching and running across the dark landscape, toward a rocky out-cropping nearby. They fell behind the rocks and settled the bulky detonator box on a flat space. Once again they looked at each other; they were boys, and this was their fun, their amusement. The older boy flipped his chin slightly – it was their signal – and the other slammed down on the detonator, with both of his hands, with all his strength.

There was a vast explosion, with fire shooting up into the sky. The boys, hiding their eyes, were surprised by the noise and the flames flashing in every direction. This was their biggest explosion yet – they were just boys. When they looked up the flames were red and yellow and tall. They looked at each other in a sudden moment of fear. But then, quickly, they stood in a crouch, and ran into the darkness. They did not stop running until they were well away from the place, then continued, walking rapidly, in the same direction. The fire burned on dramatically, lighting up the plain as far as they could see.

53. Kabul

"A piece of the pipeline was blown up," said the Wilde Oil agent for the northern section of the country. He was talking by phone with the company office in Kabul. "We turned off the gas, but it's still burning. Probably will burn out later today." There was a silence at the other end of the line.

Finally there was a question: "Anybody hurt?"

"No. It was out in the desert. A pumping station. There was no one around. We shut down the pipe. We'll be able to fix it within a few days. One week, max."

"Okay, thanks. Keep us posted." The Wilde Oil duty officer hung up the phone and called the Project Manager. It was six o'clock in the morning. He explained briefly what had happened. The project manager called Houston and informed the 24-hour operations center at the company headquarters of the incident, and the operations center informed the senior executives, the operations unit, and the press office.

The press office prepared for questions, and the company president, Pendleton Highsmith, was informed. He called Joey Torino, who had returned from the excursion to the Wilde Oil offshore rig in the Gulf of Mexico, and was just waking up at his hotel, in Houston.

"Hello, Joey," said Highsmith, "I'm afraid we have problems."

"What kind of problems?" asked Joey. He was already guessing, running through the long list of things which could go wrong.

"Someone blew up one of our pumping stations in Afghanistan – out in the middle of nowhere, thank heaven, so no one was hurt. But the press will be all over this, especially in view of the explosion here, and our Afghan visitors!"

Joey understood Highsmith's concerns. He was already thinking ahead – of how he might be able to cut the Afghan visit short, and get the visitors back to Afghanistan. That would minimize risks and there might even be some positive reactions to the visit. Wilde Oil did not need to have its pipeline project produce casualties, and the Afghan visitors would be witnesses to the seriousness of the company. He decided to talk to the leaders of the Afghan group, to ask if they would agree to an early return to Kabul.

It was approaching dinner time in Houston, so Joey knocked on Malek's hotel room door. The door was opened by Malek himself, who greeted Joey with a broad smile and a warm handshake. "Hello, Joey!" he shouted over the noise of the television, which was on full volume in the room. "Great trip we make to oil-well in ocean! I cannot believe all we see! Very great!" He patted Joey warmly on the shoulder, but then paused when he realized that Joey was in a somber mood.

"What is problem?" he asked. "We have a problem? Not that bomb on our bus! That was nothing! And we were lucky!"

"Yes," said Joey, "We were lucky. But now we have another problem. Not that bus. Someone attacked our gas pipeline last night, in Afghanistan. Blew it up." He looked Malek in the eye. "Luckily no one was hurt. But this is not good." He paused.

"I will talk with people," said Malek. "I think I know who does this! I will talk! Not good to do this, just when we are here! Not good!" He frowned and looked Joey in the eye. "I will do this." He stood for a moment, awaiting Joey's response.

"I think we should cut this trip short," said Joey. "I think we should go back. We should not be here while we are being attacked in your country."

Malek looked at Joey intently. "I know you not afraid," he said, "I know you never afraid. So I think: why Joey want to go? It will look like we afraid! Not good to look afraid!" He frowned. "Not for you. Not for me."

"Too many explosions," said Joey. "People can get hurt." He paused. "It's not important whether you look afraid or not, frankly. It's being careful that counts. We will look like we are being careful. That is important."

"Yes," said Malek, "Is important to be careful. Is very important! But if they think you afraid, they push you, and push you again, until you leave! But if you say you being careful, then, maybe okay"

"I think we should go back," said Joey. "It's your country, all of you. It is normal to be concerned about what happens in your country!"

"Yes, our country! Our country! But not to blow up!" He gestured with his hands. "We build pipeline for us – not for you! We need pipeline for us!" He seized Joey by the arm. "You think we accept this pipeline for you? Not for you! For us!" He saw that Joey was listening.

"Okay," said Malek, "we go back, if you want. But we say we want pipeline. We say we need pipeline, that not good to blow up pipeline! We say that! I mean WE say – not for you to say! WE – all in plane – we say we need pipeline. We say not good to blow up pipeline!" He put his hand on Joey's shoulder. "We will say this when we come to Kabul!" He gave Joey a fierce look. "All of us on plane; we say this! Everyone in our country will know!"

54. Houston

There was a soft knock on the door, and the young man opened it slightly – just enough to see through the opening. "Mr. Kandur? Mr. Mahmed Kandur?" The man outside the door was wearing a suit and tie. He looked respectable.

"Yes?"

"Can I come in?" asked the man at the door, holding up an identity card which showed he was an official of the US Immigration Service. "I'd like to ask you a few questions. Only take a moment."

"I do not have much time," said the young man, "I must go to a meeting."

"Well," said the man at the door, "we'll have to talk before you go anyplace." The young man noticed that there was another man next to the door. He stood back, and the two men entered the apartment, looking left and right, and closing the door behind them.

***

The old man was on time, he was sure of that. He double-checked the time on his watch; yes, he was on time. Also, the meeting place was certainly correct – they had a series of meeting places which changed weekly. But, unusually, the boy was late. Or perhaps ... the old man kept walking and turned the corner. At the next intersection he slipped into a small street and disappeared.

It was the agreed course of action – to be followed if there was any doubt ... . He would ask a friend to check on the boy.

55. Enroute from Houston to Kabul

The return flight to Kabul was somber; no one wanted to talk. The Afghans whispered among themselves from time to time, or slept. Joey also kept to himself; he was deep in thought.

Before leaving Houston, he had given his personal advice to Highsmith in a very brief private meeting at the Wilde Oil building. "Pen," he had said, "maybe the most important thing in life is knowing when to walk away."

He was talking about his trip back to Afghanistan, but was expressing a broader feeling – an approach to life in general. "If you walk too soon, you can lose. But if you decide too late, walk too late, you can also lose. You can lose big time." He had lowered his voice, looking Highsmith in the eye; "You could lose big time on this one, Pen. Be careful!"

Highsmith admired Joey's approach to life, his distance and detachment, his independence and freedom. But he was not someone who could "walk away," as Joey could. He was responsible for Wilde Oil – the Afghan pipeline project, the whole pipeline scheme, – all the Wilde Oil pipelines, the wells in the Gulf of Mexico, and all over the world. The company was heavily invested in all this. And he was Pendleton Highsmith! He could not "walk away."

***

The Wilde Oil company plane landed at an airport outside Moscow to refuel. It was after midnight, and the passengers stayed on board for the brief stopover. Most of them were sleeping.

The plane took off in the darkness for the final leg of the trip – across a dark and silent Central Asia to Kabul, landing early in the morning. There was no arrival ceremony, but Max Anders, the Project Manager for Afghanistan, was there to meet the returning group, along with a small fleet of cars to take the Afghan guests to their homes or to places where they would spend the night before returning to their own cities.

There was a brief gathering of the group, as they said farewell to each other, and thanked Anders warmly for the trip – they genuinely appreciated the hospitality, in spite of the ugly attacks against the company which had occurred both in Texas and, as they had just learned, also in Afghanistan.

One by one the cars left the airport with the company's Afghan guests, leaving Joey to ride with Anders back to the Wilde Oil building. The mood in the car was somber – neither man spoke for several minutes.

"Our pipeline was hit while you were in Texas," said Anders. "I suppose you heard."

"Yeah, said Joey, the Wilde Oil guys in Texas told us. How bad was it?"

"Not too bad. Fixable." Anders clearly had more to say. After a few minutes of silence, he continued, "But it's surely just the beginning. I'm certain we will see more. More attacks, and bigger. We will have to prepare for it." He paused to hear what Joey had to say, but Joey was silent, looking out the window at the dusty outskirts of Kabul.

"We'll also have to discuss, and make some plans. Already there are some guys who want to leave. It will be hard to keep them here." He made a vague gesture with his hand. "We'll get replacements – there are always volunteers when the pay goes up – but they won't be the same. And they won't stay long. I guess the price will double, more or less."

"The price for the workers, or the price for the pipe?" Joey asked.

"Both. Even more, would be my guess. I haven't started doing the math just yet." He was silent for a few minutes. "Of course I'm just talking about the personnel," he added. The rest is going to get real costly, too. I mean security, fencing, training, transport, insurance, you name it. All of it, everything!" He paused again, watching thru the car window as they entered the outskirts of Kabul.

"And that isn't even the main problem. The main problem will be the company! The shareholders! You think they'll want to keep their money invested here? Don't count on it! They'll be running for the exits!"

"So what happens now?" asked Joey.

"Oh, it'll take some time to sort it out," said Anders. "Maybe a month or two." He had clearly been up all night and his nerves were starting to wear thin. He had been talking to Houston on the phone, giving reports, news, damage estimates, analyses, predictions. His voice was course and dry.

The car pulled up to the gate of the Wilde Oil office building, where there were four armed guards, and some concrete blocks which made vehicles slow down and turn several times to get through. Joey realized that the car's windows were an inch thick – they were bullet-proof – but, as he also knew, they would not withstand bombs.

The guards, in bullet-proof jackets, asked to see ID cards, and the men in the car showed their cards through the windows. The guards opened the gate and waved them thru, allowing the car to pull up in front of the main entrance. Joey and Anders got out and showed their ID cards to get into the building. There were sand-bags stacked everywhere, against the doors and windows, and around the cars parked in the courtyard.

The building was empty – it was still only 7:00 AM, and no one had yet come to work. Joey went to the room which had been designated as his office; it too was filled with sandbags which were blocking the window. There was a note on his desk; Page had called and had left the number for her office, in Mazar-e-Sharif. Joey called, and let the phone ring for some time, but there was no answer; it was still only 7:15.

There was a paper memorandum on his desk, a copy of the memo sent to all Wilde Oil employees, advising on security measures that were required for all foreigners in Afghanistan. The office was filled with sandbags, furniture, and company-wide safety/security instructions.

There was a knock on the office door, and Josh Mills came in. "How was your trip?" he asked.

"Pretty bad, if you include the bombs," said Joey. "But I guess you had just as much fun right here!"

"Yeah, pretty bad." He was silent for a moment. "I stopped by to say adios."

"Adios? You mean you're bailing out?"

"Yep! I'm a married man! My wife says get out, I get out!" He smiled. "And she REALLY said 'get out!'"

"When?"

"Tomorrow, if not sooner!"

Joey shook his head, but said nothing.

"How about you? When are you leaving?"

"Me? Oh, I don't know. I don't have a wife."

"No, but you got a girl-friend! You think we don't know? Everyone here knows! It's not so awful!" He smiled. "If I were you, I'd get her out of here as fast as you can. I was in Iran when it started there. All the ex-pats had their wives, even their families, with them. But when it started, everyone was scrambling to get out! It wasn't easy!" He smiled and gave Joey a friendly punch in the arm.

"I gotta go, Joey. Take care of yourself." And he was gone. Joey heard his steps echoing down the empty corridor.

56. Kandahar

The mullahs sat in the small room in Kandahar, waiting for someone to arrive. At last the person they were waiting for knocked on the door, opened it, and stepped inside. He was a young man, sweating and dirty. He put his hand over his heart and bowed his head slightly, as the others in the room signaled for him to sit down. He was exhausted, and his djellaba was covered with dust. One of the mullahs gave him a glass of tea from the big samovar in the corner. The new arrival thanked him and sat with his tea in the place for outsiders.

"We are waiting to hear your information," said one of the older mullahs, gently.

The young man touched his forehead and his heart, and began to speak. He had a hard time talking, and drank tea from time to time. He had not eaten, and one of the mullahs passed him some cakes.

"It was dark and cold, but there were no guards, no one there. We did our work swiftly, because sometimes there are trucks that come, with the guards, to inspect. But we know how to do it. We have done many. So we arranged our material and ran the wire out to some rocks. We hid behind the rocks.

"There was a big noise, and flames, and much fire and smoke. There was much wind. We ran, fast, as far as we could. We could see it from very far. Very, very far!"

There was a silence in the room. "Inshallah," said one of the mullahs. "You have done well." He passed a plate of sweets to the young man, who eagerly took two, then three.

"Go home, young man, and rest. You have done well." The mullahs all nodded in agreement, their faces stern and silent. The young man rose stiffly, bowed with his hand over his heart, and was gone. There was a silence.

"We must do this more," said one.

"Yes ... more!" said another.

57. Mazar-e-Sharif

In Mazar-e-Sharif, Page got to her office early. She saw from the old local telephone that she had received a call, but there was no message, and the calling number was not indicated. She thought Joey was still in Texas, so she could not imagine that it was from him. After a few minutes the head nurse came in, and the two started their morning round of the small children's hospital. The doctor would arrive later – he was very busy. And there was much to do here, too, in the Center for Wounded Children for the Northern sector of Afghanistan.

In Kabul, Joey was reflecting on his situation. He had been in similar circumstances before – major forces, even massive military forces, gathering to face each other, with Joey somewhere in-between. Since he did not like military forces, it was a place he did not like to be.

New explosions had been set off – in Texas and in Afghanistan – they were signals that conflict was coming, and all his instincts were telling him to get out. He hated conflicts, had had his fill of conflicts, and fled them whenever he could.

Joey knew he owed a personal debt to Pendleton Highsmith, the President of Wilde Oil, who had helped him years ago, and he was always determined to repay his debts. It was a key element in his personal code of ethics. But he could not stop conflicts, could not change history, nor even the way history evolved. The best thing he could do for Highsmith in these circumstances would be to warn him of what was surely happening here, and what was coming.

And he thought of Page. If some form of war was coming to Afghanistan, she should leave. Even if it was just a war between Afghan factions, it would bring harm to many people, especially among the many foreigners who were here in the country, trying to help the people.

As he thought of the situation – of his own situation – he understood that for him the most important thing was to get Page out of the country – away from the danger, away from Afghanistan. He would leave, but not without her.

58. Kabul

Joey knocked on the door of Max Anders' office, which was open, and walked in. Anders was at his desk, deep in thought. He looked up at Joey and said, "There have been attacks on two American embassies in East Africa. They say it's the work of a terror group based here, in Afghanistan. If that's the case, it's only a matter of time before they hit us here."

Joey sat down opposite Anders. "What group?" he asked. "There are many groups here."

"Al Qaeda, they say. I never heard of it before." Anders was a petroleum engineer, very focused on his work. He was not someone who followed the local political scene – except when it touched on his pipeline project. He was clearly now thinking that these attacks might relate to the pipeline project, might even put it in jeopardy.

"If they are based here, and they are attacking American embassies in Africa, I guess it won't be long before they attack us," said Joey.

"Yep," said Anders, deep in thought. "I guess we have to plan for it. For how to deal with it."

"We should have a discussion with Highsmith," said Joey. "It's not a local issue. If there's a group here which can attack embassies in Africa, then we are like sitting ducks. Even worse – because we are more tempting targets than embassies – especially embassies in Africa!"

"Yep," said Anders again. He picked up his phone and the Wilde Oil operator came on line. "Can you call Wilde Oil in Houston," he said, "and leave a message with the operator there. I need to talk to Mr. Highsmith as soon as possible, as soon as he comes into his office there." He knew that it was still the middle of the night in Texas. He looked at his watch. "I guess he won't call back until this afternoon, so we have a little time to prepare." He buzzed an assistant and asked him to call a staff meeting as soon as possible. There were many things to discuss.

Joey said they should go to the US Embassy, to see what information they could get, and how they saw the situation. He called, was connected with the Political Counselor at the Embassy, and asked for a meeting. The Counselor suggested that Joey and Anders come to the Embassy as soon as possible; they would set up a meeting with the relevant officials of the Embassy staff.

Joey told Anders what he had arranged, and the two of them walked downstairs to leave for the Embassy. There was a crowd in front of the Wilde Oil building, so Joey and Anders took a company car and left by the back gate.

The Embassy was under heavy security, with Afghan guards outside and armed U.S. Marines in battle gear inside the gate. Joey and Anders were met at the entrance and taken to the "tank" – the "secure" conference room which resembled a transparent plastic box the size of a medium-sized room, with a conference table and chairs inside.

There were three people already waiting in the tank – the Acting Ambassador (the embassy was still awaiting the nomination of an official ambassador), the Political Counselor, and the "Station

Chief," who was the head of the CIA branch for the country. There were introductions all around and the group sat down.

Anders explained that his team had just learned of the bombing attacks on the two US Embassies in East Africa, and that they were attributed to an organization which was said to be based in Afghanistan. Since Wilde Oil's pipeline project had already been attacked, with one of its pumping stations destroyed, the company was concerned about this new expansion of terrorist activities that seemed to be based in Afghanistan. He and Joey had come to learn whatever the Embassy could tell them about the security situation and how it was likely to evolve. He said that he had a phone discussion with the leadership of the Wilde Oil corporation in Houston set for that afternoon, and they would certainly ask what measures the company should be taking in these new circumstances.

The Acting Ambassador, who was a career diplomat from the State Department, was fluent in the Afghan language and was considered an expert on the country, welcomed the two visitors. He said that the Embassy had been watching the company's work for some time, and had frankly been wondering when there might be some form of attack against their project. The Embassy was well aware of the company's efforts to build a base of support in the country – the schools and training programs they had sponsored, the briefings for local groups along the path of the pipeline, the employment of numerous Afghans, including women, and other examples. They also had considerable respect for the company's security efforts. And the excursion to Houston was a real gem – it was a really great idea.

At the same time, they had been watching the growth of hostility toward the project from some elements of Afghan society who were viscerally opposed to the growth of foreign influence in the country. The most active, and perhaps also the most hostile, was a group called "al Qaeda," which the diplomat explained meant "the base" in Arabic. The leader of this recently-emerged group was from Saudi Arabia, and had significant funds at his disposal. Although he had only emerged in this role recently, he had considerable personal wealth, and seemed to be a determined, ruthless and inventive terrorist leader.

Frankly, he said, he could not be optimistic about the Wilde Oil pipeline project. The Acting Ambassador echoed this thought. The Embassy anticipated more incidents – and the pipeline project was a very attractive target for them – it appeared to many Afghans as a physical symbol of Western intrusion into the country, and was an easy target because it crossed hundreds of miles of empty land. He thought that the attack which had already taken place would surely be repeated, and that the company should take the necessary precautions – possibly even review their decision to undertake construction of the pipeline in the first place. The situation could become difficult if these hostile groups persisted, and gained support, as the Embassy thought was very likely. The Embassy itself would be undertaking a significant security up-grade.

Joey asked about the effect of the visit by some Afghan leaders to Texas, and the Embassy representatives agreed that it was a positive initiative. But, they said, Wilde Oil should be realistic; it would take a huge effort to have any real impact on public opinion in the country. And meanwhile groups like al Qaeda were building on the already-existing suspicions of foreigners, which were strong at all levels of Afghan society, and in every part of the country.

The attacks in East Africa signaled that al Qaeda was going to become more active, more destructive, and the Wilde Oil project was out there as an existing, in-country, target – and a particularly easy one because it aroused all the Afghan suspicions regarding foreigners and foreign ideas, which were latent in the country. The Wilde Oil pipeline was already a visible target, and the recent blowing-up of a pumping station was a signal that there would be more destructive attacks.

In the opinion of these well-informed observers, it was only a matter of time before al Qaeda targeted Wilde Oil and its pipeline project – more aggressively and more openly. They were probably planning attacks against the project right now.

Joey and Anders returned to the Wilde Oil offices in silence. There would have to be a frank talk with the Wilde Oil leadership when the company offices opened in Houston.

59. Kabul and Houston

"Hello, Pen?" said Joey.

"Yes, hello Joey! I can hardly hear you, but I can imagine what you are calling about. No need to worry! No need at all! Everything is under control!" He paused, then added: "You're on the speaker phone. I have all the top people concerned with this matter here in my office, so you can get the best advice possible. So go ahead, and we will respond."

Joey could hear some discussion going on in the background. "Well," he said, "we are already worried, and if you were here you would be too. We think the attack on one of our gas pumping stations shows that we are already in the sights of these people. It may be just a matter of time before we are attacked in a major way! We just came back from the Embassy, and they advised us to get out! They take the threat very seriously."

The chief security official for Wilde Oil came on the line. "We need to know what you think it would be useful to have, to assure your security, so we can start sending you everything you need."

Joey and Anders looked at each other, sharing the same thought: it was not a matter of sending some additional stuff to them in Afghanistan – the problem was just beginning in Afghanistan. A war was likely to break out, in which the Wilde Oil pipeline project would be a prime target – perhaps the prime target. The company had become a symbol of foreign influence and exploitation which provoked resentment toward foreigners wherever they were working.

"Pen," Joey began, "I don't think you understand the situation we are in, out here. The main terrorist organization in this country just blew up two of our embassies in countries which are on another continent, and blew up one of our pumping stations here. We are a much easier and cheaper target, here in Afghanistan, and we are not so popular with the people here for us to expect anyone to stand up and defend us. And they have already signaled that we will be a target here, by blowing up one of our gas pumping stations. We are sure to be the central targets here."

There was some discussion in the background at the Houston end of the call. Then the chief security officer of the Wilde Oil Corporation came on the phone. "We will be reinforcing our security there, as soon as possible. No need to worry," he said. "I'm sending my chief deputy out to your place as soon as he can get on a plane. He will make some recommendations, based on what you show him, and tell him. And we will take it from there. We will assure your security. You can count on that!"

"Okay," said Joey, although he was skeptical that the visit of one of the company's senior security planners would change the vulnerability of their exposure any time soon. "That sounds like a good step. But you may also have to take some personnel actions. Josh Mills just resigned and left – he said his wife would not let him stay in this new situation. He will be hard to replace. So It is not just a security question."

There was a silence on the line. Then Highsmith's voice said, "We will replace Mills as soon as possible." He paused, then added "I will work with our specialists and we will add a "danger bonus" to salaries. And I'll talk to the State Department, so you can coordinate with the Embassy there, get their views on what is happening and how we can assure your security. Send me all your recommendations, and we will try to match them as quickly as possible."

There was some further discussion about specific items and adjustments, and it was agreed that there would be a conference call by phone every morning, Houston time, as long as the situation was of concern.

60. Mazar-e-Sharif

Page heard of the incidents in Africa and in a nearby region of Afghanistan, and she understood that they had been sponsored by a terrorist organization based in the country. But she did not want such matters to interrupt her work with handicapped children. She began to hear of Americans – some of them were her friends – who were leaving their work in Afghanistan and returning to the USA, and the Consulate sent a notice to each American citizen in its area of responsibility, recommending that they leave the country.

But she was devoted to her work, and did not see how terrorists would want to interrupt the work of people who were helping handicapped Afghan orphan children. She was determined to stay, and to continue her work.

Joey managed to reach her two days later, over a phone connection which was very bad – they could hardly hear each other.

"You should leave, go back to America, as soon as possible," said Joey. Page recognized the tone of urgency in his voice, but did not see how she could leave her work.

"What would they do here?" she asked. "Who would run this place, take care of these children?"

"There are plenty of Afghan women who can run your clinic. You have some working there now. They can stay – it's their country – but Americans will have a hard time. They will be targeted! You should leave." There was a tone of serious concern in his voice, which Page recognized.

Page did not say anything for a moment. Then she added "Anyway, I have no place to go."

"What do you mean, no place to go?" said Joey, alarmed by this new element. "You go to your parents, your relatives, your friends!"

There was a silence on the phone line, then Page said "My parents are dead and I don't have any relatives. Nor any friends, really."

Joey was stunned. He knew Page well, but he knew nothing of her family, or her background. He only knew of their life together – as colleagues, friends and lovers. They had never discussed her family. Page had always understood that Joey was a "loner", and she did not want to bring any "complications" into their relationship.

"You go directly to my house," he said, "the key is under the step. It is your house too. You stay there, and wait for me. For as long as it takes!"

There was a silence on the line. Page was reflecting. "I have to think," she said. "I can't leave these children alone!"

"When you decide, you go," said Joey. "Decide quickly! Take the easiest route, and leave. When you get to the States, go directly to our house, and wait for me." His voice was filled with emotion. Page could hear it. He was never like this.

"But you?" she said, tears forming, blurring her eyes.

Joey paused. "I will come. Don't worry about me. I know how to take care of myself. I will be there. Just go. As soon as possible! We will be there, together. Soon! I promise!" He had to go, there were things happening, things to do. He hung up the phone.

Page sat for a moment, immobile, listening to the buzzing of the disconnected phone. Then she hung up. There was so much to do.

The next day a suicide attack using hijacked airliners destroyed the Twin Trade Towers in New York City.

61. Kandahar

In Kandahar three men met outside a mosque to share the news. When they separated, each one walked away in a different direction. One went to a run-down building with outside steps leading down to a shabby basement door. He knocked on the door – a special knock – and the door was opened by a young man with a Kalashnikov sub-machine gun. The man pushed his way past the guard and rushed to the back of the basement, where he opened a door. A group of men looked up at him as he entered.

"Salam," said the newcomer. "There is news. From the city called New York, in America. There has been an attack – a great attack! The biggest buildings, in the biggest city, have been destroyed. An attack from the air, has destroyed them. It is said to be the work of something called Al Qaeda!" There was murmuring among the men gathered in the room. All were dressed in black robes, with pakol hats and scarves. Tea was brought by a boy, and the men talked excitedly among themselves.

Small groups of men gathered in mosques in cities throughout the country, in spite of the late hour. They were somber but excited, not knowing what this news might mean for them. What could it signify? What new developments could it foreshadow? How would it affect their country, their lives? Could this be good news? Or could it bring some form of disaster for their country, for themselves?

And the same questions were being asked, in small groups, throughout the Muslim world – across the Middle East, Central Asia and Africa. What did it mean, and what would it bring? What new convulsions would the World now face?

62. Kabul

Joey tried all day to reach Page, but the telephone lines were overloaded and were not working. There were urgent meetings at the Wilde Oil offices in Kabul, and long conference calls with Houston – urgent measures were being arranged, with rapid increases in security, and the immediate transfer of all families and non-essential workers back to the US. The Wilde Oil offices in Kabul were surrounded by police and private security agents.

In Mazar-e-Sharif, Page visited the American Consulate, fully covered by her black jellaba, with its ample hood and face mask. She asked to see the Vice Consul and waited in a small waiting room. Soon he was free and opened his door, signaling to Page to come in.

"You need to get organized and leave," he said without any preliminaries. "We have instructions from the State Department to encourage – to insist – that Americans leave. You are in a very visible position, and you could be targeted. You really have to leave. I will help in any way I can, but we are also going to close – as soon as we can organize it." He was clearly alarmed, and somewhat overwhelmed. It was a small Consulate, and he was already taking the steps to permit immediate closure.

"But I have responsibilities here," said Page. "How can I walk away from the children in my clinic?"

The Vice Consul gave her an imploring look. "You have to understand, Page. Everything is going to change. We will go to war here; it is inevitable after the attack in New York. Civilians just have to get out, as quickly and as safely as they can. You have to listen to me; make your plans as best you can, and leave."

He paused for a moment. "It's already difficult just to get to Kabul. And after that, too! All the departing flights are full. Half the people in the country are trying to leave."

He gave Page an imploring look. "Don't you know what is happening?" he asked. "Listen, you will probably have difficulty even getting to Kabul – the roads are jammed! I will be leaving tomorrow, in a special convoy. After that, you may well be alone here! You might be able to get into our convoy. I will check that. But if you stay on after that, you will be alone. The Consulate will be closed."

Page was stunned. She could not have imagined how quickly all this would develop. She needed some time, to ensure that the clinic would continue to operate. She could not simply walk away from the children there.

She looked at the Vice Consul in silence, not knowing what she should do. He pressed her: "Page, our convoy is leaving tomorrow morning. You can come in my car if you want, if you decide to do it. We will leave from the courtyard at dawn, at about 6 AM. I will save a place for you in my car – just a small suitcase, please!"

He smiled. "You knew there would be risks when you decided to come here," he said, "and so there have been risks." He opened his hands. "You have done the best you could, you have done a lot of good things. But now you must think of yourself. Be in the courtyard by six!"

Page left the office in confusion, not knowing what she should do, what she could do. She put her black vail across her face, and covered her hair with the hood of her robe, as she left the Consulate. There were excited crowds everywhere. People were shouting, moving very fast, carrying huge packages on their heads. She was bumped and shoved as she worked her way through the crowds, back to her clinic, her tiny office, her small world.

Aiea was waiting in Page's office. She saw immediately that Page was in shock, and she understood why. "All the foreigners are leaving," she said as Page entered the room. "I know it is very difficult to leave." She paused, trying to understand Page's vague look – it seemed as though she was miles away, not listening and focused on some distant thought. "You should leave, too!" she blurted out with some emotion. "You should not be here. Americans will not be safe! Foreigners will not be safe!"

But Page was not listening – and seemed lost in thought as she sat at her desk. "The little one, who came in last night?" she asked. "Is she alright? Will she be alright?"

Aiea responded immediately. "She is fine! All of them are fine!" She understood Page's thinking. "They will all be fine, even if you go! You have made this clinic," she said. "It will continue when you leave. You must not worry about that! You must go. We all want you to go, to be safe." She took Page's hand. "You must go, and leave this clinic. We will take care of the clinic, of the small ones here!"

Page moved her hand, asking Aiea to leave her alone, and the young woman slowly left the room, sitting outside the door in order to help if Page needed her. It was where she always sat, what she always did.

63. Kabul

Joey went with an armed convoy to visit the pipeline construction site, to evaluate the security there in this new situation. It was an all-day trip, with many new security check-points and other delays. It seemed as though half of Afghanistan was moving from one location to another, after the attacks in New York. Everyone wanted to be somewhere else, anticipating an American response, but uncertain what that might be, or where to go to avoid it.

The convoy included armed guards, with military vehicles leading and following the American group. Joey's car included Max Anders and two company engineers who had been asked to evaluate the status of construction and to come up with some alternative choices for the company in the new security situation everyone knew they would now face.

There was now an assumption that the American government would retaliate against the group which had attacked the Twin Trade Towers in New York, and that this would mean that some form of warfare would engulf at least parts of Afghanistan, especially where the Taliban were strongest. It was just a matter of time, and there might also be symbolic responses immediately – including missile attacks which could be targeted on several regions of the country. The Wilde Oil company had to try to foresee what might happen, and at the same time evaluate the possible options for their pipeline construction project.

Joey was not in a very positive mood for this trip. He was pessimistic about the future of the Wilde Oil pipeline project, but was reluctant to say anything in this sense among the people who were actually working on the project. Their job was to come up with suitable options for continuation of the construction – just closing it down was not really possible because of the huge investments the company had already made in it. Delays in construction would be much more expensive than continuing it.

He was also very concerned about Page – now cut off and isolated in the northernmost part of the country. He knew she was resourceful and would manage her situation well, but he also knew that she was a very determined person, and might well try to continue the work of her clinic in Mazar-e-Sharif, in spite of what looked increasingly like a broad and dangerous looming war. She might even consider it essential to stay, in spite of the obvious danger.

He had tried repeatedly to reach her by telephone, but the lines to Mazar-e-Sharif were not functioning, and even the Consulate there had been closed. The most news the Wilde Oil team got was from satellite TV broadcasts, and their daily discussion with Houston by satellite phone, and this was at best incomplete.

No one was yet certain of what the US response to the attack on the Twin Trade Towers in New York would be, and anything greater than a symbolic retaliatory strike would take time to prepare. Even the choice of a target for such a response was difficult – the attackers were known to be agents of an elusive terrorist organization – not a government, nor a country – just a band of terrorists. The very form of warfare in such a situation would need to be developed, almost from scratch.

But Joey was slowly coming to a decision of his own – on how long, and to what extent, he would continue to support the Wilde

Oil project. Following the attack on the Twin Towers in New York, he was concluding that the pipeline project in Afghanistan was dead – at least for the foreseeable future – and that would mean that his obligations toward Pen Highsmith would also be concluded. He had responded positively to Highsmith's request for help, but now the situation was well beyond his abilities as an international "fixer."

In this new situation it might well be time for him to go home to Maine, once he had given Highsmith his recommendations on what to do with the pipeline project in these new circumstances. It was, he thought, a whole new set of world security challenges – after the attack in New York and other terrorist actions around the world. It was the opening of what might well be a very long period of international conflict, with a new type of global warfare, based on new objectives and rules which would take time to fully understand. In any case, he could do no more for Wilde Oil in Afghanistan, in this new situation.

64. Mazar-e-Sharif

Page tried repeatedly to reach Joey, but the phone lines to Kabul were not working. After dark a messenger came from the Consulate with a short message from the Vice Consul, saying that the Consulate motorcade would leave earlier than planned; it would leave the courtyard of the Consulate at midnight. She should be there no later than 11:30.

But Page was still organizing her departure – designating who should be responsible for the many activities of the clinic, in her absence. By the time she felt that everything had been resolved, and that the clinic would function without her, it was already past midnight, and she knew she had missed the departure of the Consulate staff. She slept badly in the small bedroom attached to her office, not knowing what would happen next.

When she awoke, early the following morning, she tried another time to call Joey, but once again the inter-city phone lines were not working. Aiea had also slept in the clinic, and came to Page's office early. The Consulate convoy had left as planned, Aiea reported, and the consulate was now closed for the foreseeable future. Page was despondent and Aiea was concerned.

"It is maybe not so bad that you miss the convoy," she said. "They could have much trouble on the road to Kabul. That road is controlled by Taliban. They will stop convoy." The young woman had heard this in the morning gossip, which was sometimes well-informed and foresighted. Both she and Page knew that the women's gossip often turned out to be true.

"There is another way," said Aiea, thoughtfully. "Another way for you to leave." She looked intently at her boss, her friend. "If you want, I can see what is possible." She looked inquisitively at Page.

"What are you talking about, Aiea?" Page asked. "What other way?"

The young woman was silent for a moment, then approached Page and whispered into her ear: "The northern route." She put her index finger to her lips, to indicate that Page should not say anything, and took Page by the hand.

Slowly, she got Page to follow her out into the corridor, and the two walked in silence toward the stairs leading to the second floor. Halfway up the stairs Aiea stopped, leaned toward Page, and whispered into her ear, "If you want, I can get you out of the country, to Dushanbe. I can arrange it for tonight." She put her finger to her lips. "Think about it," she added.

65. Kabul

Joey was awoken by the phone in his hotel room in Kabul. It was Anders. He told Joey that the convoy from the Consulate in Mazar-e-Sharif had been ambushed by the Taliban, and that it seemed many of the people in it had been either killed or taken as prisoners. The young consul had escaped, and was coming to Kabul. Joey was stunned – it was possible that Page had been in that convoy. He called the Embassy to see if he could find out, but no one could tell him anything; they were waiting for news themselves.

When the time came to leave on their daily round of visits to Wilde Oil installations, Joey could not find Anders. He asked the office which managed all the company cars, and was told that Anders had already left for the pipeline work site. He tried a few more times to reach Page, then took another car and told the driver to catch up to the convoy carrying Anders.

66. The North of Afghanistan

Page and Aiea took a taxi to the north-east, heading to a small village near the border. Aiea knew the driver, who was a distant cousin of hers. She tried to explain the family relationship, but got lost and dropped the matter. "You get the picture," she said.

They drove for two hours without seeing many cars – the border crossings in this part of the country were all closed. In the midst of a very barren landscape of rocks and flat desert stretching to distant mountains, Aeia told her cousin to turn off on a side road. They followed a sandy track North for some miles and were soon out of sight of the main highway. Ahead was a tiny village – just two or three yurts standing well apart from each other.

As they neared the village they passed among small groups of tethered Mongolian camels – the two-humped Bactrian camels which were native to this region. Some were lying down while others nibbled away at stacks of grainy grass. They were tethered, and some had bits in their mouths as well as reigns slung between their two humps. These hardy Bactrian camels were patiently chewing their food or relaxing in the sand.

Soon the taxi pulled up in front of a large Central Asian yurt, the home of the owner of some of these camels. He emerged from the yurt – a bearded older man with a cap on his head and boots which came up to his knees.

"Salam," shouted Aiea, and rushed to embrace this imposing figure. "My uncle!" she shouted over her shoulder to Page.

Page had learned that "uncle" could mean many different blood relationships in this part of the world, but all of these relationships were honored and sacred. The only people anyone would trust were their blood relations. The two women, plus the taxi driver (also a cousin of Aiea's uncle) were all invited into the yurt with great ceremony – there is no greater honor in Central Asia than to be invited into a person's home.

Inside, the yurt was a comfortable retreat – the ground was covered by several layers of colorful carpets, and a fire burned in a stove with a long chimney leading out of the canvas roof. The roof also contained an adjustable opening for light and fresh air. Aiea's uncle's wife was there, and quickly organized some hot tea and bread for the two women and the taxi driver-uncle.

There were smiles and conversational exchanges in all directions, and Page was relieved to find such a comfortable retreat in the middle of this Afghan desert. Aiea withdrew from the tent with her uncle to explain that she wanted him to take Page to a safe place on the other side of the border with Tadjikistan – to the other bank of the Amu Darya, the mighty river which divides Central Asia, all the way from the Aral Sea to the Hindu Kush.

Her uncle thought for a moment, considering the many technical elements – and possible challenges – involved in such a journey, at this time of the year, and then nodded his agreement.

67. The North of Afghanistan

Soon twilight faded into a moonless Central Asian night, and Page, Aiea and her uncle set out on camels, traveling directly north and navigating by the stars, across a seemingly endless desert, flat and hard. The night was cold and windy, but the camels seemed to know where they were going, so the three plodded on thru the sandy terrain, under the starry, moonless sky.

After two hours of travel, the land ahead spread, broad and flat under the dark night sky. In the distance they could see the edge of water – it was the Amu Darya, the vast river system which divides Central Asia into North and South, and which has shaped nations, races and civilizations for time immemorial. Page knew they would come to this river, and could only hope that Aiea's uncle had some way to cross it. On the other side was Tajikistan, where she had colleagues who would help her.

But it was the camels who knew best. When they arrived at the edge of the water they drank, and then turned Northwest, wading through the shallow water for a mile, then two miles, then still farther. After they had been advancing along the shoreline for some time, they could see a few yurts on the bank of the river, and came to a stop near one of these dwellings. Aiea's uncle dismounted, approached the biggest yurt and gave a soft whistle.

After a few minutes, a man came out of the yurt, and greeted Aiea's uncle as an old friend. The two men disappeared into the yurt for some time, while Page and Aiea waited outside. Finally the two men came out of the yurt, smiling and patting each other on the back. Aiea's uncle explained that his friend was a wise and experienced river-man, and that he would take them across the broad Amu Darya river.

Page was somewhat apprehensive, but at this point it would be difficult to back out of this plan – or to return to Mazar-e-Sharif. The group walked to a nearby storage area, near the water's edge, and the two men pulled a flat river boat across the sandy bank and into the shallows. Page could see that it was more of a flat barge, with short sides and a long rudder for steering. It had several long oars, which could also serve as poles, for pushing the barge through the shallow waters of the broad river, vastly diminished and narrow at this time of year.

The men pushed and pulled the barge into the shallow water at the river's edge, and pulled the two camels onto it, then motioned for Page and Aiea to come on board the floating craft. Page was apprehensive, but knew that there was no turning back at this point, as the two men poled and pushed the barge out into the slowly flowing river. Gradually, they moved forward thru the water, at first very slowly, but faster as the barge caught the slow current and moved northward toward the center of the river.

The boatman was experienced and knew his craft. He pushed the barge into the current, and used the moving water to advance across the river, while he steered it toward the nearest place on the opposite bank – a place where the water was shallow and the camels could take over and walk onward to solid land.

It was slow going, but gradually they could see that they were progressing, across the broad expanse of the slowly-flowing Amu Darya. At this time of year, the river was lowest and narrowest, and the current was also at its slowest.

The seemingly endless water stretched out before them, shimmering in the moonlight. But it was not deep in this dry season, and soon the camels knew they would be able to walk. They stepped carefully from the flat boat onto the sandy river-bottom, and shuffled their way through the remaining expanse of water – no one could even see the other bank – splashing and plodding as they stepped their sure-footed way across the still, shallow water at the edge of the riverbed.

Aiea's uncle, who was in the lead, turned and smiled at the two women. He had great confidence in his camels, and had crossed this river many times – often at night, under the moonlight, as they were doing now – during the season when that was possible.

After some time moving northward they could see a low ridge of land rising gently out of the water, just visible in the moonlight – they had reached the other bank, the northern shoreline of the riverbed. The camels clearly knew that they were leaving the river, so they paused to drink again, and then plodded ahead, up a flat incline away from the river, under the stars. The two women thanked the riverman, who was smiling and proud, and once again mounted the camels, with Aiea's uncle taking the lead.

Within another hour the land became greener and less flat, and soon there were a few scattered lights ahead. Page looked at her watch; it was three in the morning. They found a trail and moved steadily toward the lights, which turned out to be a small village with no one visible anywhere.

Aiea's uncle continued to lead slowly, through the small village and out the other side. When the village was out of sight, behind them, he explained that this was the first village in Tadjikistan, very close to the riverbank – and the international border – and he preferred not to stop there. It would be safer farther along the trail. The small group continued to move northward over the seemingly endless rolling dunes.

An hour later they entered a narrow valley and plodded forward thru some sparse trees. Ahead there was another village, and the first light of dawn was appearing over the mountains which formed the horizon to the East. "This village is 'Avin,'" said Aiea's uncle, with Aiea translating. "This is a town of Tajikistan, where there is a main road. I take you to my friend's house. He will take care of you."

Dim lights were coming on in the small windows of the village houses, and the first light of dawn was visible in the East, over some high mountains. The modest houses were scattered nearby, each one set far back from the dirt road, with low farm buildings attached. Roosters were beginning to crow, and here and there dim lights were appearing, with smoke rising from chimneys. In the East the sun edged slightly above the mountains which formed the horizon – it was the first light of dawn, and Page felt as though she had somehow escaped to safety. She had.

***

Later that day Page said an emotional goodbye to Aiea and her uncle as she climbed aboard a shabby bus headed to Dushanbe, the capital city. They would return that very night to his home yurt, crossing the river again. And Aiea would travel back to Mazar-e-Sharif and the clinic, where she would continue Page's work.

The two women were in tears, hoping to meet at some point in the future, but not really believing they would ever see each other again. Page gave her friend the bracelet she always wore, and asked her to write, care of the US Embassy in Kabul, to let her know how the clinic was doing, how her favorite patients were getting along. Aiea was nodding her agreement, thru her tears.

And then Page was gone, as the bus drove away through the dust. It had not rained for a month.

68. Kabul

When he got back to Kabul Joey was finally able to get through to the clinic in Mazar-e-Sharif, and was surprised to learn that Page was not there. He left a message asking that she call him back, wondering what had happened. But he was very busy helping Wilde Oil to sort out its new, and very disturbing, situation.

Some key people, both within the company and among its important share-holders, were advocating complete withdrawal from Afghanistan, and cancellation or sale of the pipeline project. This was because of the very troubling situation the company now found itself in – a terrorist organization based in the country where it was heavily invested had carried out the most damaging attack in the history of the company's home country. It was a brazen and ruthless attack against civilians in the heart of America's biggest city. The views of key stock-holders could not be ignored, and the top management was reviewing the possibility of sale, or even simple cancellation, of the project, in spite of the monumental losses that would entail.

In addition, the strategic and international situation had changed overnight, and the US was now headed toward war. There was no way the country could avoid going to war, to defeat and destroy the organization, based in Afghanistan, which had attacked the Twin Trade Towers in New York. The Wilde Oil company, and its shareholders, wanted nothing more at this point than to extract the company from this pipeline project, which was having a devastating effect on its sales and the market value of its stock shares.

Pen Highsmith was at the center of this vortex of issues, and was under pressure to either produce some convincing evidence of the solid future value of the Afghan investment, or to find a face-and-money-saving exit strategy. Unfortunately, neither of these options seemed to be readily available, and he was getting desperate. He thought Joey's presence in Kabul had been helpful, but unfortunately they had all been surprised by the attack in New York – which no one could possibly have foreseen.

Highsmith's strategy for moving out of this difficult situation was to bring Joey back to Houston and let him explain it to the key Wilde Oil shareholders. He was banking on Joey's credibility, as someone who knew how to face difficult situations, and who could regain the confidence of key shareholders. This would be done in a private session and would at least help to show that the company had been legitimately caught by surprise, and was keeping its key shareholders informed. No one could have foreseen the attacks against US Embassies in Africa, nor the destruction of the Twin Trade Towers in New York.

Joey could confirm all this in his tough and candid personal style, which would be reassuring in an open meeting with the company's leading shareholders. Highsmith was convinced that this would ease some of the pressures on Wilde Oil's corporate leadership. He asked his secretary to get Joey on the phone, or to ask him to call back, which she did. Joey called back the following morning, Houston time.

"Hello, Pen," said Joey. "I was wondering when you would call. What can I do for you?"

"Hello Joey," said Highsmith in his usual celebratory style. "I thought we should have a little talk. Our top shareholders are asking for an explanation of what's going on in Afghanistan, and why we aren't just cancelling the pipeline project there.

" Of course that would be very difficult to do, as I'm sure you realize – there would be heavy financial losses! I thought that you might be the best qualified person to give them a briefing on the situation in-country, and to explain the way forward. To reassure them, you understand?"

"Sure, I understand," said Joey, "But what is it you want me to do? Come to Houston? There's a lot going on here, you know, and maybe I should stay here – everyone is very nervous. If I just fly off to Houston some of my colleagues might, well, resent it."

"Just for a couple of days," said Highsmith. "For some informal talk, you know?"

"Okay," said Joey, "It's your show. Just tell me when you want me there."

"Great," said Highsmith. "We'll get back to you with some proposed dates. As soon as possible!"

Joey hung up the phone. "I wonder what that's all about," he thought.

69. Kabul

Joey asked the Embassy if they had any information about Page, and whether she had left Mazar-e-Sharif with the other Americans. The Embassy found the young man who had been the Vice Consul at the Consulate there when the evacuation took place – he was still in Kabul, awaiting evacuation to the USA – and he told Joey his story; how he had arranged for Page to join the evacuation convoy, and then had waited for her to arrive.

He said he had to leave to keep the long convoy of Americans together. Page had not arrived in time to join the convoy. The young Vice Consul knew she was hesitant about leaving, and just assumed that she had decided to stay, to manage her clinic in this time of crisis. The convoy had been ambushed on the way to Kabul, with some shooting, but they had managed to get to Kabul.

"So she may still be in Mazar," thought Joey, and resolved to go there to see what had happened, and to find Page. The Embassy was advising against any such "unnecessary travel," but Joey had his own ways of doing things, and started to plan an excursion to Mazar, even though it was now officially off-limits for American citizens.

He contacted his war-lord friend in Kandahar, — and asked if he could arrange for some sort of 'safe passage' to Mazar. His friend laughed, and asked "What you afraid of, Joey? You think anyone can do anything to you? Like they say in your country, "I don't think so!" and he laughed. Nevertheless, he contacted some friends, who agreed to allow Joey to visit Mazar – for just one day – without harassment.

When his war-lord friend gave him this news, Joey said, "Thanks, pal. I owe you one," right out of a cheap gangster movie. Joey reasoned that these Afghan war-lords had only seen their idols – American war-lords – in cheap American gangster movies, so they would only take seriously the language and motives they would recognize from those old films. And that seemed to be the case.

Joey "borrowed" a Wilde Oil car, and just drove by himself to Mazar-e-Sharif. He was stopped multiple times, but when he said who he was and who had approved his visit, he was simply waved through. Even so, it took him a full day to make the trip, because of the back-ups and delays resulting from the expanding hostilities between the Taliban and the Government.

When he arrived in Mazar, Joey drove to the city center and parked his car. He had a private word with a nearby thug, who he thought might have something to say about the matter, and explained that his visit had been approved by the local authorities. No one bothered him.

He walked to Page's clinic, and was shown to her old office, now being used by a couple of Afghan nurses. Joey asked them what had happened to Page; where was she? But the two nurses simply looked at each other and shrugged their shoulders. They did not know; one day she had been there, and the next day she had disappeared. That had taken place on the same day that the Consulate had been evacuated, so her colleagues at the clinic had simply assumed that she had left with the other Americans, in the convoy organized by the Consulate.

Joey was disturbed and worried, but he was at a dead-end, and returned to Kabul, where it would be easier for him to continue his efforts to find Page.

70. New Orleans

The old man walked slowly thru the urban park, waiting for his newly-designated contact to appear. He sat on a park bench, opposite a broad expanse of grass. There was almost no one in the park, other than himself, so he had taken the decision to sit down. It was not his usual way, but it was a hot, humid day, and he needed a brief rest. A well-dressed man crossed the park, and the old man thought this might be his new contact. But the man continued walking, right on out of the park – he had simply been taking a short-cut.

After a few moments a young man in a jacket – but no necktie – entered the park. This was the prescribed dress code for his meeting. The young man walked directly to the bench, and sat down next to the old man. "Salam," he said.

"Salam aleikum," the old man responded.

"Do you have something to tell me?" said the young man, a little too directly for the Old Man's traditional approach. But, he thought, probably typical of the younger generation.

"Go to the city called Houston, and wait," said the Old Man. "Go to the meeting place there – every day, as foreseen. I will see you there – perhaps not on the first days, but soon. I will give you details then. This will be an important mission for you."

The young man nodded, rose slowly, and walked away. The preparations were now in place, and the action itself would follow. The new man was young, but he would have to carry the responsibility. He looked like he could do it, and he was said to have knowledge of explosives. That was the important point; the rest would not matter much. After the event, it would not matter at all.

The old man sat for a few moments longer, then rose and left the park in another direction.

71. Kabul

The dates for Joey's trip to Houston were fixed, and he told Max Anders about his trip, explaining that he had been convoked by Highsmith to brief a number of key shareholders on the situation of their pipeline project in light of the new security situation in Afghanistan. They discussed what Joey should say, and which points were best left out; which information was for shareholders and which items were just for the senior management. There were lots of such items.

Anders told Joey that he was personally very pessimistic about the pipeline project in the new situation. He did not see how it could be completed in the face of broad and determined hostility from the Taliban, especially after the terrorist attacks in New York. Those attacks would encourage increased local hostility to the pipeline, to any American projects, and there was now a growing probability of US military action right here in Afghanistan. This was being considered – even openly discussed and planned – in Washington.

Anders could not see how the pipeline project could be continued in such a situation. He thought it could not be sustained, and would have to be abandoned. Joey assured him that he would be frank in his discussion with the Wilde Oil share-holders, and with Pen Highsmith.

Anders also confided that he personally did not see how he could stay on, leading the development of this project, in Kabul. His family was in Houston, pressuring him to return to the USA, and he was pessimistic that the project could even survive. He was looking for some way out. The energy business was broad, and he had many contacts in other places, other companies.

The two men had a long discussion over dinner in the company's favorite Kabul restaurant, talking until late in the evening. As they said goodnight, both of them wondered whether they would ever meet again. The oil business is like that, Anders said – you work closely with someone and then the situation changes, and you may never see that person again.

Joey left Kabul before dawn the next morning on a company plane to Karachi, to connect with a direct international flight to the USA.

72. Houston

"I know just how you feel," said Highsmith over the phone. He was talking to Wilson Warner, a key Wilde Oil shareholder. "It is certainly a very touchy situation, Will." He looked at the ceiling, listening to a list of complaints and concerns from the other end of the call and rolling his eyes toward the ceiling. "I could not agree more!" he said. "I talked to the State Department this morning, and they told me the options they are looking at." He listened and then replied, "Yes, all the options!"

There was another question over the phone. "No, I don't think they're considering that. I hope not. But short of that, they're considering all the options. I can assure you." He listened again. "We are getting a report on that. Yes, a new report, on the new situation. Very soon, and I will share it with you."

He listened again. "Well, as a matter of fact, we have asked our key man in Kabul to come back to Houston just for that, just to inform you – and some of our other friends – of the situation there. He will be here tomorrow. Can you come to hear him out? You can ask him all the questions you want." After a few moments he closed the conversation and hung up the phone, simultaneously buzzing his secretary.

"Where is Torino now?" he asked, and then added "See if you can reach him on his plane." A minute later he buzzed his secretary again. "See if you can get Ambassador Rudolphus in Washington. Elaine Rudolphus. If she isn't available tell her assistant that I need to talk to her, as soon as possible."

After a moment he buzzed again. "And have the conference room set up for some VIP visitors tomorrow morning at ten. And ask the Shareholder Liaison folks to organize a reception for some of our top owners. Yes, tomorrow morning at 10. And get me the full list of VIP owners. I'll tell you who to invite."

A few minutes later he buzzed his assistant again. "And arrange for me to meet Joey's plane. I'll talk to him in the car."

73. Flight to Houston

Joey's flight from Karachi landed in London just in time for him to make a last-minute connection to a direct overnight flight to Houston. He was in business class, so he immediately converted his seat into a bed, drew up a blanket, and slept. He was used to long-distance travel and could sleep on trans-Atlantic flights.

He was worried about Page – hoping she was safe – it was really the only thing on his mind. But he knew she was resourceful, and that the Taliban did not usually target women. The most important thing would be for her to get out of Afghanistan. She was determined and loyal, and would not leave her clinic easily. But he thought she would understand the risks of staying in Mazar-e-Sharif after the Consulate was closed, and was probably getting out right now. It was the only explanation he could think of for the fact that she had not joined the Consulate's motorcade when it left Mazar-e-Sharif for Kabul. She must have found another way to travel. But this did not sooth his anxieties, and he could not help being concerned; he had been unable to reach her from his portable phone.

When he awoke it was dark outside and his flight was nearing North America. He went to the Business Class Galley, got some snacks and a beer, and returned to his seat. He opened his portable phone and tried calling Page again, on her portable phone. After a few rings, she answered. "Where are you?" he asked.

"In Dushanbe."

"Where?"

"Dushanbe. Everything is fine. I got here yesterday."

"How?"

"Too complicated to explain. Anyway, I'm here, I know some people here, and I have some money left." She paused. "Where are you? I've been worried."

"I'm in a plane. Headed to Houston. You should get back to the States as soon as you can. No one knows where this situation may lead. And don't worry about me. I'm just fine."

"Houston?" She paused. "I will go back to America, as soon as I am sure my clinic is safe, and my staff."

"Don't wait too long. Things will get complicated – all over the region – after the attack in New York. Do you have enough money for a ticket to the US? Flights could start getting crowded."

"I need to ensure that my colleagues, and our patients, are safe. Then I can leave. Anyway, I'm fine here. Don't worry."

"Do you have this number I'm using?" Joey asked.

"Yes."

"Call me. About anything. Just call me. I'm arriving in Texas this afternoon."

"Why are you going to Texas?"

"Company business. When you travel, let me know. And be careful."

"Alright."

They said goodbye, and ended the call. Joey ate some snacks. He was suddenly very hungry.

74. Washington

In Washington, the Secretary of Defense was annoyed as he returned to his office in the Pentagon. All the possible options he had put forward to respond to the attack in New York had been rejected by the President. They were either too small or too big, according to the tense discussion he had just come from at the White House. He was supposed to come up with more choices, more options, immediately!

He had already alerted his staff, and expected new options to be on his desk when he arrived. When he did not see them he buzzed his chief staff assistant.

"Where are they?" he demanded.

"They're coming," said the assistant. "I just checked. They're coming up now."

"I'm waiting," said the Secretary. He looked at the motto, inscribed in big letters on his wall: "Never give up; never give up; never give up," it read. A buzzer sounded on his vast desk. "Yes," he said, pushing the button.

"They're here," said his assistant. The door opened and in walked an Army General, carrying a set of briefing books.

"Good afternoon, Mr. Secretary," he said as he crossed the broad space to approach the desk. "Here are some more possible options. Personally, I favor the first one; destroy their nest. We should definitely do that, anyway, and maybe add one or two of the others, just for good measure."

He laid a series of papers on the Secretary's desk, and pointed to the "Summary" – a one page layout with four options, any one of which could be chosen by scribbling a check-mark in the indicated square, and signing at the bottom of the page. These would only be recommendations, of course, but the President had a strong history of approving the Defense Secretary's recommendations, so the assumption was that what he recommended would be the approved course of action.

"What's this fourth box?" the Secretary asked.

"Do nothing," the General replied. "No action. We would just make a statement. For example, 'we are studying possible options;' or 'we will respond in due course;' – stuff like that."

The Secretary scrutinized the options paper. "All the options are in there?"

"Yes."

"Then I'll sign it." He signed at the bottom of the page. "Send it over right away. He's waiting for it."

The General took the signed document and handed it to his assistant, standing behind him. The assistant, a Colonel, rushed out the door to the transmission room, to send the signed memo to the White House.

"I hope that's what they want!" said the Secretary. "It's always so difficult; you have to list every option you can possibly think of, and even then they aren't happy!"

231

"I think it's a great options paper, sir," said the General, "They're sure to like it!"

"Let's hope so. What happened to that other thing I was looking at? The one about the command structure? I thought that was pretty good."

The General left the office to find the missing memo, leaving the Secretary alone for the first time that day.

75. Houston

Highsmith finally got thru to the office of Under Secretary Rudolphus. He was sitting in his car at Houston Airport, waiting for Joey Torino's plane to land.

"Hello, Elaine?" He shouted to be sure he could he heard at the other end. The secretary was putting him thru. "Elaine?" he shouted again, against the noise of the all-pervasive air conditioning fans. Again there was no response. Finally the Under Secretary came on the line.

"Hello, Pen," she said over some background noise. "You'll have to speak up. I'm at the Marine Academy." There was the sound of a marching band in the background, playing a John Phillip Sousa March. "What can I do for you?"

"Hello Elaine, I'm sorry to bother you in the midst of some sort of ceremony."

"It's not a ceremony," came the reply. "It's the normal routine. They do this all the time!" She was annoyed to have to talk on the phone in the middle of a parade. It didn't look good. On the other hand, it looked very busy, so it wasn't that bad.

"Look, Elaine, I'm getting calls from our biggest stock-holders, wondering what's going on, what's going to happen," said Highsmith. "What can I tell them? Are we going to war in Afghanistan? Is that a real possibility? I need to know because of our project out there. You know, the big pipeline project?" He paused, to get some reaction, which would give him a hint as to how he should slant his question.

"War? Who said we were going to war?" exclaimed the Under Secretary. "We'll do a little clean-up. That's all! No war! We're not going to Congress for a declaration of war over this terrorist group!" She paused. "Where are you? There's a noise like a hundred whirring fans!"

"Well," said Highsmith, "That's because I'm surrounded by a hundred whirring fans!" He thought this was a very funny response, and started laughing. The door of his car was open, and passengers coming out of the Houston arrivals terminal were looking at him with some curiosity.

"Fans?" asked Elaine Rudolphus. "Where do you get fans? Is Wilde Oil that popular in Houston? I'll tell you, Pen, your outfit is not that popular here in D.C.! Some people are pushing to get you to withdraw from Afghanistan altogether, to cancel your pipeline. That might make the situation a little easier to deal with! Or at least a little clearer, and simpler! So – you don't have many fans here!"

"No," said Highsmith, "I meant cool air fans! Not fans who admire you! Fans just to keep cool!"

"Well," said the Under Secretary, all I can say is that I hope you can keep your cool when we get a little deeper into this Afghan mess, because it's going to take a lot of good-old US fire-power to sort this one out, and things are going to get, well, a lot warmer over there, too!" She snorted, which was not very lady-like but which she liked to do anyway because it was very ... expressive.

"I know what you mean," said Highsmith, realizing that he might have been a bit ... casual ... in his remarks. "Look, we will have a big share-holders meeting tomorrow, about Afghanistan. What can you tell me that I can use ... to calm them down, I hope."

"Tell them we've got the situation under control," said the Under Secretary. "Tell them it's an amateur terrorist outfit that has bitten off more than they can shoe. I mean chew! Damned retainer!" She fixed her dental bridge, which had come loose.

"I'm not talking to you, Pen, I meant my DENTAL retainer! Ha Ha Ha. Damned DENTAL retainer!" She snorted, as usual when she thought something was very funny.

Highsmith wondered what this was all about, but decided to cut the call short. There was some confusion there, and his instinct told him it would be best to terminate the call.

"Talk to you soon!" he said, and turned off his phone. Joey's plane was off-loading its passengers, and Highsmith was watching the exit closely.

76. Houston

"Joey!" shouted Highsmith, waving as he spotted Torino in the crowd of passengers coming out of the customs area. "Over here!" Joey gave a gesture with his hand, and headed for Highsmith.

"This is quite an honor," said Joey, "Being met by the President of the company!"

"What about your luggage?" asked Highsmith.

"Just this," said Joey, gesturing to the canvas bag he had slung over his shoulder. "I prefer to travel light."

The two men exited the building, where the Wilde Oil driver was waiting for them. Two minutes later they were in the airport traffic, heading for Houston.

"I thought I should brief you in the car," said Highsmith, "because we will walk right into a meeting when we arrive at the office. There will be a mix of Board Members and key stockholders, and they will all want to hear what you have to say. It's a very tricky situation, and I wanted to brief you in advance."

Joey nodded.

"Everyone is wondering what will happen next, of course. And they're also wondering whether the pipeline is sustainable after these attacks, whether this terrorist group is supported by the Afghan people in general, and what it will take to defeat them so they are no longer a threat. They are all looking to you to provide the answers."

Highsmith's voice was a bit hoarse from all the explaining he had been doing in the last few days – to investors, contractors, family groups and the press – trying to maintain that the Wilde Oil pipeline in Afghanistan was still a viable project after the attacks, which had been openly claimed by a terrorist group aligned with the Taliban. The terrorists were now warning that the pipeline would be a target, and were threatening all foreigners in the country.

Joey waited until Highsmith had come to a logical stopping-point before responding. "Look," he said, "I can answer some of these questions, but not all of them. No one knows the answers to most of these questions. Probably not even the Taliban."

"Well," said Highsmith, we need to reassure them, we need to show our confidence, to show that we can ride out this storm! You see what I mean, Joey? These are our major share-holders, so they need to be reassured. We don't want them selling out!"

"I will try to reassure them, as best I can, Pen. But the truth is that we don't really know what these terrorists want. Or what they might do. Or even who they are! If you believe the people who know them a bit, they just want all Westerners to leave the region, to leave them alone, to return to some sort of primitive version of Islam, and close off the outside world." He paused.

"I personally don't believe this version," he said. "I think most of them are being manipulated by a few cynical people, who just want to gain control of the country. These people want to return to some sort of fundamentalist Islam, as a convenient means of controlling the country – maybe the region."

Highsmith was anxious; "Yes, yes," he said. "That's very good! Very good! We can develop that! So we just want to expose them for what they are – just trying to gain control! That's very good! Our investors will like that – they know exploitation when they see it!" He laughed.

"Very good Joey, that will help! We can build on that." He paused. "And in the end it will prove to be a good investment, stabilizing the country, helping it to develop, supporting progress!" He was rubbing his hands together in his enthusiasm.

"Well," said Joey, "I don't know as I would be as optimistic as that, Pen." He looked, grimly and directly, at Highsmith. "These Taliban, their first objective is to get us to leave, and to isolate the region from the West, from Western influence," he said, in his soft voice. "I think they will be relentless in pursuit of that objective, and we will either have to find a way to live with that ... or we will have to get out!"

"Get out?" said Highsmith, alarmed. "Joey, we can't get out! We are invested up to our ears! You know this! We cannot leave! You must not say this to these investors! We have to maintain our position, our investment! You understand what I am saying? You can't say – 'Or get out!'"

"Don't misunderstand me," said Joey. "I'm not talking about the terrorists, the bombers who attacked New York. Those are cynical killers, taking advantage of simple, honest people." He looked Highsmith in the eye. "We must make it clear that what we are trying to do is in the interest of the Afghan people, not of some terrorist group. That's the challenge!"

Highsmith was alarmed, but was also trying to understand what Joey was saying, what he would be able to say to the key investors who would be waiting in the Wilde Oil conference room when they arrived. And how these investors, trying to protect their own interests, their investments, would react to what he was saying. He could not be in a position where Joey might appear to be contradicting him!

"We can say the pipeline is in their interests," said Highsmith, "in the interests of the Afghans. That is what we have been saying all along. But we must separate them from this terrorist group, which is pursuing its own objectives." He seemed satisfied with this. "If we can manage to do that, to keep that separation, maybe we will be okay." He thought for a moment. "But it will be difficult. These guys don't know the difference between a mullah and a terrorist!" He was not confident that they would be able to convince these cynical investors. "Just let me do the talking, Joey. I'll ask you to speak on specific issues; otherwise, stay silent. Okay?"

Joey looked at Highsmith and smiled. "Okay, Pen. They're your investors."

77.

The meeting with Wilde Oil's leading investors began soberly, with a briefing by the company's political analyst and the head of their Washington office. They focused on what the US government was doing, the current options under consideration in Washington, and how they would affect Wilde Oil's project in Afghanistan. None of these options was very positive; one way or another, there would be a military response against those responsible for the attack in New York — what was now being called the "9/11" attack. This would very likely focus on the locations in Afghanistan, including some which were close to the pipeline project, where the Al Qaeda group was known to have their bases.

All Americans were under government instruction to leave Afghanistan as soon as possible, and military transport planes were being sent to the country to carry out this withdrawal. Wilde Oil had many Afghan employees — engineers and some project supervisors, but work on the pipeline would have to be closed down and all Americans would have to leave the country. There was no way to continue work on the project if transportation and normal commercial relations with the country were restricted.

When the discussion started, there were numerous questions from the major shareholders, but they were careful and understanding of the situation. These investors understood the plight which the company found itself in, and did not want to add to its difficulties. They would surely reduce their investments in the company, but they would do this over time — it would not be a total and immediate sell-out. Wilde Oil was a big company, with investments and infrastructure world-wide. The situation in Afghanistan would affect its investments, and its major project there, but those were just a small part of the company's overall assets, which were substantial, and largely stable.

Joey did not play much of a role in this briefing – it covered financial aspects that he had nothing to do with, and the emergency withdrawal and shut-down plans, which did not involve him. He listened closely, hearing many things of which he was unaware, with a growing appreciation for the careful contingency planning and emergency action scenarios which were evident in these plans. Since he was a newcomer to the company, these were aspects of its organization which he knew little about.

The shareholders who were included in this briefing were also understanding of the situation the company was in, and did not give the impression that they would suddenly withdraw their support. On the contrary, they seemed to appreciate that this new situation was totally unforeseen, and was not the company's fault. It was a challenge to the country, and they all felt a patriotic solidarity with Wilde Oil and its far-sighted pipeline project.

At the end of the meeting there was an informal gathering of the shareholders, talking with the company's experts and senior executives as they sipped coffee. The mood was grim, but Joey sensed a feeling of solidarity and a firm determination to get through these difficulties. He found himself in a casual conversation with one of these major company share-holders – an elderly man, clearly quite wealthy, retired and living in Florida. He introduced himself, and the man said, "Ah, you are the famous Joey Torino!" He gave Joey a focused, intense look.

"I've heard a lot about you!" He paused, leaving Joey to wonder what the man might say. "We need more people like you! Too many desk-jockeys in this company! Need more people who understand the places where we invest!" He chuckled. "But I guess they're hard to find!"

A secretary interrupted Joey's conversation, saying she had an urgent phone call from Washington. Joey left the room, following the secretary. As they crossed the corridor the secretary said "It's Ambassador Rudolphus. She wanted to talk to Mr. Highsmith, but I can't find him. So she asked for you." Joey took the phone in another room.

"Hello," he said, "this is Joey Torino." There was a silence on the line, so he added, "The secretaries are looking for Mr. Highsmith, but they asked me to take the call in his place, until they can find him."

"Ah," said Elaine Rudolphus, in her sharp voice, "The famous Joey Torino! I guess you don't remember me from our meetings in Moscow! Or maybe you do! Probably you do! Well, I certainly remember you! How could I forget! What a mess!" She laughed, giving a sort-of nasal snort at the same time.

"Anyway, I wasn't calling to discuss that! That's all in the distant past!" Joey waited for her to finish. "I just wanted to give Pen a head's-up: we are instructing all Americans to withdraw immediately from Afghanistan.

"There will be some sort of military action. I can't say what – I don't even know what – but it will come shortly. Very shortly!

"I guess everyone will know very soon what it will be. But Americans should get out – fast. It could get dangerous for anyone who stays there! Can you pass this on to Pen?" She paused, waiting for Joey's response. "Did you get that?" she asked.

"Yes, I understood. I will pass on your message. We were pretty sure that would be the next step, so it's not a surprise." He waited, to see if there was more.

"Well, that's it. That's what I had to pass on. Not what you would call good news."

"No," said Joey, "but we were all anticipating it."

There was a further silence, then she added, "How are you doing, Joey? I hear you retired to Maine. Must be nice up there, this time of year!"

"Yes," said Joey, "I'll be heading back there – now."

"Good luck," said Under Secretary Rudolphus. "You deserve it. You've done a lot for your country. More than most of us!" The line went dead, and Joey hung up the phone.

Joey left a message for Pen Highsmith with one of his secretaries, and asked the secretary to call a taxi, left the building, and headed straight to the airport. He would take the next plane going east – any plane heading in the general direction of Maine. He would call Highsmith enroute, so no one at Wilde Oil would wonder what had happened

78. Houston

The fountain outside the Wilde Oil Building in Houston was destroyed by an explosion during the night, after Pen Highsmith's reception had finished and the key investors had gone home. The glass doors of the entry to the building were seriously damaged, but would be relatively easy to repair. The bomber, who was evidently not very experienced, had been killed in the explosion. The police were still trying to determine his identity, but they were sure he was from the region of Afghanistan, and that he was an illegal alien. They had no previous record of this individual.

Many of the shareholders who had been at a reception in the building the previous day were relieved, and thought they had been very lucky to have left the building promptly, at the end of the reception. The Wilde Oil President, Pendleton Highsmith, was thankful that no one was hurt, and was said to be more determined than ever to maintain the company's policies and programs, without yielding to intimidation.

79. Boston

Joey heard about the bombing as he was walking through the arrival terminal at Logan Airport in Boston. He was not surprised.

As he stepped out of the terminal, looking for a taxi, he heard his name called. It was H. R. Wilson, who had come to ask Joey to contact Highsmith, some months before. He said he was there to drive Joey to his house, in Maine, courtesy of the Wilde Oil Corporation. Joey smiled and thanked him, climbing into the car next to him. The two set out northward, heading toward Maine. A few minutes after they left the airport, Joey fell asleep in the car.

***

The sky was a bright blue, and at certain places it was possible to smell the ocean through the open windows as they drove north along the coast.

Sometime later they turned into the dirt road which led to Joey's house in the woods. Joey asked Wilson to deposit him at the bottom of his modest driveway. He wanted to walk up to the house by himself, to get the feel of the trees, the forest, the air of Blue Hill. He could just barely see the sea in the distance, through the trees, as Wilson's car disappeared, driving out toward the main road.

He turned the bend in his driveway, and there was his modest house, with the broad porch and the overhanging pines, just as he had left it. He was glad to be there. It was, after all, his chosen place.

As he opened the door with his key he heard some noise upstairs, and someone came running down the stairway. It was Page. She threw her arms around his neck without saying a word. He was home.

***

PART TWO

80. Houston. (date – a few months later)

The organ music drifted out from the open doors of the church, under the shade trees and across the small, tidy lawn. The people walked directly into the main entrance when they arrived, greeting others but not stopping to talk. It was a hot and humid summer day, and people everywhere were anxious to get into an air-conditioned space. The church had its air conditioning on, even though the main doors were open; there were two more swinging doors just inside, which kept the cool air within the church itself – most churches used a system like this in Houston – an easy way to keep the cooler air inside, while making it easy for the faithful to enter.

Joey was not a regular church-goer – certainly not here in Houston, but also not where he lived, in Maine, where there were fewer churches, and many fewer people. He had his own beliefs, which formed his philosophy of life, his way of dealing with other people, and he was, after all, a generous and open person, who tried to help others when he could. He was also warm and loyal toward his friends and colleagues; that was why he had come to Houston, for this funeral of his friend and former colleague, killed in an attack near what had been a Wilde Oil pumping station in Afghanistan. Max Anders had been the manager of the project, based in Kabul. But he often traveled far out in the barren mountainous areas of the country, which is where the company's pipeline project was under construction. And it was more dangerous in the field.

Anders had been in a convoy of several jeeps, with armed guards in the lead vehicle as well as the following armored truck. The convoy had been ambushed by a heavily-armed group, hidden behind a rocky ledge. There was a bloody exchange between the Wilde Oil guards and the attackers, but it was a well-planned ambush, and the Wilde Oil group was wiped out. The Afghan army recovered the bodies several days later, after scouting the area by helicopter. Anders' remains were returned to Kabul and shipped to his home in Houston, for burial. His family – wife, elderly parents, two brothers, and three small children, were all present for the funeral – a strong tradition in Texas, and especially in the oil business.

The company was also strongly represented at the funeral, led by its President, Pendleton Highsmith, who joined the family in the first rows of pews in the church, which was full, with people standing in the aisles. Anders was a respected and popular oil man – a lifelong member of the industry's broad fraternity of professionals, based here in Houston. The other people in the church were almost all from the same profession – tough men, darkly tanned from work in the field, with their strong and independent wives, and with a few oil-women, a relatively new feature in this demanding and far-flung industry.

Joey did not know many people in this group – he was not an oil man – but he had known Anders, and had worked closely with him on the Afghan pipeline project. He had respected and appreciated Anders' steady leadership in Afghanistan, in the face of growing physical challenges and security risks. Joey had come from Maine to be here, in this church, for this moment, to pay his respects to a colleague he valued and respected. Joey was not a talkative person, but he had his own code of values, and that was why he was there.

The ceremony was difficult to sit through – with the family holding on to each other, and colleagues of all kinds struggling to master their emotions. Joey always found such events difficult, and he was relieved when the family finally said a prayer by the coffin and slowly made their way to the entrance of the church, accompanied by the company's president, Pendleton Highsmith. The coffin was carried out of the church to a hearse, waiting to depart in a long cortege for the cemetery. And then the hearse slowly left, in a procession with family and friends in following cars.

As he moved to his car to join the procession, Highsmith spotted Joey, and went out of his way to pass closely. He shook Joey's hand and thanked him for coming. "Glad you came, Joey! He was a really good man; we will miss him." Joey said it was just normal to come; Anders had been a close colleague and friend in Afghanistan.

"How long are you here for, Joey?" asked Highsmith.

"I'll go back this evening," Joey responded.

"Stop by my office," said Highsmith. "I need to talk to you." He moved away rapidly to join the motorcade heading to the cemetery, leaving Joey unable to make any excuse. He really did not want to prolong this visit to Houston, was anxious to get back to Maine. But he had a long relationship with Highsmith, filled with mutual respect, and he realized immediately that he would have to "stop by" his office, as Highsmith had asked, especially if he "needed" to talk.

81.

The Wilde Oil building had recovered from the bombing attack, some months earlier. The fountain in front of the main entrance had been repaired and new trees planted. The broad glass facing of the building had been renewed. Joey was expected when he arrived, and the receptionist immediately called the President's office and accompanied him to the elevator for an express ride to the top floor, where Highsmith was waiting.

"Wonderful to see you Joey," he said, with a somber tone in his voice. "Not the circumstances I would want, of course!" He gestured for Joey to sit at the small coffee table near his desk, and sat opposite him as his secretary brought coffee for them. "Of course you know the difficulties we are having in Afghanistan. I'm sure you have followed what is going on there. But perhaps you don't know what is happening to the company. We are merging – it is unavoidable – and we will soon be known as "Insto-Wilde Inc." Don't laugh, please. I know it sounds ridiculous!" He took a sip of his coffee. "But we are not in control. Insto-oil is! They are buying control of Wilde Oil! Such a sad day for old Mr. Wilde!"

He chuckled ironically. "They are taking control – for the moment it is just financial control, but over time – not much time, either – they will take over everything. Our projects, our production, all those oil wells out there in the Gulf! Everything!" He took a sip of coffee, let out a long sigh, and waved his hand with a sweeping gesture. "That's the oil business, Joey! One day you are running things, and everyone is envious, and the next day someone buys you out on the market, and then they are the ones who are telling you what to do!"

"And I'll be out, too," he said, looking down into his coffee cup. "In these takeovers, they never want to keep the top people – everyone else is okay, but not the bosses. So I will be out, too." He picked up his cup, and stirred it carefully with a spoon, lost in thought.

"It's actually not bad for me," said Highsmith, looking Joey in the eye. "The State Department wants me back in Washington. Or at least they want me – probably not in Washington. In fact, definitely not in Washington! Ha ha!" He laughed a kind of artificial chuckle. "They want me to take on an Ambassadorial position! Not Paris, you can be sure of that! Or London, or Rome! No, they want me to take on something a bit more ... challenging ... than that. I don't yet know where I will wind up, but you can be sure it will be ... challenging." He chuckled ironically.

Joey listened with some sympathy, knowing from his own observations how Washington could treat officials who were returning to government service from prominent positions in the private sector. "But you still have connections in Washington," he said, "so I guess they will take care of you."

"Well, I can't really count on that, Joey. Times change, people change, and there are always some who have their knives out for you." He reflected for a moment. "But I wanted to tell you this because, well, because it is possible that I might call on you!" He looked Joey in the eye, trying to catch the sense of his reaction, but Joey was, as always, emotionless. "If they send me to a place which has ... problems. That is always a possibility, you know! If they send me somewhere where I face serious problems, then I may call on you! You are the best "problem solver" I know, Joey, so I might ask you to come and help!" He looked Joey in the eye, relying on his sense of responsibility, on his awareness of the ways in which he, Highsmith, had helped him in the past. He was reminding Joey of this, and putting down his marker. Joey, the number one "problem solver," might be called on again.

And Joey, grateful and loyal, was always ready to respond to such calls, though he did not always want to say that in advance. He always wanted to know what was expected before committing to help in some complicated situation. So he did not respond with a broad acceptance of the "problem solver" role which Highsmith was hinting at. But he also did not refuse it. He just listened.

"Of course," said Highsmith, "I know you are happy in your retirement, up there in Maine. But one can never know what the future will bring. And I just wanted to make you aware of this situation, before you head back to Maine. I'll keep in touch, and be in contact, as things go along, especially when I know where they want me to go. I'm a senior Ambassador, you know, so they can't send me just any place! But sometimes the most difficult posts are considered prestigious too! And I suspect that's what they will want me to undertake!" He finished his coffee, and stood up.

"Anyway, I wanted to tell you this before you go back to Maine! I'll have a company car take you to the airport, and we'll keep in touch – especially when I know where I'm going! I'll be sure to let you know where I go!" He laughed his ironic laugh, and offered his hand for a hardy handshake. These two men knew each other well, and had considerable respect for each other, in spite of their many differences. On the contrary, they respected each other because of those differences – each one of them could do things which the other could not.

Joey said goodbye, and left for the airport in a Wilde Oil car, reflecting on this meeting, and what it could mean for him.

82.

"Hello, Elaine?" Highsmith was calling on Under Secretary Rudolphus's private line, which rang directly at her office desk.

"Hello?" The voice was unfamiliar – Highsmith realized that it must be a secretary. "Is the Under Secretary in today?"

"No. She's in London. For the Group of Ten."

"Do you have a number where I can reach her there?" The secretary gave him a hotel number and he called, calculating from the time difference that she must be returning to her hotel at about that time.

The phone rang, and a woman's voice answered: "Hello?"

"Hello Elaine! It's Pen Highsmith. Sorry to call when you are at a high-level meeting abroad! But as we both know, sometimes that's the best time to talk on the phone!"

"I'm sorry, who did you say you were?" asked the woman's voice, and Highsmith began to think it was not Elaine Rudolphus after all. Perhaps he had a wrong number! The voice seemed a bit strange.

"This is Ambassador Highsmith, calling from Texas!"

"I'm very sorry," said the voice on the line, "but you will have to speak more clearly. The line is not very clear. I thought you just said you are the Ambassador of Texas! But everyone knows that

Texas is a part of the good old USA. Doesn't have Ambassadors, you see." There was laughter in the background.

"No, you don't understand," said Highsmith, raising his voice. "I'm not an Ambassador OF Texas, I'm just calling FROM Texas. To speak to Ambassador Rudolphus. Do you understand now?"

"Well, I certainly understand very well, old boy! The problem is not my understanding of the English language! It's our language, you see? Over here in England! We actually speak English here! Always have! Look here, are you sure you dialed the right number? Easy to get it wrong, you know. If I were you I'd try it all over again, maybe even try to get it right this time!" There was a click and the line went dead.

Highsmith, mustering his diplomatic patience, asked his secretary to find Ambassador Rudolphus, wherever she was, and arrange for them to have a telephone conversation.

He was well aware, from his long experience of Washington, and the way it operated, that it was a very bad signal when one could not reach the person one wanted to speak to there. If a phone call was considered important – if the caller was considered important – the other person was always find-able and available to take the call. Not getting thru on the phone was definitely a bad sign.

And that was not the only bad sign. A few minutes later Highsmith's secretary buzzed; there was a call from the Chairman of the Wilde Oil Board of Directors. Highsmith took the call. "Hello Gerry," he said, "It is a really positive coincidence that you called.

Great minds think alike, and I wanted to have a chat with you. In fact, I was about to call you!"

The voice at the other end of the call was somber. It was The Honorable Gerald Imbaldwell III on the line, calling from his weekend retreat on Long Island, a first in Highsmith's experience – it was well known that the man never touched a phone on weekends.

"Hello there, Pen," said a deep-throated voice at the other end of the line. "How are things in Houston?" There was some sort of conversation going on in the background, seemingly among several other men. "I'm sorry we haven't had a chance to talk in the last few days – lots going on – but I did want to talk to you personally, and I was finally able to get through. I think you have been quite busy."

"Yes, you could say that!" said Highsmith. "We have been stabilizing the situation, pretty well in the circumstances. And then the death of our man in Kabul hit us. Very sad. But we are organizing and dealing with the situation, and I think we are managing it very well!"

"Yes, well, that is what I called about, Pen. The situation." There was a pause, and Highsmith waited for the Chairman of the Board to explain the meaning of his call. "We think we may be a bit over-extended in Afghanistan ... in view of the circumstances there."

It was the "we" which hit Highsmith most strongly. It meant that there had been a consultation among the key Wilde Oil shareholders, including Jerry Wilde, the playboy grandson of the company's founder, still a major shareholder and an inescapable figure among the company's owners as the grandson of its founder. Highsmith waited for what might come next.

"We think the situation may merit some re-thinking, and maybe some urgent measures." So that was what this call was about, Highsmith found himself thinking; "urgent measures."

"Yes indeed," he said. "We are definitely moving, very fast, to do what is needed. We will be closing down – temporarily of course – the Afghan project, especially in view of the unfortunate death of our company manager. I just came from his funeral, by the way, and got a quick up-date on the situation from a couple of his colleagues, and the ..."

"Well," said the Chairman of the Board, "That's not exactly where we are headed, I'm afraid to say. And by the way, may I say how unhappy we all were with the very sad death of our esteemed colleague. We all had a lot of respect for him." The Chairman paused again, before resuming his presentation.

"We think the situation demands really major adjustments. Major." He sighed, and cleared his throat. "I had a discussion this morning with Wilbur." Highsmith knew immediately who the Chairman was referring to: Wilbur Anglesea Jr. was the Chairman of the Board of Directors of the Multinational Oil Corporation – MOC – Wilde Oil's ancient competitor and fierce rival. "We agreed to open some discussions – just discussions ... for the moment – but I wanted you to know this, and also to ensure that you would be represented in these discussions. We will meet tomorrow ... out here." Highsmith understood that this would mean at the Chairman's Long Island estate, which was clearly another alarm bell – these people never held discussions on weekends, and certainly never at their Long Island summer estates.

"Well," said Highsmith, "I'm grateful that you have informed me of this, and I will certainly try to join you as quickly as I can. I'm sure I can get to New York this evening."

"Okay, that might be useful. But the main thing is to get someone here who knows the situation on the ground ... I mean in Afghanistan. Just in case the subject comes up. Who do you have who might be able to fill this role – answer questions I mean? About ... local matters."

Highsmith thought rapidly – with the assassination of the head of the Wilde Oil project in Afghanistan, it was not obvious who could fill this role with a group of senior investors in the energy sector. He needed someone who could talk to these people about the project, and the situation in Afghanistan, and impress them – dazzle them – with expertise, determination, and – most important – the ability to take responsibility for such a formidable project. Someone tough and "from the front line."

"Torino," he said, almost inaudibly.

"Who?"

"Joey Torino. He's our expert. I'll try to get him there. With me, of course."

"I don't think I know that name," said the Chairman of the Wilde Oil Board of Directors. "Who is he?"

"He's an expert," said Highsmith. "He just came back from Kabul. He knows the country, the situation out there. I'll try to get him — - to come along with me."

"Well I certainly hope he will come. He sounds like just the person we need to talk to. Is there a problem?"

"No problem. He's just in Maine — he lives there. I'll have to get in touch with him."

"I see. Yes, please do that. And let my office know when you can get here, so we can arrange things. And be flexible! We may need a day or two of discussion!" He hung up, leaving Highsmith wondering if he could manage all these details. He buzzed his assistant, and asked her to come into his office.

83. Near Kandahar

"Allah Akbar! Peace. I come in peace, to see the Master." The man had a heavy beard and wore a turban. He was dressed in a black jellabah.

"Who are you?" said the voice behind the sandbags.

"I am Ali, a friend, from Kandahar. The Master knows me."

"Do not move. I will see." There was a sound of movement behind the barrier of sandbags, out of sight under the rock overhang.

"Mohamed! Ask for Ali, from Kandahar!" shouted a voice behind the barrier.

The gun braced against the sandbags did not move. No one moved.

The light was very dim, here in the area under the rock overhang, at the entrance to the cave. It was a wide, flat area, sandy, with sandbags piled high near the back, covering the entrance to the cave. The guards were behind the sandbags, in the dark shadows.

The outer guard had already stopped the visitors, checked their identities, and searched them for weapons. He had accompanied them, with his Kalashnikov armed and pointed at them, to the entrance of the cave. Now he stood nearby, his weapon still pointed at the visitors. They stood, motionless, in the dim evening light, waiting to be admitted.

After several minutes, a different voice came from behind the sandbags. "One person only. Advance slowly. Hands out." The man did as he was told, stepping carefully, his hands extended to the sides. He stepped into the space between the overlapping sandbag barriers, and a man felt his body, through the material of his jellaba, across his shoulders, down his back and chest. He felt the legs, the body, front and back, and the neck, and then signaled to remove the shoes. He motioned to the visitor to advance, still pointing his Kalashnikov machine gun at his stomach. The two marched slowly into the darkness under the overhanging rocks.

At the turn they had to duck their heads under the low rock overhang, but beyond that it was easier to walk on the sandy desert floor, where the space widened. There was a dim light farther back, and another barrier. Finally they came to a full wall of sandbags, with a low door, where the guard knocked.

The door was opened from inside, and a woman's hand motioned for the visitor to enter. Inside it was even darker, but there was a dim light in the back of a domestic space.

"Salam, Master," said the visitor as he entered the space. On the opposite side of the open cave was a man, reclining among some massed pillows, with veiled women on either side. He was smoking from a water-pipe, and did not move. "I come from Kandahar, to inform you of events there, if you approve."

"Go ahead, speak, inshallah. I am listening to you." said the reclining man, continuing to smoke from the water-pipe.

"The foreigners are leaving the city," said the visitor. "Also other cities, throughout our land. There is much fear among them." He paused to gauge the Master's mood, then continued. "In Kabul, too, the foreigners are leaving. All the planes are full. Foreigners are going there from all parts of our land, to get on the air planes to leave."

"This is good," said the reclining man. "We will continue on our path."

The visitor hesitated to continue. There was a pause, a silence.

"What else do you have to tell me?" asked the reclining man, taking the water-pipe from his mouth.

The visitor hesitated before speaking. "It is said that the Americans are preparing to attack us, here in our land," he said carefully. He did not wish to offend or anger the reclining man. That was always dangerous.

"It is said that they are preparing a mighty attack, with airplanes and bombs, and other weapons that they have." He paused to judge the effect of this report. It was sometimes dangerous to be too frank, to report too directly, too openly, too honestly.

The reclining man frowned. "They will surely strike back," he said. "But they can do us no harm." He inhaled from his water-pipe. "Should they destroy our cities? They will only kill our enemies! Should they destroy our deserts? They will only kill our sheep! Inshallah!" He waved his hand at the visitor, signaling that the conversation was over.

But the visitor hesitated to leave. "You have something more to tell me?" asked the reclining leader.

"Yes, inshallah, I do."

"Go ahead! Say what you have to say! Tell me!"

The visitor hesitated, then continued. "There is a man here in our land, a visitor among us, and it is said that he can help us, that he can carry a message to our enemies. It is said that he knows our ways, and that he could help, so that our enemies might not destroy our land." He paused. "As they will surely do after our attacks on them." He was quiet, and looked down, fearful of the reaction to this news. But it was not as angry as he had expected.

"We do not fear the reaction to our attacks!" said the leader. "We will continue them! Until the infidels understand that they must leave us alone! Leave us alone in our lands! We are stronger, more determined, than they are, stronger than they know! Soon they will lose their will, and withdraw. All will see! They will leave, and we will still be here, in our lands, Inshallah! They will lose, and will withdraw in fear! And we will be here, in our lands!"

The visitor had conveyed his message, and was fearful of the anger of the leader. He bowed and said "Inshallah," backing toward the door to leave. The meeting was over.

The guard escorted him to the entrance, out through the sandbagged barriers. The sun had set, and darkness was advancing rapidly across the barren landscape. He knew the path to follow, and would reach his destination before midnight. There was nothing more he could do; the way forward had been confirmed.

84.

Aiea was preoccupied by the health of one of the small children in her care. He had suffered from a minor wound, but it had not been properly cleaned and disinfected, and had festered before he had been brought to the clinic. Now the wound was swollen and red. One of her assistants had brought the boy to her office, and she was showing the girl how to sanitize the wound. The boy was crying, his face was red.

"You must always clean any wounds when the patient arrives in our care," she instructed the young woman, showing her how to do this with a swab and sanitary cotton.

Just then, the door of the office slammed open, surprising the two women, who looked up, and the baby, who suddenly went silent. A Taleb militia man stood in the doorway with a submachine gun, which he held aggressively, making a sweep of the room silently. He was a young man, but heavily bearded, and dressed in white, with ammunition magazines strapped over his shoulder. He was clearly surprised by the scene of two women cleaning a wounded child.

"Allah Akbar," he said. "What are you doing?"

"As you can see, we are cleaning the wounds on this small baby!" said Aiea indignantly, in loud Pashto. "What are YOU doing in my clinic? This is a medical service center – a hospital – and you have no right to be here. This is my clinic; I am the Director. Please leave!" She was furious, stunned by the presence of an armed combatant in a clinic for children.

"There is a foreign woman here," said the Taleb. "We know this. Where is she?"

"There is no foreign woman here," Aiea replied firmly. "Just my colleague and myself, as you can see. You are mistaken."

"No! We know. We have been told," said the young man. "We know this." He looked around. "And you should be properly covered, inshallah!" He was indignant, as Aiea could see. But he was also nervous, a teenager, Aiea thought. His beard was straggled and soft, his eyes nervous, looking quickly to left and right. Aiea thought quickly – he could easily shoot, because he was young and nervous, and surprised. Better not to embarrass him.

"It is good that you have come," she said, "we need your help, as you can see. This poor child has an infected wound. Please help us. You can hold him for a few seconds while I sanitize his wound! Please!" she looked at the boy, appealing to his good-will.

The young man looked around the room, carefully, then slung his machine-gun over his shoulder. "What do you want me to do?" he asked. "I will help if I can."

"Just hold him under his bottom, please, so I can clean his wound. I need two hands to do it." The boy took the weight of the child in his hands, and Aiea proceeded to swab the wound, while her young assistant was paralyzed with fear. When she had finished cleaning the wound, with the baby crying, she put down the swab and covered the wound with tissue, taping it around the leg to hold it in place. The child quieted down, realizing that his ordeal had ended, and Aeia took him in her arms, rocking him gently and looking him in the eyes while she talked in a whisper.

"That is better, no? That's what we needed!"

The boy with the machine-gun backed away, looking embarrassed. "Will he get well?" he asked.

"Yes, of course. It is just a slight wound. He is lucky; someone brought him to us. Many others are not so lucky! But we do not know who he is. We will have to find his mother ... or someone from his family. It is always like this. It is the children who suffer."

The boy backed away sheepishly. "I will leave you to your work," he said, nodding, and left the room, closing the door behind him. Aiea looked at her associate, who was still trembling in fear, and the two women shared a few moments rocking the baby to sleep, then placing him in a crib.

"I'm surprised he didn't make us put on our face coverings," said Aiea quietly. "That's what they normally do." Her young assistant was still shaking with fear, so Aiea gave her a warm hug. "Don't worry. You see, they are not as tough as they look! You just have to be careful with them!"

85.

Highsmith finally reached Joey in Maine, as the sun set and darkness surrounded his house in the woods. "Joey?" he said with some relief. "I've been trying to reach you for the last hour!"

"Sorry, I was out walking. Just getting used to being back. Something urgent?" He was wondering why Highsmith would be calling him so soon after he had returned to Maine. Whatever the reason, it could not be good.

"Joey, I need to ask your help once again. I must meet with the big Wilde Oil shareholders tomorrow – to explain the situation in Afghanistan. And they want me to bring along someone who is an expert on the situation there. So I thought of you. They are a very important group – needless to say – and they want to know what is going on out there, want to get a first-hand version of the challenges we face. I really need you to be there, to give a first-hand description, a kind-of oral report. And to give them a sort of – you know – a prognosis, an analysis of what will happen, going forward. You understand what I mean?"

Joey considered this new situation briefly, but it was not in his nature to refuse a call for help.

"I can be there," he said, "if you think you need me." He paused, as Highsmith breathed a sigh of relief. "Just tell me where I need to go, and when."

"They are out on Long Island – must be about an hour's drive from the city. I can meet you at the airport – whichever airport you can get to – either Kennedy or LaGuardia. My secretary looked at the flight times, and there is one from Boston to LaGuardia – leaves Boston at about 10 AM. Could you make it?" He paused, anxious to pin down the needed arrangements for this meeting.

"Ten AM from Boston? A little early, but I can probably make it. Will your secretary make a reservation for me? If she makes the reservation, I will be there. You can count on it."

Highsmith said he would take care of the reservations and would meet Joey at the airport near New York, to drive out to the Hamptons, where the meeting would take place. He gave Joey all the information he had on the time, place, and the likely participation in the meeting, and asked him to be prepared to give a sort-of executive presentation on the situation in the country.

Highsmith hung up the phone breathing a sigh of relief. He had confidence in Joey, and especially in his ability to project a full and confident understanding of the situation – and what actions would be required. Unforeseen developments were a normal part of the energy business, especially in remote parts of the world, where they always formed a part of the risks investors had to foresee, and take into account. The challenge for managers was to deal with unforeseen developments, and to find ways to maintain the investment projects which were threatened by them. Investors wanted to see confidence and readiness to deal with such threats, to overcome them, and to bring investment projects to completion, and to profits.

Highsmith asked his secretary to make his own arrangements to get to New York, and to be at the airport, with a car and driver, to pick up Joey when he arrived from Boston. He would have time in the car to explain the full situation to Joey, and to coach him on how best to present the situation in Afghanistan to these key Wilde Oil investors – the Chairman of the Board, and the son of the company's founder – the two largest shareholders.

86.

Highsmith waved when he saw Joey emerge from the arrivals section of the airport. It was almost noon – the plane was a little late – and he was getting just a bit nervous waiting for it to land. He was casually dressed, looking like he had come directly from the Maine woods, but this immediately struck Highsmith as useful – it made Joey look even more like a real "field man."

"Hello Joey," he exclaimed as they shook hands. "I apologize for interrupting your private time, but this is, well, a real emergency. These are the principal owners of the company, and it's not every day that they ask to dig into the specifics of a situation. And it has become a potentially dangerous situation, so they are concerned about their investments." They were walking briskly toward the car, where the driver was holding the passenger door open.

"No problem," said Joey. "I like to get up early." They both got in the back seat, since Highsmith had to explain the situation the company was in, which would be on the minds of the investors they would be talking to. The press was filled with articles about the situation in Afghanistan, and it was clear that most major investors would be concerned about investments in the country, following the take-over of the government by the Taliban. In this situation the company was vulnerable, and the major shareholders faced the prospect of significant financial losses. No one knew what the attitude of a Taliban government would be toward investments – especially foreign investments – in the country, and many investors were simply cutting their losses and leaving the country.

There were many things which Joey did not know – about the investors, the history of their involvement with Wilde Oil, their personal considerations and the history of their involvement with the company – all of which would surely be factors in the current situation. Some might feel a loyalty toward the company, while others would judge the situation solely on the basis of the financial factors. And it was clear that the company faced very substantial losses – most, and possibly all – the value of what had been invested thus far in the pipeline project. No one in the company had yet done the math to determine this investment value, nor to weigh the possible value of what the company might recover from the sale of assets relating to this project. But it was already clear that the situation threatened the very existence of Wilde Oil.

Joey was not familiar with the financial situation of the company, and was not very experienced or knowledgeable about investment finances – his biggest investment had been buying his cabin in Maine – and even the terminology was a challenge for him. But he easily understood the logic and the effect of the situation on the company's investors.

"They want us to explain the situation in Afghanistan," said Highsmith, "and the way that situation is likely to evolve. And they want to know what the attitude of the Taliban is toward the whole idea of a pipeline, the involvement of foreigners, the effect on the country, on their way of life. All of that. And they want someone from the company, who has been there in the present situation, to tell them what it is like and how it is likely to evolve. So they will want you to tell them about all that, in very plain language. I know this is right up your alley, Joey – that's why I called you!"

"Well," said Joey in his soft, unassuming voice, "I hope I can handle this. I will just tell them the truth of the situation. They will have to judge for themselves what it means for them, for their investments."

"Yes," said Highsmith, "That's very good, just what they want. They want to hear it from someone who has actually been there, seen it, and can give them a first-hand account. Just tell it like it is – of course not exaggerating things either – we don't want to look like idiots for having gone into the country in the first place! The energy business is by definition a risky industry! If you're going to invest in it, you have to take that into account, in your personal investment situation."

He thought for a moment. "And we have to do a careful analysis of the new situation – the costs of trying to pursue the project in the new circumstances, versus the costs of trying to extract ourselves from it, which would be substantial."

"Well," said Joey, "That's your area, Pen. I don't really know anything about costs. I can talk a bit about what I see as the risks, okay. But the costs are your department."

"They will surely want to pull out," Highsmith mumbled to himself. "The risks are too high, that's for sure." They were driving along the shore, with broad beaches stretching away toward the horizon and big waves of surf rolling in from the south. A bright sun was making the water sparkle, and there were few people visible on such a cold day, in the off-season.

He was thinking of the likely outcome of this meeting, and preparing for the worst. They would have to look at the company's basic situation, whether it could survive such a catastrophic setback. They had poured capital into the opening of the project, betting on what looked like a very positive return. But they had not foreseen such a complete change of control in the country – to a radical government whose likely policies where impossible to predict.

Uncertainty was the worst enemy of an investment project, and the stock markets were already judging Wilde Oil's situation as catastrophic. They would have to find the best way out, and it would surely be a financial disaster, under any rational scenario. Highsmith knew he faced a difficult session with the company's shareholders. He had not been President of the company when the first decisions were made to pursue the project in Afghanistan, but he had continued the project, and he would be held responsible. He understood this, and was preparing himself for what would surely be the outcome of this meeting with the key investors – the owners of the Wilde Oil Corporation.

87.

There was a long driveway through the dunes toward the beach, with a low hedge separating the paved drive from the dunes. There were few trees in the sandy soil, but up ahead there was a vast country house, surrounded by carefully-tended bushes and stone walls, all designed to fit into the overall beach-side atmosphere of the mansion overlooking the broad beach beyond. The drive formed a circle which arrived in front of a substantial doorway, under a long porch designed to give the building a casual beach-side look. The main door opened as the car circled to stop, and a butler in uniform stepped out to open the passenger door.

Highsmith, the experienced diplomat, got out of the car and motioned to Joey to come along with him, as he entered the doorway, with another servant holding it open. They were in a large entryway which maintained the beach-side decor of the house, and were led directly toward the back of the house, which faced out across the sand toward the water's edge. There were few people on the beach beyond – it was a windy day – and those in view were clearly walking, getting their exercise, close to the water's edge.

They were shown into a small library, with books lining the shelves on one side and closed glass doors on the other side facing the sea. Another servant was waiting there, with a tray of drinks, and some snacks were laid out on a small table. Highsmith had entered many waiting rooms in his long career, and immediately took a small snack and a drink – motioning to Joey to do the same. "Better prepare for a long meeting," he said quietly. "We may be here all day." He placed his file folder on a chair, and took another snack while looking out at the beach with the eye of someone who had seen many such mansions, and many similar beaches.

After a few minutes a door opened and their host – Gerald Imbaldwell III – came into the room. He was dressed casually and had a folder in hand, which he had clearly been reading – it was well-thumbed and had place-holders sticking out along the top edge. He was clearly over sixty years old, but was also well-tanned and fit – it was well-known that he spent a part of every day pursuing some sport – tennis or golf, but also long walking or jogging sessions on the beach. The choice of sport related to the season, and the weather, but he was active every day. And he approached all his activities – exercise or investments – with the same careful thought and preparation. He had multiple advisors, but was as studious as any of them and was famous for making his own decisions on major investments. He was a life-long investor in Wilde Oil, and was thought to be its biggest individual stock-holder.

Imbaldwell greeted his visitors warmly, but this was his well-known style, so Highsmith, who knew him fairly well, did not attach any importance to this – he was waiting for what would surely emerge at some point: a succinct statement of the issues which faced the company in light of the situation in Afghanistan. After that, there would be a review of the options for possible action. The views of the two visitors would be interesting, and would be heard carefully, but would not be decisive – final decisions would be based on the economics of the matter, and these were only partially rooted in the actual facts, the analyses, and the expectations of experts.

This discussion was obviously only a preliminary meeting – a full gathering of major investors was planned for later in the afternoon. Highsmith and Joey were shown their rooms – they were clearly expected to spend the night there – and it was suggested that they might want to "freshen up" before luncheon, which they did.

Two other men arrived at the beachside mansion a little later, and all five were shown into the luncheon room – a bright sunny place which extended out toward the water – for drinks before sitting down for lunch. Much of the discussion was casual, and included a broad variety of other subjects – golf, football, cars, latest jokes, exotic travel destinations – and Joey followed it only partly.

It was over coffee, with the guests seated in the library, when the difficult subject which was the reason for the meeting, first came up.

"What do you think is going to happen in Afghanistan, Pen?" asked the host of the meeting flatly.

Highsmith was not surprised, and had been waiting for just that occasion. "Of course, we have to look at all our options," he said carefully. "But I am always cautious in situations like this." He paused, then added "We will be looking – are already looking – for a rational exit strategy, and measuring that option against the risks of holding on."

"By "holding on," what exactly do you mean, Pen?" asked one of the guests.

"Yes, well, frankly that depends on many factors – most of them unknown, for the moment. We are watching carefully, while also protecting our investments as best we can, and looking for possible opportunities – across the board." There was a silence as the other men in the room reflected on this formulation.

" 'Across the board,' – what does that mean, exactly," asked one of the key Wilde Oil share-holders? "Does it mean selling out? Getting out? We've got a lot of capital – not to mention the company's reputation – invested out there. And it seems to be in considerable danger right now. Am I mistaken here?"

"No, you are not mistaken. Of course one option is selling out. But that would take time – and frankly there would be no buyers in the present circumstances. At least no buyers who would offer an acceptable deal. We will need a little time to identify possible options or buyers, and also to get to know, and to evaluate, the attitude of the Taliban to our project. We really don't know that. We have some information, but we have never really had a discussion with them on this." He paused, then added "I brought with me today our best expert on the situation there, and on the Taliban. I thought you all might be interested in hearing his thoughts on this. He knows the situation better than anyone – at least better than anyone in the company, and anyone here in the US. Maybe you would be interested in his thoughts on this – he just returned from Kabul a couple of days ago." Highsmith looked at Joey, then at their host, to see whether he would pick up this offer to have Joey speak.

"Yes, certainly," said Imbaldwell. "We can have our coffee here at the table." He gestured to the server, indicating that the group would remain at the table, and then signaled to Joey that he had the floor. Joey leaned forward to speak.

"The situation right now is pretty chaotic, but it will surely settle down shortly. Right now it is still difficult to judge just how radical the Taliban will be – in power as a government, as opposed to just talking and fighting. Most rational people think they will be more moderate than they sound in their statements, but we will see as the situation evolves.

"I don't think the situation is necessarily as bad as it may look right now," Joey continued. "Once the Taliban are more used to carrying the responsibilities of government they may adjust some of their policies. They will discover that things are not as simple as they seemed – when they were on the outside. But it will surely be a difficult period.

"It is often thought that the Taliban are all the same, and that they all belong to a single organization, following the same program. But that is not really the case – they are a collection of different groups, with different leaders, and lots of strong individuals. They will take some time to really develop into a single, united government authority. So I guess the real question for you is how long your company can hold out, to see how things are going to develop, and to judge whether, in the end, it will still be worth it to keep your project in a sort-of "stand-by" situation. And I don't think anyone can answer that question right now – it will just take some time."

"How much time?" asked one of the Wilde Oil shareholders. "We need to have some idea of that so we can judge whether it is worthwhile to hold on to the company's shares."

"Unfortunately, no one can answer that question right now," said Joey. "At some point I would suggest sending a small delegation – all arranged in advance, of course, with guarantees of safety – to discuss the whole project with them, to explain the objectives, and the advantages, for themselves and their people – the benefits that will come from the pipe."

"Mr. Torino has spent considerable time in Afghanistan," said Highsmith. "He has traveled widely there, and has met with some of the leaders – of the Taliban – and also some of the so-called warlords. He knows the country well."

But Joey quickly contradicted this: "I don't know the country well, and would not claim to. No one does. It is a country which is a continuing puzzle. Whatever seems to be true today turns out to be false, or exaggerated to the point of being – for all intents and purposes – false. I don't mean it is impossible to do something there – it is definitely possible, and worth the effort. But you have to be prepared for shifting currents, the many factions, the shifting moods of the place, and the mix of ethnic identities and tribal traditions. You must engage the Afghans themselves – as we tried to do when we brought a delegation to Houston, to the Wilde Oil headquarters. That was a big plus for us, a real success, especially the visit to the off-shore rig. The Afghans were really impressed – they understood that we could do things which they could not even imagine."

"But none of this trades in the market," said one of the men, who had not spoken up to that point. "Our share value is crashing, and there is nothing positive on the horizon. This is a business, not a missionary church!"

The door opened and a late-comer entered and pulled an empty chair up to the table. "This is Gerry Imbaldwell," said the host, "our Chairman, arriving late, as usual."

The new arrival nodded his head once, grunting and flashing a half-smile. "Don't let me interrupt the discussion," he said.

But the host, in whose house they were meeting, had a different idea. "I think this may be a good moment for a coffee-break," he said, standing up. "Gerry," he called over to Imbaldwell, "Can we have a word?" Imbaldwell got up slowly, and the two went out of the room together.

"What's that all about?" asked one of the other share-holders, indicating the exit of the host of the meeting and the son of the company's founder. There were general shrugs among the other people in the room as they rose to stretch, get coffee, and have private discussions around the table.

After a half hour had passed, the Chairman of the Board, Gerald Imbaldwell III, and the son of the company's founder, Gerry Wilde, came back into the room, and the Chairman resumed the meeting. " I hope everyone has had time for a cup of coffee," he said, "and I am glad that Gerry has joined us. I brought him up-too-speed just now, and we have a proposal to put forward to the Board."

Everyone nodded with interest, and the Chairman continued. "We propose that the Board ask our new friend, Joey Torino, to visit Afghanistan on our behalf, to talk to the Taliban leadership and anyone else he thinks is relevant, about the continuation of our pipeline project. He will try to convince them that our pipeline will be beneficial to the country, and, if he manages to convince them, he will seek responsible assurances that our project will be allowed to continue without any problems. I don't know what exactly such assurances will look like, but we will judge that when we see them. I would hope for something in writing, but we may have to be flexible."

There was a silence around the table as the participants reflected on this proposed course of action. There were a few questions about the duration of this process and other procedural details, but at the end of this round of discussion there was a silence, and the Chairman asked if all the participants could agree to this special mission. There was a general nodding around the table, and the Chairman said the idea had been accepted. Joey nodded to indicate that he was also in agreement, and several of the participants came around the table to wish him well. The meeting then seemed to come to an end, as several participants began to leave. They all wished Joey good luck as they left, and soon the host was alone again with Joey and Pendleton Highsmith.

The three men sat in a bay window overlooking the sea. It was late, and the Chairman, who was also their host, suggested that they both stay overnight, indicating that there were two rooms ready and available if they could stay. And so that is what they did, having a friendly dinner overlooking the beach, and a good night's sleep with the sound of the waves in the distance, and the fresh sea air all around them.

88. Kandahar

Malek was furious, but knew he had to restrain himself. He had an appointment with the leader of the Talebs who had occupied Kandahar. All over the country this was happening, as the Taliban seized control. Malek had been caught by surprise, like so many other prominent people – the Taliban had slipped in without firing a shot – or at least with minimal resistance. Now he was faced with a very unpleasant situation – his home city, where he was regarded as one of the leaders, was controlled by the Taliban, and he was viewed with suspicion because of his recent contacts with foreigners and especially his trip to Houston, which was very hard to explain.

The appointment was to take place in one of the inner rooms of the Mosque, and Malek had taken the precaution (which was very unusual for him) of coming on time. Now he waited alone for the Taleb leader to arrive, trying to exhibit total nonchalance but actually somewhat nervous; you could never know what to expect from these savages, he thought as he sat, indignant at being made to wait.

Soon the door opened and the designated Taliban leader for the city came in, followed by several armed lieutenants and bodyguards. All were dressed in white robes and turbans, and had full black beards. The leader sat in a chair opposite Malek and stared at him. He looked vaguely familiar to Malek, but he could not place him among all the men he knew in the city. The Taliban leaders were from all levels of society, all ages, and sometimes from other parts of the country, and their full beards made it harder to recognize individual persons. Malek studied this man's eyes, trying to identify him from the past.

"You have asked to see me," said the Taleb leader. "I know you are a prominent person in this city, but I also know that you have been friendly toward our enemies, and that is not what we want to see in our country. We are the Afghan people, the Afghan state, and we are proud of our identity, our history, our culture." He paused, and let this negative first statement sink in. "We hope you will join us to make our country totally free from the foreigners. We will have a country – our country – which is free of foreigners, of their ideas, of their presence, of their influence. If you support us we will welcome that, but if you are still under foreign influence, we will consider you an enemy." He looked steadily at Malek in silence, surrounded by his armed guards, all with black beards and turbans.

Malek quickly understood the situation, and was not at all inclined to get himself into a confrontation with these determined and well-armed men. He was someone who knew how to accommodate to change, how to make friends in order to strike a deal, how to make something positive out of even the most difficult situations.

"And I am very pleased to meet you face-to-face," said Malek in a friendly tone of voice. "It is good that we meet now, so soon after you have seized control of our city. As I am sure you know, I can be very helpful to you and your friends. This is my city, the city of my fathers, and we have many relatives and friends in this place, in this region of our country. I will be most pleased to work with you, with your friends, for the good of our city, our people, here in Kandahar. There are many things we can discuss which will be beneficial for our people here, and which can also be very useful for your leadership." He paused to gage the reaction to his words, but the Talebs remained stony-faced and silent, following the behavior of their leader.

After a few long seconds of silence, the leader broke into a smile. "That is very good," he said, nodding his head. "We will welcome your ... cooperation." He looked around him with a smile, and the others in his group nodded and smiled with him. "We will have some tea while we talk!" He gestured, and young boys appeared in the doorway with trays, and a samovar, which were placed on a carpet between Malik and the Taleb leader. The boys served tea in plain glasses, and offered pastries on a brass tray. Malik and the Taleb leader raised their tea glasses and looked each other in the eyes. An understanding had been reached – the details would be worked out later.

89. Kabul - Five years Later

"God-damned burka," came the voice from behind the veil. "How can they wear these things?" It was Ambassador Rudolphus, struggling with her Afghan robes as she prepared for her first meeting with the Taliban authorities, newly installed as the legitimate government in Kabul. They had been ... reluctant ... to receive a senior American envoy, but Ambassador Highsmith had managed to arrange a meeting. The sole condition of the Taliban had been that the high-level visitor be clad in an acceptable fashion – acceptable by Taliban norms, that is.

Elain Rudolphus had managed the travel program – involving stops in Germany and Qatar – pretty well, but this unforeseen dictum regarding the way she should dress for her meeting with the Taliban, including a face-to-face "courtesy call" on the Taleb who had been named Chief of State in the new governing line-up was a bit too much for her. She had been prepared for almost anything – physical danger, long waiting, inconvenient hotels, and driving to diplomatic meetings in armored Humvees – but not this! And the real problem had been that no one in the American community in Kabul had any burkas!

"Why not?" she asked, incredulous, when the Deputy US Representative at the Embassy had informed her of this "little problem."

"Well," said the young man, "almost all the women have left." He was nervous.

"What difference would that make?" asked Rudolphus. "American women don't have burkas! What a dumb thing to say! You don't have any burkas because all the American women have left? And anyway, they haven't all left. I've already met two women from the Embassy staff!"

"No," said the young man, getting seriously nervous, "I didn't mean to say that there aren't any women in the Embassy! Of course we have women! Of course we do! The dependents have left – that's all! The Embassy staff is still here! Of course!" He wiped some sweat from the back of his neck – he always sweated at the back of his neck when he was nervous.

"Well," don't just stand there! Help me get this thing on!" She had to pull it over her head, which seriously risked disturbing her hair, annoying her even more. "Who does this guy think he is, anyway?" she growled from under the long black robe, as she adjusted the arms and neck.

"He is the Foreign Minister of the new Taliban government," said the young man evenly.

"I know who he is!" said Rudolphus, annoyed even more. "I was a professor of international relations, you know! Should have stayed there!"

The young man was worried – trying hard not to offend this senior official, in Kabul for a brief visit, trying to establish more normal diplomatic relations with the new Taliban government. He was an expert on Afghanistan, but not on the attitudes of senior women officials. In fact, his main qualification for his urgent assignment to the Embassy in Kabul had been that he was unmarried, which "simplified the paperwork," as his personnel officer had explained.

Now Ambassador Rudolphus had the burka in place, and was adjusting the head-ware she had been advised to wear for this meeting. It consisted of a sort-of hat, which had a long tail falling to the shoulders, and a button-on face cover hanging in front.

"So," she exclaimed, turning toward the mirror. "Not bad, if you ask me! What more do they want?"

It was time to go, and she walked to the lobby, with its complicated security arrangements based on huge walls of sand-bags forming an overlapping barrier with a narrow entrance in between. She was grumbling as she walked, escorted by the young man. They were joined in the lobby by Pen Highsmith, newly arrived as the first American Ambassador to the Taliban government of Afghanistan, waiting to escort this senior diplomatic visitor to her first meeting with the Taliban government's new Foreign Minister.

"Well," said Highsmith in his usual optimistic tone, "You look splendid! Right out of the Thousand and One Nights!" He chuckled at his humorous remark. "They will be delighted!"

"Oh shut up!" said Ambassador Rudolphus, "I can't imagine why I am doing this! Should have stayed in Washington!" Highsmith could sense that she was not in good humor. And why would she be? She had traveled for two days, coming from Washington, and was now made to dress up in this ancient garb to meet a Taliban Foreign Minister. He adopted a very professional tone – they were diplomats, after all, and this was one of the highpoints of diplomatic life, of diplomatic tradition: the diplomatic visit of a first Senior Official to a newly-formed government of an ancient, remote, tradition-laden country.

"Shall we go?" he intoned in his supremely diplomatic style, holding out his hand, palm upward, toward the door of the bullet-proof limousine, squeezed between two armored hum-vees manned by marines in combat-dress and carrying battle-standard machine guns. He entered the limousine a little awkwardly – he was, after all, wearing shoulder-to-hip body armor, which forced a certain stiffness of posture.

The gates of the Embassy swung open as two Afghan government police motorcycles led this "convoy" out into the avenue, heading for the Foreign Ministry.

90.

The Chief of Protocol of the Afghan Foreign Ministry stood outside the ministry's ornate entrance doors, awaiting the arrival of the American envoy. He had recently returned from his most recent overseas posting, which had been as the Taliban representative in New Orleans – not a role which had been announced, of course – with responsibility for the organization's activities throughout the southern half of the USA.

He knew American society well, and was looking forward to receiving this first senior visitor from Washington. He was an older man, and believed he understood American thinking – especially of people in the areas he had often visited, in Louisiana and Texas. He spoke English well, and was planning to use his language skills to greet the visiting American official. He was wearing his specially-embroidered robes, reflecting his seniority and the distinction of his position.

The motorcade entered the grounds of the Ministry through the ancient gates leading to the main entrance. The gates had been retained, even though the legendary building of the Ministry, destroyed by a bombing during an earlier civil war, had been rebuilt in modern style. A caravan of police on motorcycles was followed by two hum-vees with Afghan soldiers peeping out of open hatches. American security officers surrounded the limousine as soon as it came to a stop in front of the entrance of the Ministry.

The motorcade had stopped with the limousine positioned exactly at the bottom of the steps leading to the main entrance, and one of the security officers put his hand on the door-handle, waiting for the signal to open. When everyone stopped moving, the door was swung open, and the Chief of Protocol stepped forward to greet Elaine Rudolphus as she stepped out of the limousine in her Afghan robe, head-cover and face-mask. "Welcome to Kabul," said the Chief of Protocol in his New Orleans-accented English.

"Oh," said Elaine Rudolphus, "Thank you! I'm so glad to be here!" She was having trouble speaking through her face-mask, and kept adjusting it. "Damned mask!" she said softly as she pushed it one way, then the other.

Ambassador Highsmith came around the car from the other side, smiling warmly, and stood next to the Under Secretary. He was an experienced hand in this formal diplomatic exercise, and smiled benevolently as if to confirm that the various people present were indeed doing the things they were supposed to do.

The party entered the open doors of the Ministry, escorted by the white-clad Chief of Protocol. "Don't I know you?" asked Ambassador Rudolphus, who was sure she had met the older man somewhere. "Haven't we met before?"

"I do not think so," he replied. "I have visited the USA, but we have never met. I would remember."

"Ah, so you have been to our country? Where?" asked the Under Secretary.

"Uh, well, the south," said the Chief of Protocol.

"The South! I love the South! Where were you?"

"Uh, well, Texas," said the Chief of Protocol, so softly as to be inaudible.

The great double-doors swung open, and the group entered the formal reception area, surrounded by portraits of previous rulers and other Afghan figures. At the other end of the long room stood a figure dressed in traditional Afghan ceremonial robes. It was Kabel Malik, the newly-named Foreign Minister of Afghanistan, making a last-minute adjustment to his headdress. It was his first function as Foreign Minister.

"Hello Mr. Ambassador, hello Mrs. Ambassador!" said Malik loudly, in his broken English. "We are so happy to see you here! In our country!" He shook hands with Highsmith. "Welcome again, Ambassador Highsmith. So happy to see you."

Highsmith was happy to show off his knowledge of the country to Elaine Rudolphus; "Yes, indeed Kabel," he said, "And I am so pleased to present my colleague, Ambassador Rudolphus. She is here for a visit – and of course she is covering herself in order to respect your traditions!" Both men looked at the figure covered in robes and face-veils.

"Well, I would also be happy to say hello," said Ambassador Rudolphus, "but frankly it is not that easy to see through all these veils, believe me! I can see you … vaguely … but I can't really say "what a pleasure it is to see you," when I can't really see you at all! At least, not very well."

"Boy!" shouted the Minister to a nearby Afghan, "bring a woman!"

A young man rushed out of the room by a side door, leaving it open, and reappeared in an instant with a veiled woman in a black jellaba. The woman bowed and helped Elaine Rudolphus to un-wrap her face-veil. "Whew!" said Ambassador Rudolphus, "I didn't think I would ever see the light of day again!" She reached out to shake hands with Malik, who hesitated briefly before taking her hand.

"You know," he said, with a confidential air, "it is forbidden!" They all laughed.

Malik gestured toward an ornate conference table at one end of the room, and they all sat down for a lengthy, disjointed discussion, with Afghan interpreters intervening when needed. Tea was served midway through a polite conversation which did not get into any serious issues. As the meeting was breaking up, Highsmith was able to speak privately with Malik: "I'm so happy to see you in this position," he said, "I recall very well our meeting, when you came to Houston!"

"Oh yes," said Malik, "Was wonderful trip! I learn very much! That oil well, out in ocean! Very good!" He laughed. "Now, we must make oil wells, too! Not in ocean! We have no ocean! Ha ha ha! But we will have pipes! Pipe ... lines! We will have much, much pipelines!"

"Now they make me Foreign Officer ... no!" He corrected himself, "Foreign Secretary, yes?" He smiled. "But I will change, become Secretary of Pipelines! Ha Ha Ha! Secretary of Pipelines!"

"What's this about pipelines?" asked Elaine Rudolphus. "If there are going to be any pipelines, we will do them! We do pipelines better than anyone!" Everyone laughed. The meeting was over. Official American relations had been established with the Taliban government of Afghanistan.

As the American group left the courtyard in their cars, an Afghan government spokesman briefed the press: "The two sides had a frank and fruitful discussion, covering all the current issues between the two governments. It was an open discussion and clarified national positions on both sides. The hope was expressed that this sort of open dialogue will continue, and will lead to better mutual understanding."

91.

It was a moonless night, just as they had expected. They worked only on moonless nights. But it was cold, with a strong wind blowing the sand across the flat plain. In the distance they could see the silhouette of the mountains, against the dark, star-filled sky. Nearer, there were rocky areas around them, under the light of the stars.

They stopped for a brief rest, and ate a handful of biscuits out of their big pockets. It was all they would eat this night, but they had water. They were young, and enjoyed these risky missions. The hardships never bothered them; they had known hardships all their lives.

In the distance they could see the pipe. It crossed the flat, scrubby land mounted on square platforms; a few miles further on it had been buried underground, but for some reason the builders had left it above ground here, for the few kilometers where it crossed this flat area. They knew this, had scouted the place months ago, had noted it as a possible target area. And now the time had come.

They ran in short spurts across the sandy ground, the dust swirling in their faces, covered with the cloth from their robes, and thrown over their shoulders. They had traveled all day to get to this place, and had hidden among the rocky hills, waiting for darkness. Now there were no lights anywhere, but they could find their way by the tracking the shimmering stars.

They were hungry, but it did not matter. They drank from their leather water-bags – not the best water, scooped up from a wide spot in a dried-up stream, where there was a left-over puddle – but not the worst they had found. They knew how to survive in this barren region; it was their home – these stark, sandy flats – and they could survive here even when the water was muddy, when the sand blew, and when there was nothing to eat. It was their place, their piece of the world; and it was for no one else.

They had lived like this ever since they had finished Koran school. It was their only education – they had memorized the entire Koran. The mullah who had taught them had done the same; he also knew the Koran. It was the tradition. It was the way.

Under the stars they mumbled the words they knew, from the Koran, before they started their work.

Crouched low they ran across the open space to the rocky stand which supported the pipe. It transported gas; they could hear its faint hissing sound inside the rounded steel. They fumbled in the large pockets of their long black robes; they had just two sticks of dynamite, and had to use them well. But they knew their work, knew just how much they would need, and where to place it.

They felt along the pipe, seeking just the right place for the charge – it was at the joint, where one pipe overlapped the next – just there, where there was an edge! It was the edge which would be blown away, leaving the tiny opening hissing in the dark night as the gas escaped. And then the gas would ignite from the spark. That was all. That would be enough.

They fiddled with the pipe, found the place for the explosive, ran the wire out fifty meters, where there was a big rock outcropping they could shelter behind. When everything was installed they crouched behind the rocks and turned the crank for the spark.

The flash was small, but the sound was deafening, out in the middle of the dry sand plain, under the stars. The boys looked at each other and smiled. They could see the first flames, hear the hissing of the gas now, coming from the damaged tube, blown by the night wind.

They got to their feet; there was black smoke curling upwards. And they ran – across the flat, dusty plain, toward the distant shadowy horizon, in the direction they knew.

92.

At the airport in Kabul there was a chaotic crowd, leaving their cars everywhere and dashing for the entry to the passenger terminal – families with children, sometimes too small to walk, carried by their parents, and other family members, some of them old and moving slowly. The women wore long robes, with their faces and hair covered, carrying bags and suitcases of all kinds. Cars had been left chaotically, and were now blocking the traffic in front of the terminal. There were armed soldiers on each side of the entrance, watching the stream of people entering the departure area, which was already jammed with people and luggage of all kinds.

There were barricades around the entrance area, with a line of people waiting to have their documents checked, snaking back and forth along the lines of cars which had been left randomly, pointing in various directions, sometimes with empty luggage compartments left open. Armed soldiers were posted around the entrance to the terminal and also on the roof of the entrance area. Other people wandered aimlessly among the scattered cars, dressed in Afghan jellabahs, vests or other parts of Western clothes, crossing paths with armed Western soldiers or Afghan militia men with automatic weapons slung casually over their arms and long ammunition belts slung over their shoulders for quick use.

There was an enveloping silence in this area, interrupted randomly by the sound of a plane, taking off in the distance. After a few seconds of the roaring noise of the engine at takeoff, the plane would appear over the roof of the terminal building, climbing steeply away from the airport, headed toward the distant mountains, the distant world, far from Kabul and the mountains of Afghanistan.

Joey was headed in the other direction, back into the country, on the new mission he had been asked to carry out – to determine whether the new situation in Afghanistan required a complete shut-down, or outright abandonment, of the Wilde Oil pipeline project. There were very few people going into Kabul from the airport, but the Wilde Oil office was still functioning, so someone there had sent a car to pick him up. There was a driver waiting outside the empty arrivals area holding a sign with the word "Torin" inscribed on it in shaky Western lettering. Joey nodded to the driver, who was leaning against the car, and got into the passenger seat.

"You are Meester Jo-ee?" asked the driver.

"That's me!" said Joey, signaling with his hand that the driver should put the car in motion.

"Hello, Meester Jo-ee," said the driver. "I wait long time, not sure you coming."

"Well, I'm here," said Joey, as the soldier guarding the car entrance waved them thru. The road into Kabul was crowded with the usual walkers, carrying heavy loads on their heads, or pushing carts, sometimes with hand-written signs indicating whatever they had to sell. There were a few women, entirely covered, including their faces, in the hot sunshine, sometimes carrying infants, or followed by small children. It was the usual Afghan crowd, heading into the city, as Joey could see as his driver picked his way slowly through the traffic.

Here and there were groups of armed men, in the usual mix of Taliban outfits. They were never alone, always with dark beards and massive cloths wrapped around their heads, weapons and cartridge belts slung over their shoulders, watching carefully as the crowds passed by. Some sat in vehicles at cross-roads and intersections, in twos or threes, while others were positioned at street corners or the entrances to buildings. They watched Joey's car pass by, looking at him carefully but not stopping the car.

After a long, slow drive into the city, the car was admitted to the Wilde Oil office building through the back entrance – the main gates were barricaded with piles of sand-bags and could not be opened. Joey looked around, and then approached the back entrance to the building, which was opened by a guard from the inside.

"Meester Joey?" asked the guard at the door. Joey nodded. "We expect you today!"

"Where is everybody?" asked Joey. "The place looks empty."

"No people here," said the guard. "Just us. The guards." Joey noticed that he was wearing a bullet-proof vest, and that he had a helmet on the table he used as his desk. He asked Joey to sign in, and pointed to a place in his log-book for visitors – an empty page with only the date inscribed awkwardly at the top. Joey signed "Torino."

Joey walked alone to what had been his office, on the first floor – his name was still on the door. Inside, he found his desk, also unchanged, with maps and charts relating to the pipeline rolled up on a shelf to one side. There was an envelope in the center of the desk, with "Mr. Joey Torino" inscribed on the front. He opened it and took out a hand-written note.

"Dear Joey Torino," it read, "Welcome back to Kabul. I am sorry I am not their to welcom you, but our office was closed by police, and we are not aloud to use. We are only aloud to come to office for emergensee. Plees call me when you want at my own house where I am stay becaus of new regulasions." It was signed illegibly, and there was a telephone number inscribed in careful lettering below.

Joey dialed the number. A woman answered in Afghan. "Hello. This is Joey Torino." The woman hesitated a moment, and then shouted to someone else, in Afghan. There was a silence on the line, and then a man's voice.

"Yes, hello?"

"This is Joey Torino."

"Ah, good! I am so happy to talk with you, Meester Torino! I await your call. You are at the office, I think. I hope we can meet, so I can explain a lots of things. There are many things to explain. The situation is very ... different." There was a moment of silence. "Is very difficult to move around city. Very difficult. You understand?" There was another silence on the line.

"Where are you?" asked Joey.

"I am not in center of city. Not good to come here. I meet you. You stay at Metropole Hotel. I reserve for you already. I meet you there. We can talk there."

"Okay. When?"

"You go there, register. I come as soon as possible." There was another silence. "Is difficult. I come as soon as I can."

"Okay. I'll say goodbye now. I will see you at the Metropole Hotel. I will wait for you there."

"Yes. Good." The line went dead and Joey hung up. He sat down, thinking.

After a few moments, he got up, examined the papers and maps in the room, and walked down to the back entrance. The car and driver were still waiting for him in the back courtyard of the building, and he got into the seat next to the driver, saying "Metropole Hotel." The guard opened the gate and the car set out for the hotel.

The streets in the center of the city were calm. There were armed Afghans in robes at the major intersections, and few people or cars. They reached the hotel quickly in the light traffic, and Joey entered the empty lobby. At the main desk he rang the porters' bell, and a Desk Clerk came out from a back room. It was clear that there were no guests. "Yes?" asked the Desk Clerk.

"I have a reservation," said Joey. "The name is Torino."

The Desk Clerk looked through a file and found the reservation. "I apologize, Mr. Torino. You understand – we have many reservations, but the people do not come. They just do not come. You understand?" He gave a shrug of the shoulders and made a facial expression of helplessness, while turning the registration book for Joey to sign.

"No problem," said Joey as he signed in. The clerk looked at the passport which Joey had presented. He noted some things from the passport, completed the registration, and handed the passport back to Joey.

"We have no porters at the moment," said the Desk Clerk. "It is a strange time. Can you find your room on your own?"

"Sure," said Joey, slinging his back-pack over his shoulder. "The elevator working?"

"Oh! Yes! That, at least, is still working!"

Joey picked up the key, and took the elevator up to his room. It was still his favorite hotel in the city. He opened the window, anticipating the call of the muezzin shortly, and slumped down on the bed. It had been a long trip.

He knew that this would be his last visit to this place, understood the situation very well. There was no future for the pipeline; it was a failed project. He would talk to people, would probably visit the construction site, contact a few government officials. He instinctively knew that they would not be able to tell him anything – how could they predict the future?

But Joey was a realist, and he knew there was no future for this project – it was simply too much, too big, too costly, too complicated. And the Taliban would be hostile to it – how could they take any other attitude? It was a foreign intrusion, intended to take advantage of the local people, their ignorance of the way modern commercial systems worked, and their suspicion of anything they did not understand, anything which was beyond their knowledge. He would talk to people, look around, make some practical recommendations, but he knew where it was all headed. It could not come out any other way.

The timeless call of the muezzin floated through the air, and echoed against the surrounding buildings. Within a few minutes he was asleep.

93. Paris, Two Years Later

The speaker went over her time limit, but the chairwoman did not stop her. After she had gone on speaking for another three minutes, the chair started waving the name-card in front of her to signal that her time had expired. The speaker nodded but continued to speak, without any indication that she was coming to a conclusion. The other speakers on the stage started to move in various ways, signaling their unhappiness – the speaker was going well beyond the allotted time. Finally the chairwoman tapped her gavel lightly and started to say something, and the speaker looked at her, nodding her head but continuing to speak. The Chairwoman tapped her gavel again, signaling with her hand, and finally the speaker paused and concluded her presentation. There was no applause, the next speaker was recognized by the chair, and a began her comments.

Page waited patiently for her turn to speak, listening carefully to the comments of the other women on the stage. The auditorium was full, with some people even standing at the back of the hall. Practically all of the audience were women, with only two or three men in the room – a steeply-inclined lecture hall at the Sorbonne university, in the heart of the "Left Bank" of Paris. It was a conference of the international association of women in public service, and the room was more than full. At the back of the lecture hall women stood in the aisles, and all present were listening attentively to the speakers. It was a very international group, with delegations from every world region, and each subject featured a distinguished list of speakers – professors, political figures, and women in other leadership roles in their countries.

Page was attending as a US representative, chosen because of her experience working in developing countries and her active participation in women's organizations. She had been asked to speak on her experience in Afghanistan, as the leader of a clinic for children which was near an active war zone. The clinic had been cited for its work more than a year before the conference, but Page had been unable to attend at the time, and had come to the next annual meeting, one year later. It was her first attendance at such a large conference for and about women and their place in society.

The discussion ended and the meeting was adjourned for a coffee break. Page, who did not know any other conference participants, wandered to a coffee stand and filled a plastic cup with black coffee. It was, after all, Paris, and even a plastic cup of conference coffee was not bad at all. But she had no one to talk to and found herself wandering through the crowded lobby. A bell rang, indicating that the next session was about to start, so she found her way back into the hall, and sat in one of the rows of seats nearest to the lobby.

The speakers in this new session of the conference were announced, and Page was surprised to hear the name of her former Afghan assistant, Aiea, who she had not seen since leaving Afghanistan, almost a year earlier. She struggled to see her friend, who was now on the stage, but could hardly see her face from so far away. She listened carefully to the discussion, and found herself feeling proud and pleased with Aiea's presentation, in English, about the activities of the clinic, and her own life in Afghan society. The audience was attentive and clearly interested in what life was like for a woman carrying out such an important and challenging role in Afghanistan, in the midst of the on-going difficulties there. She knew the clinic very well, and could understand better than anyone else what the real situation was like, from Aiea's very general presentation.

At the next coffee break Page squeezed through the crowd to the front of the room to say hello to her old friend and colleague, and when Aiea saw her she smiled broadly and the two young women embraced warmly. Neither one had expected to ever see the other again, and they were both in tears.

When the meeting resumed for the next session, Page and Aiea slipped out into the lobby, talking rapidly and intensely about the clinic, what was happening there, and also about Page's life in Maine, where she was a volunteer at a local hospital, and was hoping to join the management team.

"I cannot believe that we just meet like this – in Paris!" said Aiea. She asked a stream of questions about Page's life, while Page asked Aiea about every detail of life at the clinic, about the small patients they had tended to while they were together there, and in Afghanistan in general.

The conference resumed, but the two friends continued talking, sitting alone in the lobby and sipping coffee, laughing sometimes, but more often talking quietly and seriously, exchanging information about patients – some known, some not. They were somber part of the time, but laughed together at some stories, or at shared moments from the past.

When the afternoon session of the conference adjourned for the day, Page and Aiea walked together, slowly, through the streets of Paris, still talking, sometimes very serious and at other times laughing together over some shared impression or experience. They passed monuments and striking urban vistas, but noticed nothing – they were so concentrated on each other, on catching up with the activities of their friend. It was clear to Page that Aiea had grown and matured with experience and responsibility. She was sure of herself and confident, and said repeatedly that she had learned everything from Page.

They sat in a sidewalk café, and as the Paris evening settled across the city they ordered some light dinner dishes – more snacks than a real dinner – but they were so interested in talking that they hardly noticed what they were eating. They had so much to say to each other, and both of them wanted to know everything about the other one's life. They asked endless questions of each other, and smiled or laughed at the answers. There were so many things they agreed on, and which they found amusing, or silly, or frightening, or all of these things together.

After lingering over coffee Page walked with Aiea to her hotel, which was very close to the conference site – it was the hotel which the conference was using for its invited speakers. They sat in the lobby for another hour, exchanging news and trading addresses, phone numbers, gossip. They did not want to end their discussion, did not even notice the time passing. But it was late and the small Left Bank hotel dimmed the lights in the lobby – hinting that it was time for them to end their long discussion.

Page asked Aiea about the possibility of her coming to the USA, but Aiea immediately said she would never leave Afghanistan. She said firmly that the country needed her, and she needed to stay in her own land. She was deeply motivated by her work, by her role in her own country, carving out a space for women to take their share of responsibilities in a society where that was new and not yet fully accepted. She was a pioneer, and knew that what she was doing was important – for her country, and for women in general.

The two exchanged contact information and promised to keep in touch – they felt like sisters together, and each one knew the other felt the same way.

Aiea was leaving early the following morning, to start the complicated travel back to Afghanistan, from Paris to Dubai to Kabul by plane, and then by bus back to Mazar-e-Sharif. She could not be away from the clinic for more than a few days. The two young women embraced warmly and said their tearful farewells, promising to stay in touch. And then Page left to walk back to her own hotel, nearby. She was programmed to participate in a discussion group the following morning, and to leave Paris to return to the US that same evening.

***

Epilogue

Page and Aiea never saw each other again. The clinic in Mazar-e-Sharif was closed when Aiea disappeared during a riot in the city. She had been the target of many groups which opposed foreign influence in Afghanistan – and were hostile to women taking up prominent positions.

Pendleton Highsmith and Elaine Rudolphus retired with distinction after holding long and active leadership positions in the State Department. Each of them was awarded the highest honors at their retirement ceremonies.

Wilde Oil sold out to its traditional rival company after suffering considerable financial losses resulting from the canceled pipeline project, and the company ceased to exist.

The United States, with its allies, fought a long and bloody war against the Taliban and Al Qaeda, in Afghanistan and elsewhere, but finally left Afghanistan without a clear result.

The planned oil and gas pipelines across Afghanistan were never built. Joey visited Kabul, years later, invited to participate in an international conference. He was surprised to run into the young man who had interpreted for the group of Afghan visitors to Houston, so long ago. The Afghan now had a prestigious position at a senior level in the government in Kabul, and had become a serious figure with the reputation of being a conservative, opposed to foreign influences in the country.

The last time they had spoken was on the flight back from Houston to Kabul. After some friendly greetings, Joey asked how Afghanistan had changed over the years; were the changes positive?

The younger man expressed his warm feelings about seeing Joey after so long, and then took on a serious expression as he started to respond to Joey's question. "There have been many changes," he said, "that is normal. All things change over time."

"But it is our country, our culture," he said. You were just a visitor. Visitors come, and then they go. Many visitors. And our country is always the same, always ours. Visitors can never understand. They can never change our ways. It is our country! We follow our culture, our laws!" He frowned and his eyes became dark. "Not yours!" he said with emotion, "Never yours!"

It was the last phrase Joey ever heard from an Afghan speaker. He left the reception quietly and walked back to his hotel, through the silent streets of Kabul. The following day he left the country to return to his house in Maine. And he never visited Afghanistan again.

Elaine Rudolphus retired from the State Department and was named President of a small college in Southern California.

Pendleton Highsmith was assassinated in Kabul when a homemade bomb, which had been attached under his official car, exploded.

Kabil Malek served for many years as a Minister of the Government in Kabul.

"Insto Oil" merged with "Wilde Oil" to become "Insto-Wilde," but the brand name remained "Insto Oil" and that logo was retained on all the company's gas stations.

"Gerry" Wilde was appointed Ambassador to London.

Joey Torino and Page Wheatly lived a private life in their secluded cabin in Maine.

THE END

***

The Taliban in Texas

Cast of Characters

Joey Torino

H.R. Wilson, Private Agent from Boston

Pendleton Highsmith, Retired US Ambassador, now President of Wilde Oil Corp. in Houston

Elaine Rudolphus, former US Ambassador in Moscow, now Under Secretary of State

Conchita Rivera, Assistant of Pendleton Highsmith at Wilde Oil HQ in Houston

Page Wheatley, Friend of Joey Torino, who runs a clinic for women and girls in Mazar-e-Sharif

Aiea, Afghan Assistant of Page Wheatley

Max Anders, Head of Wilde Oil Management Team in Kabul (dies in Afghanistan)

Josh Mills, Wilde Oil Team member in Kabul who leaves.

Azeem, Local employee/driver for Wilde Oil in Kabul

Young man US Vice Consul in Mazar-e-Sharif

Old Man in New Orleans, a Taliban agent

First Taliban Agent in Houston (later arrested)

Second Taliban Agent in Houston (later killed in an explosion)

Kabil Malek, Afghan War-Lord in Kandahar

2 young Afghans in Kandahar

2 young Afghans who blow up gas pipelines (possibly the same two who appear in Kandahar)

Afghan lady on bus to Kabul

Aiea's uncles – a taxi driver and a camel/boat man in North of Afghanistan

Old Afghan Man who goes to see head of Al Qaeda, and also to meetings in Kandahar

Hon. Gerald Imbaldwell III, Chairman of Board of Wilde Oil (and former Governor of Texas)

Jurgen ("Jerry") Wilde – Playboy Grandson of founder of Wilde Oil

Wilbur Anglesea, Jr. – Chairman of the Board of Multinational Oil Corp, which owns Insto Oil, is named Ambassador to Great Britain

"Insto-Wilde," – is the name of the merged company after Multinational Oil Corp takes over Wilde Oil (but the brand name "Insto Oil" is retained on gas stations, as the best-known trade-mark)

Edition Noëma
Melchiorstr. 15
D-70439 Stuttgart

info@edition-noema.de
www.edition-noema.de
www.autorenbetreuung.de